Nada Alic

Bad Thoughts

Nada Alic is a writer in Los Angeles. Her story "The Intruder" was shortlisted for the 2019 CBC Short Story Prize, and "My New Life" was published in the journal *No Tokens*. In 2020 she was a recipient of a Canada Council for the Arts literary grant for her debut story collection, *Bad Thoughts*. She is currently working on a forthcoming novel.

Bad Thoughts

Bad Thoughts

Bad Thoughts

STORIES

Nada Alic

VINTAGE BOOKS
A Division of Penguin Random House LLC
New York

A VINTAGE BOOKS ORIGINAL 2022

Copyright © 2022 by Nada Alic

All rights reserved. Published in the United States by Vintage Books,
a division of Penguin Random House LLC, New York, and distributed
in Canada by Penguin Random House Canada Limited, Toronto.

Vintage and colophon are registered
trademarks of Penguin Random House LLC.

Several pieces first appeared in the following publications: "My New Life"
in *No Tokens* (January 2021) • "The Intruder" on CBCBooks.ca (April
2019) • "This Is Heaven" in *Astra Magazine 1: Ecstasy* (April 2022) •
"Daddy's Girl," in different form, in *This Is Badland*, no. 5 (April 2022)

Library of Congress Cataloging-in-Publication Data
Name: Alic, Nada, author.
Title: Bad thoughts : stories / Nada Alic.
Description: First edition. | New York : Vintage Books,
a division of Penguin Random House LLC, 2022.
Identifiers: LCCN 2022005045 (print) | LCCN 2022005046 (ebook)
Subjects: GSAFD: Black humor. | Short stories.
Classification: LCC PR9199.4.A4455 B33 2022 (print) |
LCC PR9199.4.A4455 (ebook) | DDC 813/.6—dc23
LC record available at https://lccn.loc.gov/2022005045
LC ebook record available at https://lccn.loc.gov/2022005046

Vintage Books Trade Paperback ISBN: 978-0-593-46663-6
eBook ISBN: 978-0-593-46664-3

Book design by Christopher Zucker

vintagebooks.com

Printed in the United States of America
1st Printing

To Ryan Hahn
To Andrea Nakhla

Contents

Instead of pathologizing every human quirk, we should say, By the grace of this behavior, this individual has found it possible to continue.

—Sarah Manguso, *300 Arguments*

Bad Thoughts

My New Life

Sometimes I wonder, *Is this it?* and I'll look around at all the modern luxuries that keep me alive and think, *Probably.* I have no reason to complain; I have everything I need. Last night Mona and I watched a documentary about the impossibility of our planet—the strange alchemy that created life, my life, my one and only. Billions of years of molecular replication, mutant algae clawing up from the depths of the ocean, consciousness forming out of soft tissue and nerves. Instead of thinking, *What an exquisite machine,* all I could think was *What a burden. What an act to follow.* And also *Is the heater on? I can barely feel it.* When the fifty-two-hertz whale swam across the screen singing its lonely song, I cried. Mona cried, too, not because of the whale but because her mother is judgmental.

I can barely remember life before Mona. Sometimes I'll get flashbacks from childhood of someone piercing my ears with a safety pin or a wayward neighborhood girl teaching me how to throw up, but I'm not sure if I just made that up or if I saw it on TV. I met Mona two summers ago at a backyard baby shower, my third of the month. Imagine a congregation of thirty or so women in neutral linen sets presenting their offerings of homemade banana bread and hemp diapers, shrieking at one another. Personally I could never get past the image of being ripped apart, half-submerged in bathwater, while being gently instructed to breathe through it. I sometimes worry that motherhood is contagious, like a parasite or the way cohabitating women synchronize their cycles. I stood off to the side and kept my coat on. Luckily no one seemed to notice me, except for Jessa, who stared dead-eyed in my direction while she breastfed her newborn. It was so unnerving that at one point I mouthed *What?* and she finally turned her gaze back down toward her puffy nipple.

I was in the buffet line poking at the untouched vegan potato salad when Mona came in from behind for a hug, pressing her full weight into me. She'd mistaken me for someone else, a friend. Instinctively, my shoulders softened and my knees buckled and my body went limp in a trust-fall motion before I realized what was happening. When I turned around, I saw a beautiful woman wearing a tailored blue pantsuit practically levitating above a sea of homogenous white smocks. I couldn't stop staring at her face. She had a strong jaw, fat lips, and a sturdy Slavic nose. Her sculptural features were so striking that they eclipsed any of her other minor imperfections: unkempt eyebrows overgrown from neglect, a constellation of chin acne, or the splotch of melasma on her forehead. I felt as though I had been chosen, as if she had come to usher me into my new life moments before my old one imploded. She smiled and introduced herself, then pointed out the woman she'd mistaken me for, who was refilling an ice bucket off in the distance. We looked nothing alike, but I felt a strange combination of hatred and gratitude for this woman and tried to assume her posture for the rest of the party, which was difficult since I had so little to go on.

We piled our plates with hard cheeses, baby carrots, and globs of hummus and found a seat in the mildly damp grass. I knew I liked her when she told me about her heavy period before I knew anything else about her: what she did for a living or how she did that thing with her eyeliner, the way she made it smudge on purpose. She spoke in a soothing, unaffected monotone—a welcome reprieve from the shrill mating calls of new mothers manically trying to convince one another they were having the time of their lives. She lowered her voice to a whisper when talking about the other women, many of whom had worked with her at a now-defunct wellness brand for dogs. She described the cultlike conditions of the company, how employees were forced to attend wilderness retreats, where, sedated by CBD-infused teas, they sat cross-legged on colorful Mexican blankets and took turns sharing traumatic childhood experiences. Most told benign stories of divorce and life-threatening allergies, so Mona decided to wow them with a made-up story about being molested by a stepbrother. She wanted to prove how easy it'd be to expose the perversity of their trauma Olympics, but mostly she was bored. She had no cell reception all weekend and had watched too many true crime procedurals to wander off on her own at night. When she finished, all her teary-eyed coworkers snapped their fingers in gratitude. The following Monday, there was a bouquet of tulips on her desk with a note from the team that read: *To a Warrior Goddess!!*

I swallowed a laugh and nearly choked on a seed cracker. I was so relieved to be talking about anything other than inter-mittent fasting or my Enneagram number that I quickly offered up my most embarrassing qualities, beginning with my chronic night sweats and fear of birds. She agreed: most birds were untrustworthy. With each confession I felt lighter, somehow absolved. She listened attentively as I told her about my incur-able sadness, how it had taken on new gradients this year, with sharper edges that sometimes left me breathless. I wondered aloud if it was just one of those things, like getting older, and how fault lines suddenly appear across your neck and your lower back hurts for no reason. I used vivid imagery when describing my pain, to show her I wasn't boring, regular sad; I was an emotionally complex person. I was maybe even an artist. She reassured me that it was likely hormonal and no big deal, then complained about the disproportionate size of her left breast compared to her right, and her popcorn addiction, as if any of those problems were categorically similar to mine. Sometimes I wonder if her problems are even real at all. My worst fear is that she's making them up, just to relate. Actually my worst fear is being eaten alive. I don't know where it came from, but I think about it often.

As the lonely whale song played through the credits, I was reminded of a recurring nightmare I've been having. Normally I wouldn't mention it, but, unlike most people, Mona loves hearing about dreams and translating their symbolic and archetypal meanings. In this one, my husband, Liam, and I are on the beach. The midday sun burns brightly, but I'm fine because my body is covered in a thick frosting of sunscreen. I let it sit until it's caked on and hardened, like a full-body cast or a papier-mâché shell. He asks for the sunscreen, but I've used it all up, so I tell him he doesn't need it. I tell him he's overreacting and that he could use a little color. He shrugs and returns to his book as the sun proceeds to set the earth ablaze. Birds drop from the sky, leaving trails of smoke. Beachgoers boil alive in an ocean of flames. I look over and notice big chunks of Liam's skin cracking and melting, exposing muscle, fat, and internal organs. He asks again, "You sure I don't need any?" His legs have burned down to the bone. A rotting smell sits heavy in the air. "I'm positive, honey," I say from under an umbrella, "you're building a base." He rubs his face, wiping the remains of cartilage from his nose, and smoke starts to rise from the top of his head as his brain cooks. He sighs, unable to read the words on the page. "I don't feel right," he says. I tell him he's dehydrated and give him a bottle of water. He's so thankful, so moved by the gesture. "Leave some for me!" I say to what's left of him, now a pile of charred bones and a pair of flip-flops. I watch as skeletal vultures pick at his remains, and laugh. (I made that last part up just to impress Mona with my creativity.)

As with any recurring dream, there are subtle variations—sometimes it's a tsunami in the distance, or a swarm of killer bees—but the essence of it remains: willful endangerment. I know I'm doing it, but I can't stop. I'll wake up, having soaked through the sheets with a guilt that doesn't belong to me, and the only way to rid myself of it is to repent by being extra nice to him in waking life. I'll do anything; I'll open my eyes when we have sex, and I won't even do that thing where I look away and imagine his brother. When he shaves his chest in the bathroom and gets little hairs all over my toothbrush, I'll just blow them off; I won't make a big deal about it. And when he tells me we're going out with his boring work friends, I won't protest; I'll just say, "Party time!" in a singsongy voice. I'll be so accommodating, a perfect angel.

"Dreams about beaches usually mean good things are coming your way," Mona said, lazily stretching out on my sofa like a cat. "Want to hear something worse?" Before I could answer, she said, "I cheated on Greg, sort of."

She and Greg had only been married for a year. He had classic movie star features but a little more gaunt and mournful. He had sallow eyes, like someone with secrets—a troubled person. In this way, I understand him. He clings to Mona's self-assuredness in the way I do. He is so handsome that I can never look him in the eye for too long and instead rest my gaze on the hairless space between his brows. The few times I've looked, I've fought the inappropriate urge to cry.

"What's 'sort of'?" I asked.

"I made an online dating profile as a joke, just to see."

"See what?"

"I don't know, to see how it works."

Mona does these sorts of things on occasion: slips out of her own life "just to see." She's always in on the joke and treats it like some kind of performance art: always one step removed to inoculate her from consequence. She draws philosophical guidance from all manner of suicidal poets, cult leaders, and controversial feminist critics to justify her worldview. "Woman is nature and nature is unknowable. Therefore, woman is unknowable to herself and a threat to men," she's explained. She believes that nature is inherently violent and morality is an oppressive form of spiritual castration. Acting on her impulses is her way of reclaiming her humanity. All her compelling theories about womanhood make perfect sense in the moment but leave me confused once I leave her orbit. She makes me feel impassioned and manic, but I can't explain why.

Her escapist impulses led to a short-lived career as a mukbang camgirl, where she ate endless bowls of cereal at the request of her subscribers. After that she spent a year as a devout Catholic, claiming it was research for a role in a movie she would one day write and star in, but after she met Greg, her experimentation became more internal, using chemically altered states to achieve ego annihilation and get closer to God. Like that one time she called me from the bathroom stall at work after taking what she thought was a microdose of acid but was, in fact, a full tab. She called to let me know that her boss, Leonard, was her son in a past life, and wasn't it so funny? Leonard! It explained so much. Then she laugh-cried for ten minutes straight while I stayed on the line, loading the dishwasher. *I can see it all, and it's perfect. It's all perfect*, she'd said.

"So you met someone?" I asked.

"Dylan. Yes. I told him I was just looking for friends, and he said that was great because he was, too, so we agreed to meet as friends in the parking lot behind Rosewood Plaza." She paused, adding, "People do that, you know. They meet friends online."

"I believe you," I said.

"He didn't look like his photos." She laughed.

"They never do!" I agreed, not that I have any idea. I met Liam at the gym during a period of my life when I thought getting abs was an attainable goal. He would idle on the ellip-

tical behind me, and whenever I turned around, he'd pretend
to be on his phone. It went on like this for a year before he
ever talked to me. I hated being constantly watched, constantly
monitored. I felt so exposed, but I was in the best shape of my
life. One night, he followed me home. I didn't know it at the
time, but this was his way of flirting with me.

Mona went on to describe the encounter: how young Dylan
actually was, how his gangly limbs swam in a stretched cotton
T-shirt and basketball shorts, how his car smelled like body
spray and fruity nicotine. When she got in the car, he looked
straight ahead as if he'd just been caught. Nothing happened,
she swore, she just sat in the passenger seat and put her hand
over his to calm him, as if she'd done this before, but she hadn't,
Not with a teenager, god! She repeated the word *friend* in her
mind like a mantra. He closed his eyes and guided her hand to
his mouth, and she let him suck on her finger. Whichever one, it
didn't matter; looking at them, she felt they no longer belonged
to her. That's all he wanted to do, and who knows why. Maybe
nerves. Or maybe it was a dare, like one of those college hazing
initiations, a seduce-a-MILF challenge—I read an article about
it once. When it was over, she emerged from the car with her
face beaming as she tried to recall certain details about her life,
some anchor points to remind her of who she was. Greg, the
last four digits of her social security number, if she believed in
a god and, if so, was he watching? Her mind was blank. All she
could feel was the sound of her heartbeat synced up to the deep
house-music bassline blaring from his car as he drove away.

When she finished her story, I took a sip of my wine and
looked at her fingernails. They were oblong-shaped and freshly
manicured. I kept my face soft and expressionless. Being the
keeper of her secrets was a role I took seriously, because it

meant no one in the world could know her like I did. I wanted
to know more, like did she like it, and if she did, would she do
it again? Was she going to leave Greg now? Upend her whole
life?

"Ha!" She waved her hand as if swatting a fly, then quickly
changed the subject to last night's episode of a reality dating
show where contestants were blindfolded and taken to an undisclosed location somewhere remote and inhospitable to human
life. "Lisa didn't deserve to go; she was their best chance for
survival," she said, stuffing a fluff of store-bought sponge cake
in her mouth. A crusty flake remained at the corner of her lips
and she just let it be. Nothing ever fazed her. Maybe that's it,
the answer to everything. Let it be.

A few days later I accompanied Liam to an upscale wine bar for
his friend Quin's birthday. When we arrived, Quin waved us
over to join the group in the reserved balcony area. He looked
to be in his late forties, with grayish hair and neatly trimmed
stubble, which is to say: totally forgettable. Apparently we've
met before, but I couldn't place him. Now that I'm married,
I have a hard time remembering men's faces. There is nothing that makes them stand out, I guess, unless if they're hideous, I'll probably remember them as a courtesy. Liam ordered
our drinks, and I listened politely as a circle of men discussed
exotic trips they were about to take or had just returned from.
Anytime someone spoke, I would smile and push air out of my
nostrils in a polite low-impact laugh.

After a while, I couldn't remember what I was doing there.
Everything had lost its meaning and all I could think was *Don't
touch anyone's penis—don't do it. Imagine what would hap-*

pen if you did, like, right now. Think about anything else. Look up at the ceiling tiles. What is that . . . distressed tin? Elegant choice. Very modern. But once I thought it, I couldn't stop. I fixed my gaze on the assortment of black and gray dress pants before me. They all looked so vulnerable, so up for grabs. Concealed only by thin layers of fabric. I imagined them as wind chimes waiting to be struck. The impulse wasn't sexual; it was destructive. I just stood there, not touching anyone's penis, quietly frightened by who I am and what I'm capable of.

On the drive home, I didn't mention penises, but I did ask what the point of it all is, not just the socializing or the drinking per se but this whole business of being alive. Liam ignored me and instead asked if I could hear it, that churning sound the car was making. He told me it had been doing that for weeks now and he couldn't figure it out. I wanted to tell him that I no longer love him but not to take it personally because I don't love anything besides sleep and the feeling of having my hair professionally washed. I knew well before he began driving erratically up the winding narrow roads toward our home that he had very little to offer me in the emotions department. He's going through his own thing: rapid hair loss. All I can say is *It's very masculine* or *I can finally see your face.*

We pulled up to our building, a converted motel lined with drooping banana plants designed to confuse us into thinking we live at a luxury resort. I had bought into it for the last couple years, but now I can see that most of the plants are dying. "Someone should water these," I whined. Complaining about lawn maintenance was the closest I've ever felt to being rich. Liam makes just enough money for the both of us as a web developer for an accounting-software startup, but he spends his money on stupid things. For my birthday last year, he bought me a star. He printed out a certificate from a website as proof. I'd asked for a new computer.

Inside, Liam turned on the TV and began working on a pile of pistachio nuts left out on the coffee table. He doesn't just crack them open; he sucks on the shells and spits them out like a cowboy, looking so pleased with himself, so proud. I pulled out my phone to read a text from Mona; it was a link to poorly photoshopped photos of celebrities that exaggerated their hips and butts and made their torsos look deformed. We replenish our thread constantly with inspirational quotes and questions about things we can easily find out for ourselves, like: Can you eat salmon skin? How many years until the sun explodes? Through it, we explore the edges of our stranger impulses and our secret thoughts; I tell her about the vegetables I find most erotic, and she makes a list of conditions she thinks people are just making up: ADHD, for example, and Lyme disease.

I was standing next to Liam when I felt him grab my free hand and plop it on the back of his neck, signaling a request for a massage. I wondered if he was jealous of Mona, but I don't know if he could ever fully comprehend what she and I have. It isn't romantic because it's more than that. Romance is a fiction, a lonely movie that plays just for you. It passes like a mood. Mona is my witness, proof that I'm not someone else's fantasy projection; I'm a real living thing on planet Earth. I continued standing, half-heartedly clawing at Liam's back while he made little whimpering sounds like a baby animal; I fell for it every time.

"Your hands are magic," he said.

I pressed my thumb hard into his shoulder meat. I worried he might be right. What if my hands are magic? I've never used them to their full potential; I've never thought to before. Liam took my hand and guided it down to his crotch, where a hard mound had bloomed between folds of raw denim. He looked up at me with a big smile, like a child proudly presenting his macaroni art, like he'd been waiting to show it to me all night. I kept my hand limp. Sensing my hesitation, he clarified his intent by unzipping his pants, taking his penis out from its complex cotton boxer flap, and leaving it for me to tend. There it was, so pink and unselfconscious. I didn't want it. My urge to touch had very little to do with actual penises and almost nothing to do with his penis specifically, especially then, when it was splayed out so clinically, like an umbilical cord or a mollusk. It is such an unusual-looking appendage, the kind of thing that belongs on ice or under a shell at the bottom of the sea. What I want doesn't want me back. What I want won't even see me coming. I patted his bald spot. "My stomach hurts," I said. "I'm going to throw up." I told him I'd be back and went to the bathroom.

I sat down on the cool toilet seat and silently contemplated the ebb and flow of our marriage, the big and small ways a person can change. Liam got sober last year and now spends most of his time cycling in a group of Lycra-clad men with sculpted calves and father wounds. The one time I rode bikes with him, he sped ahead of me to show off how fast he could go. I could see him in the distance practicing wheelies while I labored over each pedal uphill. He's different now, like a new man. I want so badly to be new, too, but he says I'm not allowed to attend meetings if I don't have a problem. His problem is contained, like a country with clear borders, while mine is more like a cluster of hundreds of uninhabitable islands. I don't know how to explain this to him.

I returned to the living room to find Liam with his pants

zipped and his legs crossed in defiance. I sat on the edge of the sofa and lit a match for a vanilla-scented candle on the coffee table. I held the matchstick up for a moment and watched the soft orange glow expand as the wood withered and curled. For a brief second, I imagined what might happen if I tossed it on the floor, how quickly our cheap high-pile IKEA rug would be engulfed in flames. I imagined the white noise of soccer fans chanting in unison: "Let it burn!" I waited until the flame seared the tip of my thumb before I blew it out. I was so spooked, I let out a fake laugh.

"What?" Liam asked.

"What," I said. "Nothing, I'm just tired."

My heart was racing with exhilaration. I left the room and opened the freezer to feel the cool air on my face. I did my meditative breathing exercises and tried not to think, but it was impossible. Don't think about a blue dot. See? I didn't want to die; I'm not even a reckless person. I have high hopes for a future I can barely imagine in my current state. I even pray sometimes, when I get food poisoning, asking for forgiveness just in case my Catholic mother was right about everything.

I tried imagining Mona's face when I tell her about my little match stunt. She was the only person who could declaw the thought and soften it into a story. She would think it was funny, and even if she didn't, she would still say, "You're so funny," and those words alone would reassure me.

The next morning I looked over at Liam's swollen sleep face and it restored me to a place of deep gratitude. He slept on his back with his mouth slightly ajar and whistling from sleep apnea. He looked like a large baby, so pale and helpless. Most mornings start like this, with the hope that my cells had regenerated and I'd improved overnight. I quietly got out of bed and started picking dirty socks and underwear up off the floor and organizing them in a neat pile, then watered the houseplants to make up for who I had become, or who I had been this whole time, plus aging. I thought that if Liam woke up to a spotless apartment, he would forgive me for sobbing uncontrollably throughout the night. He doesn't understand what I mean when I say it relaxes me. "Let him sleep," I whispered to the invisible child we decided not to have so we could spend more time working on ourselves. It was his idea, and Mona says if you think about it, it's the most romantic thing in the world. He wanted me all to himself.

I quickly got changed and left to meet Mona for breakfast at our favorite nearby diner. She was already sitting at a booth waiting for me when I arrived. The seats were sticky and smelled of bleach, but the wholesome country-kitchen ambiance fills me with misplaced nostalgia for a simpler time.

"You're late," she said, scanning the giant laminate menu.

"Sorry, I took a detour across the playground and got distracted. There were so many kids running around, more than usual. I started doing that thing where I try to pick out the child who looks most like me, you know, one who could pass as my own," I said, tightening my ponytail, a little winded. "It'd have to be a quiet one, maybe a poor one, one who would appreciate a more comfortable life, but also a young one incapable of forming long-term memories . . ." I trailed off. "Obviously I'm not serious," I added, making nervous little origami shapes with my napkin.

"You'd be a great mother," she said, not really getting the

point. Then I told her about the penises and how close I was to really touching them, how afraid I was.

"It's not that weird," she said. "I've done it."

"What, touched one?"

"No, just sort of brushed my hand past one, over the pants so it seemed accidental."

"Who was it?"

"I don't know, some guy on the train."

She barely looked up from her menu once. She looked preoccupied, as if her mind was elsewhere. I knew this would happen. I often worry that I've depleted her, or worse, that she's finally bored with me. I honestly don't know what I would do if that happened. I'd probably fall into a vegetative coma-like state, one step removed from death, only to wake to the sound of her voice. I try my best to reciprocate by letting her talk about whatever she wants for as long as she wants, then find ways to agree with her. Like how feminism created incel culture, or how money is a social construct. Or her weeks-long investigation into a stolen sweater that she later found in the back seat of her car. "Someone clearly moved it on purpose," I assured her.

After breakfast, Mona went to work, and I walked directionless for a couple blocks, trying to figure out what to do. Most days I wander to and from the diner, the park, and home in a predictable geometric pattern that would make it so easy for someone to memorize my movements and kidnap me. No one has, but the point is they could if they wanted to. The glare from the sun burned my eyes, and my nose wouldn't stop running. I was still adjusting to my new routine, and my body wasn't used to being out in daylight. I lost my job three months ago on account of no longer showing up for it. "You were never a morning person," Mona liked to say, and it's true. After six years of working in sales at a luxury bedding brand, my motivation to work had waned. Instead of writing quippy ad copy, all I could muster was a list of reasons not to get out of bed. I was also groped by my manager during a performance evaluation, but I figure it would be tough to prove since he is partially blind, so he could have just been looking for the light switch. Exhausted and overwhelmed by the ceremony of having to say goodbye to my coworkers, I called in and told them I was very sick. I pictured them all weeping, struck by a grief they didn't know they felt for me. *But who will oversee the launch of washable rugs!* they'd cry. After two weeks, the calls stopped and they left me alone.

I slowed my pace to a sidewalk shuffle when I noticed two men in the distance. One stood in line at an ATM, and the other was across the street at a bus stop, looking at his phone. The man at the ATM was middle-aged and wore a Bluetooth earpiece, while the younger man wore a loose-fitting basketball jersey. These men were total strangers, but my mind paired them as two participants unwittingly starring in my fantasy. *Stop,* I thought to myself. *Stop, stop, stop.* But I couldn't stop. In my head, they were already fighting, *Mortal Kombat-*style. Maybe the one guy prefers the rival basketball team, who cares. The point is they were punching and kicking each other, blood oozing from their mouths and noses as they took turns and grunted like tennis players. Eventually the younger one managed to pin the older one to the ground. *Why are you like* *this?* Fine, let's say the older one called a truce and wrapped his arms around the younger one, patting his back in reconciliation. He let his hands linger on the boy's back. *Okay, the end.* Surprised, the younger one, more eager and unselfconscious, initiated a kiss. A passionate, muscular one. The mutual shock was so cataclysmic, so outside the laws of their agreed-upon universe, that the only reasonable response was submission or death. *Oh my god, no.* Slowly a crowd formed around them to watch, and how could you not watch? The crowd moved closer, huddled around the men as if gathered in worship. I bit down on the inside of my cheek and kept walking until they were out of view and unharmed.

I continued walking for a few more blocks, then sat down on an open bench to collect myself, giving polite smiles to passersby like a normal person would. As I bent down, I felt my wallet tumble out of my jacket pocket. It's one of those decorative triangle pockets that sits under the armpit, making it unreachable and useless. I looked down at the wallet and had an idea. I could empty it and throw it a few feet away to see if someone would take it. It would be a harmless experiment to prove what I believed to be true: that it isn't just me. At our core, everyone is rotten. Some are worse than others, of course. But we are all animals, guided by impulses that have been muzzled by morality—our true selves forced to recede into the subconscious, which causes cancer. Mona sent me a TED Talk about it once.

I tossed the wallet and waited to see what would happen. A young couple walked by holding hands, followed by a conga line of kindergarteners led by two women wearing soft sweaters and whistles. No one touched the wallet. Finally a shoeless woman carrying a trash bag half-filled with empty beer cans and water bottles walked over and picked it up. My cheeks flushed with righteous relief. Aha!

"Is this yours, miss?" she asked, presenting it to me.

"Oh yeah," I responded, examining it closely. "Thanks."

"No prob," she said, looking sleepy, almost bored by her own gesture.

She wandered off, and I watched her sit alone under a tree from afar. I suspected she might be homeless but quickly told myself it was unlikely given how young she looked. She was probably doing community service or cleaning up after a big party. Yes, a birthday party! Everyone had offered to help out, but she'd insisted they go home; she would handle it. That had to be it. I winced until the girl became a shape and that shape became none of my business. A nausea warmed my chest with what I understood to be shame for what I abandoned in order to live: the whole ugly world and everyone in it.

I got up and followed the sounds of birds screaming and the trails of smoke billowing from idle cars' exhaust pipes, in search of life. My own life or some version of it I could cobble together in the next few hours. I checked my phone to see if Mona had called or texted but she hadn't; she was at work. I tried not to think about her life at work, the endless fires she puts out, the people who envy her, the omnipotent authority she has over her interns. She can be cruel when she wants to be, but only out of some sense of cosmic righteousness from which I am always spared. I feel uniquely blessed; like that feeling you get driving past a car crash or hearing news of someone's terminal diagnosis: not me, not me, not me, thank God. I notice the way my cruelty unfurls in her presence like a slow and silent fart. I don't want it to, but I can't always control it. The first time I complained to her about someone else, it was a photo of an acquaintance named Laura posing nude in a bathtub with the caption *criminal justice reform NOW* or some other unrelated social cause that Laura often exploits as the loose scaffolding for her narcissistic personality disorder. Mona had responded in kind with a photo of her coworker Melissa's weird-looking baby. Gossip is collateral, deepening our loyalty and reinforcing our inherent superiority over everyone else. Once mutual trust was established, it only escalated. We judge everything from holidays to governments to abstract concepts. Time? An illusion. Those impossible little slits in condiment packages? Poor design. The "You've Unsubscribed" email? A cry for help.

I wandered a few more blocks like a tourist in a foreign country: tired, constipated, and secretly bored to death. *I could look for a new job,* I thought. I needed something to occupy my restless mind. I relaxed my shoulders with relief over contemplating this very big decision. To prepare, I'd need to come up with a list of skills and corresponding jobs that best suit those skills. I thought of my strong sense of smell, how that could be useful given the right circumstances. Or my ability to sit for long stretches of time. First, I would need tools: pens, a notebook, and so forth. I spotted a corner store and wandered in to see if they sold office supplies.

The store was empty except for an older man in his sixties who was slouching in front of the performance water cooler. From where I stood, I could see the outline of his bulge through his athletic shorts. The bulge had an unusual arc to it, and at one point I thought I saw it shift as if to wave hello. A voice from within said, "Touch it." Without hesitation, I walked toward him and slid by, letting my hand brush against his crotch, feeling the soft hump of flesh as I passed. From there I kept walking to the travel section in the next aisle, examining tooth-paste and baby wipes with intense focus.

After a while, I couldn't tell if he had even noticed. Maybe I'd done it wrong—not enough force. I forgot about the office supplies entirely and poured coffee into a paper cup and brought it to the cashier, acting like nothing even happened. I watched as the cashier effortlessly scooped up change with her long clawlike acrylic nails. She seemed skilled, as if she'd spent her entire life practicing. Hypnotized by her elegant and precise finger work, I nearly forgot about the man until I turned and noticed he was standing close behind me. I glanced around, pretending to look for someone else, but no one else was in the store.

Up close, the man's face looked old: he had bloodshot eyes and bad skin with big pinprick pores and a network of bro-ken veins around his nose. A yellow Gatorade rested on a deep scar that snaked along his forearm and bubbled at his wrist. I mumbled "Sorry" under my breath, not for earlier, but a more general sorry you give to a stranger for no reason.

When I walked out into the parking lot, I didn't feel like a new woman at all; I felt the same, maybe a little worse. I quietly rehearsed how I would tell Mona about it so that I could dis-charge it from my mind and move on. But I had no time—the man approached me, waving.

"Hi," he said. From up close I could tell he was trouble. He smelled like yeast, like something had fermented inside his mouth.

"Hello," I said while walking away. It took about twenty steps before I realized he was following me, or just walking in the same direction. I didn't want to make any assumptions even though part of me knew it was bad; I could feel it. Parts of my body began shutting down prematurely in preparation for the end. My eyelids grew heavy, and I so badly wanted to stop and lie down in the grass.

When I looked behind me, I could see him also looking back, as if someone was following him or us, like we were in this together. I tried to pick up the pace to distance myself from that narrative. I looked around in disbelief at how average the day was, how no one seemed to notice what was happening. I was still holding my coffee cup, which gave off too casual a vibe and failed to communicate the danger I was in, so I tossed it into a nearby flowerbed. A city bus whirred around the corner, blowing hot air in my face. A mother pushed a stroller past me, forcing me briefly onto the grass. I considered screaming, "Help!" but I didn't think anyone would. I heard a woman scream for help once and I just stood there, waiting for it to pass like a fire alarm. A man in a slow-moving vehicle had been following her, taunting her, alternating between sweet apologetic pleas and violent threats. What was I going to do about it? Several men had been standing nearby with their arms vigilantly crossed, but none of them meant it. No one helped her; they just wanted a show. I didn't stick around long enough to see what happened.

I could have called someone, but I didn't know where to direct them and I couldn't afford to stop and retrieve my phone from my bag. The man picked up the pace to beat a yellow light but then kept running, as if he had just discovered running was an option. I too began to run, at first quickly, then slowing myself down to a more manageable long-distance pace. At a certain point I forgot I was being chased and it just felt like exercise. I ran across a busy intersection, and once I reached the other side, I could see him in the distance: he was bent over, resting against his knees, squeezing his abdomen in pain. I could see his chest expanding and contracting with air. He'd given up. He couldn't go any farther.

I kept running; I didn't want to stop. My body was humming with caffeine and adrenaline. Pedestrians moved out of my way; groups of tourists and families separated on the sidewalk to clear a path as if they could all tell I was running for my life—not my old life but my new life that had just begun. I ran past the sushi restaurant that gave me food poisoning, past the laundromat and the sidewalk café where Liam refuses to tip because a computer takes your order. After several blocks I took a left toward Mona's apartment and spotted her car parked in the driveway like a mirage. She was on the front porch, waving at me as if she'd been waiting for my arrival. I collapsed at her feet and tried to catch my breath.

"What happened to you?" she asked.

"I did it," I said.

"Did what?"

"But then he chased me!"

"Who chased you?"

"I got away!" I said. My legs were trembling. I hadn't noticed my eyes welling up with tears until I blinked them away and she absorbed them into her sleeve.

"You sure you lost him?"

"I'm sure," I said, panting performatively.

"You've gotta be more careful next time!" she said, scooping my hair from my face and loosely twisting it into a bun. The moment she let go, it unraveled, chunks of it falling into my mouth. I let it stick to my spit; I didn't brush it off.

I was bludgeoned by those words: *next time*. There would

be a next time. We both knew it. She said she was late for yoga and had to go but that she'd call me later. She asked, once more, if I was okay. I nodded heroically.

I stayed on her front step a little while longer, trying to force more tears out of my eyes, but they were dry. I tried coaxing them out with a little whimper, but it came out as a laugh. I covered my mouth. I thought about calling Liam, but he hates the phone and we've promised not to call each other unless someone's died. And I hadn't died; I was more alive than I'd ever been. Instead I got up and walked back in search of the man, hoping to find him, hoping to accept whatever might happen once I did. It didn't even feel like a choice. I live in a world of consequence and it's foolish to think otherwise.

I walked slowly and deliberately in the direction of my fate, paying attention to everything I could. I saw a billboard for a movie about a woman who falls in love with a dolphin. No one understands their love. Below the billboard, a husky woman wearing oversize headphones was dancing to a song only she could hear. Anytime someone honked, she performed a raise-the-roof gesture in appreciation. On the next block, a teenager was selling fruit behind a multicolored umbrella. He was playing a game on his phone, and every time he won, a little song played. Towering palms lined the street, and despite the wind, they wouldn't budge. When I reached the intersection, the man was gone. Of course he was.

Can't seem to let go of the dream of being
discovered at the mall

Ever look at your closet and think, *I am a stranger
to myself*

Arranging to have NO WORRIES IF NOT! THANKS SO
MUCH!! etched on my tombstone

My idea of success is just knowing no one in my
life is currently mad at me

Unsolved Mysteries: bruises on my leg edition

My spiritual philosophy: "Thoughts aren't real,
let them pass like clouds in the sky," but also
"Thoughts manifest your reality and steer the
course of your fate," okay, good luck!

Right after I read an inspirational quote online I
think, *Wow, I will remember that forever*, and then
never do

The Intruder

When I got my friend Leon's text to come to an art opening in Culver City, I was in the middle of reading an article on "How to Wear Hats Fearlessly" and applying body lotion to my face because I had run out of face lotion, so I was, by all accounts, extremely free. I don't even own a hat but a part of me hoped there might be people there wearing hats and acting like there was nothing different about them, and I wanted to observe the kind of behavior required to do such a thing.

When Leon arrived to pick me up, he didn't get out of his car; he just honked his horn incessantly over the sound of his muffler's heaving death rattle. I used to hurry, but not anymore. Over the years, our friendship had settled and congealed into the more brutal intimacy of siblings, sparing all niceties.

Nothing else in my life could offer me that, not even my real siblings, who now seemed like total strangers to me. I got in, and he gave me a half-hearted hug and told me my deodorant was giving him a headache, even though I'd never worn deodorant in my life.

We arrived late. Almost all the people who had been wearing hats were now holding those hats in their hands, which meant that they were either too hot or not ready to fully commit to the look. Very few people could; I made a note of this. A tall man wearing wiry glasses and a public-radio merch tee waved in our direction, and just as I asked, "Do you want some gum—" Leon was gone.

I did a ceremonious lap and drank a room-temperature beer, then found Leon absentmindedly leaning against a mixed-media collage and talking to two blond women from his yoga class. I stood and waited to be introduced. I waited for the newness of the moment to wear off, but it would not wear off. The last time I felt this invisible was when I took mushrooms and went to IKEA with my college roommate and got lost so I sought refuge in a tiny village of Chinese paper lanterns and waited to be found. People had shopped around me, as if I didn't exist. I don't remember how I made it home.

Eventually the blonder blonde announced they were headed to a bar down the street and asked Leon to join them. Leon turned to me and mouthed *Sorry,* grotesquely contorting his face to communicate how badly he felt. How truly pained he was to have to leave me like this. *Good luck,* I thought, flashing him a clownish grin. In the ten years we'd known each other, neither one of us had graduated from the other, despite our best efforts. New friendships required us to be interesting people, but neither one of us could keep up the performance for very long. Dutifully I pulled out my phone and said something about how I was tired, except that I was not tired. I had just taken a 5-hour Energy, and I still had three hours of energy left. Leon then kissed me on both cheeks, even though he had never been to Europe, and took off.

I got home and tried to fall asleep, but my mind was too wired. I stayed up and thought about everything I could remember to think about. I thought about whether I was an uglier version of an attractive celebrity or a prettier version of an average woman. I thought about whether I'd already met the person I would spend the rest of my life with and if I had to choose right at that moment, who would I pick? A name appeared in my mind and it surprised me. I didn't even think I had feelings for this person, but I decided not to question it. It kind of made sense, come to think of it. I thought about emailing this person but knew it'd be best to wait until morning.

Then I heard it: a noise. An outside noise. It sounded like the panicked rustling of someone too eager to keep quiet. At first I did that thing where I decided it was the wind, covered my ears, and forgot about it. I couldn't believe how effective that was. What if I just covered my ears the next time something bad happened? What if that was all I'd ever had to do but instead I just made everything more complicated for myself? Then, just as I thought it was over, I heard it again: left, right, left, right, left, right, and so on.

I didn't know what to do, so I slowly pulled my knees toward my chest, rolled to my side, and courageously rose from bed. This felt more real than it had moments earlier, back when it was the wind. Life was simpler then. Standing complicated things; standing meant walking, and walking into what? Standing world felt different; in standing world, people died in unspeakable ways, often without warning. In standing world, men cried. They cried because they wanted to do bad things and there was nothing anyone could do about it. They tried counseling, they meditated, but still they longed to cut soft necks clean across. I thought about my life, about how stupid it was and continued to be. I thought about how I had never known love but could roughly imagine it and, from what I could gather, it was heaven. I thought about my breasts and how so few people had touched them, how I had barely touched them myself.

The noise persisted in a back-and-forth pacing motion. Step, step, step, pivot, and so forth. As if on instinct, I too began to pace around my living room as I recited the Canadian anthem in French, then in English for the parts I forgot in French. It was the first song that came to mind, as if I were invoking some ancient battle cry. I hadn't sung it since my elementary school days in rural Ontario, yet there it was, lodged in some dark fold of my brain, waiting to be unearthed for this very moment. *"We stand on guard for thee!"* I sang, with my hand on my heart. After three Canadian anthems, I waited to hear the sound again, and there was nothing. I stood for an extra twenty minutes to be sure. Finally I drew the curtains and peered out the window. No one was out there. I unlocked the front door and poked my head out. All clear. I locked the door and barricaded it with a fake Eames chair, then returned to bed and tried to sleep, but instead of sleep I played out every possible break-in scenario in my mind, in both English and French, until the sun came up.

The next morning, I got out of bed and stood in front of my bathroom mirror, splashing water on my face like they do in skin-care commercials—with the abandon of someone who truly loves themselves, someone who is glad to be alive. I wondered who it could have been out there. Was it some-one I had wronged? I had wronged so many people in my life-time, some intentionally but most accidentally. Little wrongs left unresolved and compounded over time that now seemed unforgivable: all the calls I'd never returned, all those times I told someone they had something in their teeth when they had nothing in their teeth, or that one time I lost my cousin Anthony at the mall and pretended I hadn't for an entire day until he showed up at his mother's doorstep the next morning missing a shoe and with a speech impediment that would never fully fade. He must be in his early twenties by now.

I walked outside and into my yard, which was a small com-munal grassy patch designated for smokers and for small dogs to urinate on, but it was barely used. Most of my neighbors were old and stayed indoors, so I marked my territory with a lawn chair and a clothesline strung between two lemon trees. No one seemed to mind. I crouched down and picked up a handful of dirt from the ground and smelled it. I plucked a ripe lemon off a branch and pressed it against my cheek, then rolled it around my face with my eyes closed, hoping to communi-cate with its energy. "What did you see?" I whispered. When I opened my eyes, I noticed a crushed snail near my doormat. Not regular crushed—pulverized. Someone was sending me a message. When my neighbor Linda walked by, I didn't men-tion it to her. This was none of her business. We had a shared understanding never to engage in small talk, out of respect. Our mutual avoidance was, in a way, more intimate. Free from the tyranny of unnecessary chatter, we exchanged nods.

I explained what had happened to Leon over breakfast at the faux-retro diner he loves because he swore he saw an Olsen twin there once. When I asked him which one, he got defensive and said, "Doesn't matter." He was staring at his phone, and when I finished my story, he asked me if it was all a dream. Then he started telling me about a recurring dream he had about making out with his brother. "I don't know it's him when I'm doing it." Leon's friend Dale showed up and apologized for being late. Dale worked with Leon at a bar in Koreatown called Beverly's and still lived with his parents. He told people it was because they were sick, but Leon said he met them once and they seemed perfectly fine.

"Bro, check this one out: Seventy-nine Porsche 930 Turbo, asking one hundred Gs," said Dale. Dale and Leon were the kind of guys you'd see showing up to classic car meetups without cars of their own. In other words, total losers. A better person would get up and walk away. But I am not better; in some ways, I'm much worse. When Leon went to the bathroom, Dale began telling me about dolphins. "They have two stomachs," he said, "and they get periods," as if he'd never talked to a woman before. As he talked, I softened my gaze and visualized myself back in my room. I'm surprised more people don't do this— you can think about whatever you want and watch it in your mind like a movie. I'm very discreet, too; I could do it right in front of you and you'd never know.

I visualized myself back in my room, listening to the sound of hot, sour breathing outside my window. It sounded like this: *haaah. haaah. haaah. haaah.* I try to get up but can't; each *haaah* is like an invisible force pushing me deeper into my mattress. The *haaah*s are coming from a man in a ski mask standing before me. He climbs on top of me and presses the full weight of his body onto mine. His breath smells metallic, like pennies. At first the weight feels nice, like a heavy wool blanket. I almost enjoy it until I hear bones snapping. I am flattening under his weight, which now feels dense and unmovable, like a giant boulder. I focus on making myself as inhospitable as I can. I lower my body temperature to below freezing, forcing my body hair to sprout into thousands of prickly quills. When that doesn't work, I tell him I love him. I tell him I want to die and, if anything, it's happening too slowly, so could he please get on with it? He laughs and tells me I smell bad. Even in fantasies, I worried about this. As I die, I say goodbye to all the things I love most. I can get to only the first three: my niece, coffee, and swimming pools.

"And they have their own language, too," Dale continued. I was startled by the sound of Dale's voice and returned to myself, disoriented. I took a sip of orange juice to calm down. A text popped up on my phone from Leon, who was sitting across from me: *you're blushing!!! busted!!!*

I rolled my eyes and excused myself to the bathroom but instead kept walking until I got to my car. I couldn't stop thinking about the man and when he'd come back and how I couldn't stop him even if I tried. Even if I moved to another city, I had a feeling he would find me. From the car, I called my mother and told her about it. "It sounded like this: *haaah haaah haaah*." I breathed heavily into my phone.

"This happened to your cousin Lacey," my mother said. "Same thing with the breathing. Turns out it was a sinus infection." She couldn't hear me over the sound of her dishwasher.

In the weeks that followed, nothing happened. Not even the wind. I placed a knife under my bed and waited. Next to the

knife were a pair of slip-on shoes and a whistle. Knowing they
were there brought me comfort. Up until now, my life's purpose
had been idling in the shadows, but here it was, so obvious to
everyone but me. I had a life valuable enough for someone else
to want to take from me. I was a precious thing. I needed to stay
vigilant. The world around me was a sensory banquet; I registered whatever stimuli I could as potential evidence. I became
attuned to the texture of every sound: the crunchiness of a leaf,
the mating call of a spotted dove, the sloshy hum of my neighbor's washing machine. I practiced visualizations in my mind
to anticipate various break-in scenarios. Sometimes I was covered in sores, emitting foul, toxic gas from every orifice. Other
times I was invisible, passing easily through walls, hiding in
vents and shower drains. With enough effort, I believed I could
will each state energetically. I began telling more people about
the man in case I went missing one day. "And it went like this:
haaah haaah haaah," I explained at my sister's potluck dinner,
and all the women nodded and said, "You know, that happened
to me once." I didn't believe them. Women do that—they like
to relate.

You'd think over time I'd give up hope, call it a fluke. That's
exactly what he'd want me to do. The more I thought of the
man, the more I felt I knew him. I couldn't explain it, but the
act felt personal, like a cry for help. I'd done it myself before;
slowly and dramatically picked up loose produce from a torn
grocery bag, hoping a pedestrian or passing car might see me
and hurry over to help. I wondered if he was trying to tell me
something and if I was the only person in the world who could
understand him. I laughed at how much he reminded me of my
father, a mostly absent alcoholic whose presence filled me with
dread and longing. He once threw an uncooked chicken at my

head, then scooped up my small child body in his big, veiny arms and pleaded with me not to cry, said it was an accident. I'd never felt safer than when he tenderly blotted my head with a wet rag and said, "You're fine, don't be a baby."

When I left my apartment during those crucial first weeks, I conducted myself as if the man were watching me at all times. I searched for him without knowing who I was looking for. In order to do this, I had to pretend that every man was him, and if that man was holding a baby, then he was the baby, too. Certain women were him, and so were pets and insects as well as planes flying overhead. I walked around like a cop, slowly and deliberately. I spit gum on the sidewalk and memorized license plates. At the drugstore, I bought supplies I knew I had no real use for but that made me seem prepared: protein bars, rubbing alcohol, batteries. In the parking lot, I scared off a group of pigeons by running into them, yelling, "Caw! Caw!" I'd never felt so free. Under the watchful eye of a monster, I was invincible.

I was out on one of my routine supply runs when my phone alarm buzzed. I had to hurry home to get ready for my date with Dale. Why would I go out with him? Lots of reasons. For starters, I don't like myself very much, so when other people do, it's as if they know something about me that I don't, and they suddenly become interesting to me. Leon had told me that Dale thought I was *hot* and to let me know that. He then asked Leon to change it to *beautiful*, but he refused. I thought Dale was gross and most likely suffering from some undiagnosed mental condition, but I needed someone to practice my break-in drills with. That was the only way to know for sure if I could handle it.

When I got home, I took a long shower, scrubbing every

part of my body with a lemon-scented body wash. Then I put on a white blouse and admired myself in the mirror, not for how beautiful I could be for someone else but for how beautiful I was for no one, how my beauty didn't need a beholder. Dale would do it wrong anyway; he would focus on the wrong things—my breasts, for example—and skip the best parts: my earlobes, which are perfect and squishy and pink. Or the moles on my arms, which remind me of the markings of an exotic bird.

Here, texted Dale. I made him wait for several minutes to establish dominance. I didn't want to give myself away by coming off as too eager or remotely interested. After a few minutes he texted: *It's Dale.* Shortly after, he added: *Leon's friend??*

It was time.

Dale took me to a fancy bistro where the waiters all spoke with French accents, even though some of them weren't French. Some accents were better than others, but you could always tell which were real and which were fake.

"They're actors," he said, whispering over his menu.

"That makes sense, most actors wait tables," I explained. "Have some," I said, sliding over a glass of wine to test his obedience.

"I don't drink," he said. Leon had mentioned Dale was Mormon, but I had already sensed it from his starchy short-sleeve dress shirt.

I put my hand underneath the table and rested it on his knee. "Would you try it for me? Please, I won't tell anyone."

Dale looked left and right to check if God was watching and took a sip.

"Do you like it?" I asked.

He nodded, adding that he felt "a little lightheaded."

"Why don't we go back to my place and you can rest on my sofa for a little while?" I said.

Dale motioned to a waiter. "Monsieur!" he said, writing his signature in the air. When the bill arrived, I half-heartedly shuffled through my purse while he paid for my drink with his parents' credit card. This small display of assertiveness was oddly reassuring.

When we got back to my apartment, Dale asked for a glass of water and sat down on my sofa. I wanted him to feel comfortable, so I said, "It's hot in here, you want to take that off? I don't care, I'll do it, too." He seemed unfazed by my offer, as if he'd spent his entire life following instructions from people who did not have his best interest in mind. I unbuttoned my blouse, revealing a beige satin bra. Soon we were both sitting shirtless on my sofa, acting like two people who still had shirts on.

"How did you learn so much about cars?" I asked. As he spoke, I took the glass of water from him and pulled his arm to stand. I pressed my hands against his clammy palms and interlaced our fingers. He kept talking, shyly orating the pros and cons of leasing versus buying. I gently swayed back and forth. He tried to kiss me and I pushed him away.

"Do you want to try something?" I asked.

Dizzy from the dancing "and all the wine," he said, "Sure."

I massaged his shoulders and told him about my plan. I told him about the window and the ski mask and the breathing. I told him why it was important, using words like *epidemic* and statistics like *one in four*. I wanted him to know that what he was about to do was vital and potentially lifesaving. He straightened his posture, suddenly realizing the magnitude of the exercise and his role within it. We began.

"Okay, so you've gotta do it like this: *haaah haaah haaah haaah*. Do you want to try it first?"

"Like this?" he asked, breathing hoarsely.

"You got it," I said, "just like that."

I handed him a blue ski mask and told him to go outside while I lay on my back in bed. He stood on the other side of the window and waited for my cue.

"When I cough, you can start, okay?"

I couldn't hear him from underneath the ski mask, but he gave me a thumbs-up. It took him forever to climb through my window; he entered arms first as if he were diving, then hoisted each leg over inelegantly while mumbling words of encouragement to himself: "C'mon, Daley boy, you got this, easy . . . almost there" and so forth. Once he got through my window, I told him to just stand there for a minute and look at me. My body tensed up, even though I knew it was fake, because it felt real, more real than I'd imagined it would. He stood there, quietly clearing his throat from "inhaling the mask fuzzies."

"Perfect, now walk toward me and take off my pants."

Protected by the anonymity of his mask, he grew confident and uttered "Bitch" under his breath. Embarrassed, he immediately followed with "Sorry."

He sat on the edge of my bed and unclasped my bra, then slowly unbuttoned my jeans and pulled them down to my ankles. His eyes bulged and he froze, forgetting what he was supposed to do next. He just sat there, staring at me.

"Come here," I said with my arms outstretched.

He climbed on top of me and relaxed his muscles. I could feel his heart thudding against my chest.

"Like this?" he asked.

"Yes, just like that," I said, pulling him in as hard as I could.

We lay together in silence, exchanging breaths in up-and-down motions, our chests like crests and troughs. I thought about dolphins. Dale began to cry.

"What's wrong?" I asked.

He pulled the ski mask halfway up. His nose was runny, and it was dripping on my neck.

"Your hair smells like lemons," he said. He wiped his nose on my shoulder. "Lemons," he said again softly.

"I know," I said, stroking his head. "Shhh, I know."

I just held him there like that; I didn't know what else to do.

The only thing that moves a man is when he
watches a documentary about another man
attempting to climb a big rock against all odds

So unsettling to find out what your favorite podcast
host actually looks like. Do not look! You will
never recover!

I feel generous and saintly whenever I let a man tell
me what my name means

Whoever named daddy longlegs is a sick
twisted creep!
Gonna start calling them papa longlegs

A man who is purposely bad at giving massages is
called a massaginist

Me personally? I love to watch dogs take painful
little poops

Tug, Spin, Release

"What if *this* is hell?" I'd been repeating it to myself ever since Heather's little sister, Claire, offered up her grim diagnosis of reality. It was a passing philosophical musing from a slightly buzzed twentysomething wearing cowboy boots and a sash that read BRIDE TRIBE, but it stuck with me.

"You mean the Pueblo Bonito Pacifica?" I joked, referring to the cheesy all-inclusive resort we had booked for Heather's bachelorette weekend in Cabo. Our room had gaudy Spanish-style decor and faded cream carpeting that had an Orange County divorcée–type ambiance to it, but no one cared because we needed it only for the express purpose of doing drugs and sleeping. I wanted to remind Claire that this hell seemed fairly benign compared to most people's, like the arthritic cleaning lady who had come by to unclog the toilet for a second time that day. But I knew what she meant: everyone suffers, but how that suffering is doled out is unique to each person. I was comforted by the thought and nearly offered the platitude about being kind because everyone is fighting a hard battle, but I didn't know the exact phrasing and had just taken two cookie edibles and was too self-conscious to get it wrong in front of the group. I'd met Heather through my friend Amelia, who couldn't travel due to health issues, making me a second-tier invite. I was fine with this and had committed myself to consuming twice as much of everything in Amelia's honor. It's what she would have wanted.

I was struggling to get into a rhythm with the other women, mostly because my mind was elsewhere. I was waiting for an email that was going to change my life, but the cell reception was weak and my inbox wouldn't refresh no matter how many times I tugged and released the screen. Days earlier, on a whim, I'd submitted a few poems about birds and spit and the texture of velvet to a prestigious artist-residency program in Upstate New York. The prize involved a monthlong stay in a private cabin, which was enough time for me to finally establish myself as an artist and then figure out a way to stay there for the rest of my life. I could work as a farmhand in exchange for room and board and devote the rest of my time to writing and having deep conversations and casual sex with like-minded people.

I'd been writing poems for as long as I could remember, and my only plan up until now had been to eventually die so that my work could be discovered posthumously. I thought of my poetry as my own personal *Voyager* floating through space and time, awaiting contact. My poems wouldn't even have to be great since people tend to be more forgiving of the dead. As a poet, I could think of nothing more romantic.

But the residency was much bigger than that; it was my ticket out. Being a middle school phys ed teacher hadn't been my original plan. I thought I'd be a gymnast, like one of those muscular girls who run around twirling ribbons in the air, whatever they're called. Then I turned twelve and my boobs mushroomed practically overnight. Even then, I knew it was over for me. No one aspires to teach gym; it's just something that happens to you through a series of poor choices and an inability to grasp even basic math.

The funniest part is that I would've never known about the residency if I hadn't overheard Margaret, the English teacher, discussing it in the break room. Apparently she was invited last year and stowed away in a cabin for six weeks, which makes sense, because she suspiciously returned for the fall semester with an entirely new nose. Convenient. Margaret thought she was hot shit because she graduated from an Ivy League and made people call her doctor for some reason, yet there we were in the Eastmont Middle School women's restroom, separated only by a thin partition, desperately waiting for the other to leave. I wasn't built for academia; the girls at school terrified me—they only ever wore sports bras and nothing else, and if I made a comment, they accused me of being a pervert and threatened to sue for sexual harassment. The boys reeked of Juul and did nothing to hide their erections, which were constant and hypnotizing. I couldn't take my eyes off them, if you want to talk about hell. I wrote poems about how their basketball shorts flapped in the breeze patriotically like flags, but I never showed them to anyone. No one had any idea I could write at all. I hoped that in the coming weeks, I would find out for myself.

Between the email and me were a turquoise infinity pool and a realm of endless possibilities. I did a swan dive into the deep end of the resort pool and swam around inelegantly, splashing like a toddler while the other girls watched because they all refused to get their hair wet. I'll admit, having no Wi-Fi access for the weekend was exhilarating; it meant I could live in a fantasy world of *what if?* for a little while longer. I suddenly understood the point of believing in heaven or saving dessert for later: there was no better drug than anticipation. I imagined it as my reward for getting through the weekend; the bridal-game theatrics and constant socializing would've been unbearable without my little hope and the right combination of canned wine and pharmaceuticals, which produced a kind of pleasant fugue state that made the weekend go by quickly, like a dream in a power nap.

It's not like I didn't want to tell them about my plan; I'd actually tried to bring it up the night before, sometime after the second round of spicy palomas, but everyone just kept asking me how Amelia was doing and if there was anything they could do, etc. I told them that all she wanted was for us to have fun and to live life to the fullest. Heather lifted her chalice for a cheers and made a speech about how lucky she felt to be surrounded by so many incredible women.

"So well put," said Jess.

"You have a way with words," Claire added.

I suddenly hated Heather. Words were *my* thing. *I* had a way with them. I waited for the right moment to recite a poem out loud. I imagined their faces softening in awe, the background music and chatter stopping, and time itself collapsing into the present moment. All eyes on me, for once. One of them would slow clap and the rest would join in. They would beg for more, but I'd feign modesty and say, "That's enough for one night! Maybe tomorrow." But I was thwarted by Candace, a retired pageant girl, who started telling a story about her secret email correspondence with her husband's mistress, thus setting the evening's mood, which included Claire's secret abortion and subsequent reconciliation with Jesus, followed by Jess's body dysmorphia. Then once again, back to Candace and her base-less fear that everyone in the group secretly hated her and talked about it whenever she left the room. The group hurried to comfort her, making a big show of how much they valued her, how none of them could believe she wanted to be *their* friend and so on.

The night quickly devolved into a teary-eyed indictment of All Men Ever, beginning with their fathers, who either loved them too much or not enough. Everyone's stories began to blend together. I watched as each woman drove her emotional car off the lot; the potency of each revelation depreciated as soon as it had been said aloud. I was glad I kept mine to myself. No one pressured me to participate, but I caught wind of a rumor going around that I was planning some sort of big surprise because I was "acting weird" and kept wandering off from the group. I hadn't planned anything, so when the fireworks erupted on the final night, I panicked and told Heather I had arranged for them in her honor. In a way, it was a gift. She deserved a fantasy of her own. They all did.

I instinctively checked my email as soon as my return flight landed. It was still too early for me to be getting an email, but a part of me hoped that whoever read my work had been so com-pletely blown away that they couldn't help themselves. It seemed insane that life-changing news could fit inside the body of an email. Emails were for birthday e-vites and seasonal sales, not for this. Imagining it sandwiched between spam wire-transfer requests and UPS shipping confirmations disturbed me. What about a gold-embossed letter in the mail or a man who comes to your door holding balloons? I quickly scanned through my twenty-three unread emails, and not one of them contained the subject line "Congratulations." I let out a loud sigh of relief that I'd been holding in all weekend. I wanted to be showered and well rested when I opened it. I wanted to put on a nice blouse. It would've been disrespectful and reckless to open it at the airport, among the noises and the smells of tourists and their distant relatives waving at arrivals.

I lost the bachelorette group at baggage claim and practically ran to the taxi stand with a current of adrenaline pumping inside me. Maybe my chronic anxiety wasn't anxiety at all but a state of prolonged anticipation for my true purpose to reveal itself. Maybe my hope had gone unchecked for too long and had degenerated into a neurosis. I was awake now, though; I was paying attention. All it took was some time away to clear my head.

When I got home, I unpacked my suitcase and threw everything in the laundry, which had a domino effect: I decided to empty the contents of my closet and lay it all out on the floor so I could look at everything I owned. Something about coming home from a trip made me reassess my entire life. My time away gave me a fresh perspective and confirmed my suspicion that I wasn't fulfilling my potential and needed to make some moves. I would begin by purging. I didn't have much, but I could always have less. I threw my open-toed shoes in the Donate pile along with a puffy down-filled coat and a graphic T-shirt that read CAFFEINE QUEEN that I'd never had the courage to wear in public. I tossed artifacts of a past life: a body-con dress, low-cut jeans embroidered with rhinestones (why?), and a lone platform stiletto that I had no memory of buying. *Who am I?* I thought while pushing my fist through a pair of neon fishnet stockings. I filled three large trash bags and moved on to scrubbing the scuffs on my walls with a Magic Eraser and stripping the bed to wash the sheets. Sitting on my bare mattress, I reviewed my social media profiles for no other reason than to remind myself I existed. I liked being contained safely inside a grid, a living avatar of a self.

What if *this* is hell?

"Can you read this?"

A wispy little voice startled me so badly, I screamed and threw a shoe in its direction.

"I got a concussion. I'm pretty sure—my vision is blurry." It was my roommate, Tom, whom I had forgotten existed. He was holding a tub of margarine. "I can't see the expiration date," he said.

"It expired last week," I said. I thought if I didn't acknowledge his concussion, he'd leave my room. He was always informing me of some new ailment he had.

"I was picking up an olive from under the table when my phone rang, and I sprang up and hit my head really hard."

"That sucks," I said.

"I've been in bed since you left."

"Why don't you go to the doctor?"

"I don't have health insurance."

"Right. Bummer." I sighed.

"Yeah, I just can't afford it," he explained.

I wish I could say I found Tom on the internet, but I didn't.

I'd known him for years before he moved in—not super well, just well enough to know he wouldn't kill me and that if it ever came down to it, I could easily overpower him. He had respiratory issues and slow reflexes; it wouldn't even be that hard. We'd met at an improv class years ago, and I'd sometimes watch him do stand-up comedy on Tuesday nights at Tempo Cantina. He joked about his psoriasis and his estranged father's new family. I thought he was funny in a sad way, but offstage he was just sad. No one told me this about comedians. Occasionally I would hear what sounded like a conversation happening in his bedroom until he'd start repeating the same sentence over and over and I'd realize he was recording a video of himself. "Hey guys!" Pause. Cough. "What's up, my dudes!" Pause. "What up, what up? Please like and subscribe. Yo, like and subscribe or I'll kill myself. Jk, jk, I love you guys." I considered it low-grade domestic abuse.

The longer he lived with me, the less I knew him or wanted to know him, and the distance between us grew over time like mold. When he moved in, he'd assumed we'd be more like best friends, but that seemed like too much of a commitment considering how often we passed each other on the way to the bathroom or the kitchen. Tom's life was a series of unfortunate and self-inflicted tragedies. Comedy wasn't going so well, and his dog, Churro, had recently gone missing. Tom had gotten stomach ulcers from stress and started drinking more than ever, which led to weight gain and cystic acne. No one wanted to have sex with him, which wasn't even so bad because his antidepressants made him impotent anyway. I wasn't sure how much of this was true, but I wanted nothing to do with it.

"Sorry to hear that," I said.

"It's the life I chose." He shrugged.

I checked my email before returning to my piles. It was Sunday, so I kept my expectations low. There was an email from Heather to the bachelorette thread thanking everyone for an amazing time, followed by responses from the other girls, little inside jokes about diarrhea and hot tubs. I swiftly deleted it, annoyed by the implication that we would all keep in touch. We were strangers, united only by our separate relationships with Heather, which was not enough of a shared interest to sustain a friendship.

Deleting felt good. I opened an email from the assistant vice principal alerting me to another student's near-fatal exposure to nuts. "For the safety and well-being of our student body, please help us in maintaining a nut-free environment." Delete! There was another email from an outraged mother who'd obtained an incriminating photo of a discarded bag of trail mix in my trash bin. "Traces of nut particles remain in the atmosphere for hours; this behavior is wildly irresponsible. If something happens to my son, there will be blood on your hands." Jimmy's mom was so paranoid, and it was extra disappointing to find out they were in cahoots since I thought Jimmy and I were cool; we were both *Seinfeld* fans and quoted it constantly. I guess you never really know a person. Delete.

After that, I pressed SELECT ALL and deleted all my emails, even the old ones I had kept thinking that one day, on my deathbed, I'd be bored enough to revisit them and glad I'd saved them all. All I wanted was a clean white space of nothing: unblemished by the past and primed for the future.

After that, I couldn't stop. I kept refreshing my email dozens, sometimes hundreds, of times a day. I barely noticed I was doing it; I'd be doing something else, putting in a contact or driving on the freeway, and suddenly I'd be mindlessly pulling my thumb down and refreshing. There was nothing, but there would always be a brief moment when it could be something, and I wanted to live inside that moment forever. For a couple weeks, my life glinted with an ephemeral quality. Something was about to happen. As with any high-functioning addict, everything, including my job, became more bearable. Wiping down wrestling mats and collecting used jerseys wasn't as much of a chore anymore. I was like a ghost floating above my body—*Who is this woman on her hands and knees, scrubbing wildly? Look at her go!* I was teaching my students about consent and how periods work with gusto, knowing that my life had become the eve of another life, a better one. Farewell, demons! Farewell, little shits! Except Brian: he was autistic and a real sweet boy, a total gentleman. I might've taken him with me if the circumstances were different.

One Friday afternoon, I was checking my email while the class ran laps around the track. Only a few students actually ran; most walked, and some just sat in the grass, also looking at their phones. The students and I shared an unspoken agreement that if I looked at my phone, they could also look at their phones, but I drew the line at sexy photoshoots. One time Mandy posted a photo of herself jutting her butt out on the soccer field with me in the background, napping on the bleachers in plain view. I asked her to delete it, and she said I was infringing on her rights and started quoting the Constitution incorrectly until I grew tired and gave up.

While I thumbed away at the screen, a fight broke out between two boys in the class. I let it go on for a few seconds, hoping that whatever they were trying to work out just needed to be resolved on an animal level and that my interference would ruin the natural order of things. A crowd formed, shouting as the boys tumbled, almost sensually, in the dirt. For a moment I pretended it was for my honor and quietly joined in on the chanting. But then Lisa, the class narc, started filming with her phone, and I screamed, "Enough!" The boys kept going, so I ordered the class to go inside to change and wash up while I figured out what to do. I thought about taking off my clothes to create a distraction or throwing a towel over them like caged birds, but I did neither of those things. I watched for a while until the shop teacher, Mr. Krugman, came outside. I blew my whistle and waved at him for backup. He tossed his cigarette butt and sprinted over like a cop. I could see the vein in his forehead swelling like an erection. Everyone feared Mr. Krugman, including me. There was a rumor going around that he had gone to prison for trafficking exotic animals and had loose affiliations to neo-Nazi groups online, but I had started that last one because he was such an asshole.

"Cut the shit!" he yelled, grabbing one of the boys' legs. I heard low grunts and heavy breathing as I walked away and left them to it. I continued walking all the way to my car, where I briefly dozed in the back seat until I heard the bell ring. I awoke to the disembodied voice of Principal Boyle calling me to the office over the intercom. I assumed it had something to do with giving my witness account of the fight, but there was Jimmy with the school nurse. His face was bloated and red. He looked like an adorable pug.

"Ms. Friedman, are you responsible for setting a rat trap in your classroom?"

The school had a rat infestation, and whenever I asked Rudy the janitor to handle it, he told me that as long as "these shitheads" kept leaving food in their lockers, the rats would keep showing up, no matter what, so there was no point.

"It's a humane trap," I said. I'd set up a little cage with a spoonful of peanut butter as bait.

"You can't bring peanut butter in here. This is a nut-free zone. Look at Jimmy's face."

"Who cares about nuts! We're overrun with rodents!"

"Let Rudy handle that," said Principal Boyle.

"Serenity now!" I joked, shaking my fists in the air, hoping to get Jimmy's attention.

Jimmy kept his eyes on the floor. He knew it wasn't my fault; his reaction had nothing to do with the trap. He'd acquired a taste for peanut M&M's, knowing they could very well kill him. His girlfriend, Pamela, told me about it last week after things got awkward between Jimmy and me. Pamela was a theater kid with an amazing vocal range, but there was some brooding darkness in her that I recognized as a fellow artist. I wanted her to think I was cool, so I'd promised not to say anything. She said it had started out innocently enough, just one or two to see what all the hype was about. Then a couple more. Soon, he was hooked. She said it was thrilling to see how many he could eat before his throat started to close up. If it ever got too intense, he would let her stab him with an EpiPen. "Imagine that kind of passion," she'd said. I wanted that kind of love: to love something so much, it could kill you.

"You're right. I'm sorry, Jimmy," I said, taking the blame. I had no other option. Also what's the worst that could happen to me—I'd get fired? Ha!

"I'm sorry, Ms. Friedman," said Principal Boyle, handing me what looked like a prepared termination letter.

I will admit, I did not see that coming. I had no choice but to take it as another sign that the Universe was clearing the path for my true life's purpose. I wasn't completely delusional; I was aware of the possibility that the residency might not work out. Only five people would be accepted out of thousands of submissions, but I had to act as if I might be one of them. I'd been reading a lot of books on mind power and manifesting abundance in the quantum field. I'd even packed a suitcase and canceled my gym membership and my HBO subscription as a way of saying yes to the Universe. I also planned to delete my email account once it happened. My refreshing days would be over; what a relief.

Amelia took me to lunch the next day to get the full recap of Heather's bachelorette party. So much had happened since then, I could barely remember it.

"What's with you?" she asked.

"What? Nothing."

"Can you put your phone away?" she asked, violently stabbing at a grape tomato in her salad.

"I was just checking something."

"Who is it, Jason?"

His name was an electric shock. The way she said it, too, with her mouth wide open, wet and exposed. Jason and I had dated unofficially for nearly a year until he slowly stopped responding to my messages, so I guess he must have died. I hadn't seen or heard from him in months, rest in peace.

"No, actually," I said.

She smiled with a mouth full of romaine. She looked like a grazing cow. I always suspected she secretly had a crush on Jason but whatever, we were never a couple, so it was none of my business. Weird for her to bring him up, though, no?

"I'm just waiting to hear some news," I said.

"Are you pregnant or something?"

Ha! Impossible. Jason was the last guy I'd slept with, and that was seven months ago, but seriously, why was she harping on him? She knew how sensitive I was. He was the only person I let read my poems, and he said I reminded him of Patti, as in Patti Smith, as if he knew her personally. I took that to mean he thought I was skinny. He liked to refer to our relationship status as "hanging out" because he preferred to take things slow. He approached everything in life with the same excruciating slowness, laboring over an unfinished screenplay and a novel for the last six years. He cited uncompromising perfectionism as one of his best qualities. I think he was waiting to die before he found success, too.

As a sensitive artist, he was moody and unpredictable. If he let me in too much by, say, letting me sleep over, he would over-correct by ignoring me for days without explanation. I would wait and wait for a call or a text. If Amelia or my mom ever called me during those times, I'd get a full-blown panic attack and scream at them for poisoning me with false hope. Sometimes I'd throw my phone across the room and retrieve it like a dog. Other times I'd speak to it lovingly, like an injured bird incapable of understanding human language but somehow able to sense my good intentions. I would've given anything to be with him. I would've died, but not *died* died. I don't know why people say that. Maybe what they really mean is that they'd rather be a stranger to themselves than a stranger to the whole world.

The intensity of being ignored was only matched by seeing his name pop up on my phone. It was an indescribable rush, like finally finding out that God exists and you, of all people, are his favorite. You only get a few of those moments in life, when time stops and everything is easy. Then you spend the rest of it either trying to re-create that moment or trying to forget it ever happened. I don't know which one is worse. I was trying hard to create new moments since all my old ones involved Jason, and I wasn't sure how triumphant getting someone to occasionally penetrate you was.

The last time I saw him, I didn't know it was the last time. Probably because he said, "I'll see you later." I tried contacting him for months and never heard anything. I thought I saw him once on the street, crouching down and tying his shoe. I was driving by, and when I turned my car around, he was gone. A demented part of my brain still thought he was scared because he loved me too much. I started seeing a hypnotherapist who made me perform this whole cord-cutting ceremony to let him go. She instructed me to put on ambient instrumental music and burn incense, but I didn't have any, so I just burned a Febreze deodorizing candle instead. Then she told me to bind my feet with black yarn and remember that time Jason used my bathroom and left a tiny poop floating in the toilet bowl and how gross I thought that was. I don't know if it worked, but when it was over, I felt lighter. I was better, more normal. Like, even if he texted me right now, I wouldn't even flinch; I would be like, *God look at this loser, how pathetic.* Delete! Delete!

"I'm just waiting to hear about an artist-residency thing, whatever, it's boring," I said.

"I didn't know you were into that stuff," she said.

"Yeah well, you never asked." Amelia was diagnosed with breast cancer and spent most of last year in chemotherapy, and suddenly everyone started treating her like a saint. Once I found out she had an 80 percent survival rate, I'd started resenting how everything was always about her.

"Well, I'm asking you now!" Amelia tightened the knot on her babushka. Her hair was growing in patches and she still didn't have any eyebrows. I told myself not to brag about my future until her hair reached bob length.

"I don't want to jinx it," I said. All I wanted to do was go home and stare at my phone.

"I feel the same way. I only have one more surgery to go, just to reposition my nipples," she said.

I was sucking on my smoothie straw and barely listening. I closed my eyes and warmed my face in a block of sunlight like it had been placed there just for me. I pictured the residency based on photos from the website; it was located on an idyllic farm with dogs and chickens and therapeutic mini horses. There were individual cabins and an old Victorian schoolhouse where meals were prepared and served by diabetic grandmothers. I imagined myself seated at a giant oak desk with my glasses sliding down to the base of my nose, journaling about clouds. I'd wear a coiled-snake braid on my head with furious wisps and a long skirt with big tortoiseshell buttons, like a pioneer woman. I wanted my smoothie to go on forever; I could have drowned myself in pureed chocolate banana until I threw up. I started to get teary-eyed just thinking about it: how happy I was but also how sad it was to be this happy over nothing. Over a dream.

"Are you crying?" Amelia asked. "It's not a big deal, my

doctor said there'd be hardly any downtime," she said, rubbing my back.

I wiped my eyes with my shirt. "Oh good, that's good to hear," I said. I'd keep my secret joy in my chest until I could safely enjoy it later on, in the privacy of my own space.

When I came home, Tom was cradling a small wet dog in the hallway.

"He's back, can you believe it?"

"Who?"

"Churro."

The whole apartment smelled like rum and lasagna. Tom swayed with the dog drunkenly. The dog was not Churro. For starters, Churro was a Pomeranian, and this dog was some kind of terrier. I wanted to tell Tom that he'd stolen someone else's dog, but he looked so happy. It was nice to see him like that for a change. In the morning he'd figure it out on his own, but until then I'd let him bear witness to a miracle.

"Never do that again, okay?" I watched Tom shake the tiny animal as he swung from euphoric sobbing to angry scolding. He nuzzled his head against the dog's feral mouth. "Promise?" It was some kind of emotional jazz performance, from hyperventilating to spontaneous giggling, followed by a long, self-indulgent weeping solo. It was all coming out; every emotion perfectly right and justifiably expressed, simply because it was felt. His body couldn't believe this was actually happening. Churro was alive.

"He looks hungry. Let's go find him something to eat, yeah?" I said calmly. I took Tom by the hand and gently guided him into the kitchen. I couldn't tell you the number of times I'd walked Tom to his room after a night of drinking, then rolled him onto his stomach and taken off his shoes while he lay there half dead. I patted Tom's shoulder while he filled the water bowl, using my free hand to check my phone. Knowing the email would arrive at any minute made me so aroused, I had developed a Pavlovian response to the act of tugging the base of the screen and watching the little circle spin and update. Tug, spin, release. More, more, more. Again, again, again. If Tom weren't home, I would have jerked off to it right there on the kitchen floor.

"Do you want a drink?" Tom asked, already pouring one.

"Sure," I said. Knowing I'd probably be moving out soon put me in a celebratory mood. *Farewell, dumpy apartment! Farewell, loser!* I turned on the Bluetooth speaker and played a little up-tempo Steely Dan song. *This is your big debut / It's like a dream come true.* We raised our glasses, which were filled with something brown and perfumy. Tom tried to cheers and missed; his eyes were glossy and he could barely stand upright. Suddenly shy, he put the dog down and crouched on the floor.

"I love you, you know that?" he said, looking away from me.

"Love you too, man," I said.

"No, I mean it."

"Oh."

"You couldn't tell?"

"I thought you were just depressed."

"You're the girl of my dreams!"

He sighed. Fake Churro sensed his distress and came over to comfort him, licking the spittle off the side of his mouth. The old me would have run away. The new me took pity on Tom; she knew what it was like to sit on the floor, begging to be loved. Besides, when he woke up in the morning and realized he had the wrong dog, he would be devastated. I didn't want to add to his anguish; he already had so little to live for. The heat of my phone buoyed me through the uncomfortable silence. I'd be gone soon, and I'd never have to see him again.

"I think you're a cool guy," I said.

"Really?"

"Yeah," I said, squatting down beside him. This was the closest I'd ever felt to Jason. I could see why he liked leading me on; I felt powerful and empty and godlike. I was drunk on my own magnetism and also literally drunk.

I wanted to see how far I could go with it, so I put my face right up to Tom's. His eyes were half-closed and his face was pink and puffy from dehydration. I opened my mouth slightly and waited. He pushed my chin down with his thumb and pressed his lips against my forehead. It was like getting blessed by a priest or a kiss from a baby: a wet nothing. He held me in his embrace and drifted out of consciousness. I rolled him off me and he slumped farther down, his torso bent impossibly to one side like a deflated air mattress.

I went to my room, collapsed on my bed, and rested my phone on my sternum, my body vibrating with purpose. I took the phone and started typing a text message to Jason:

Just thought you should know . . . Delete.

Last night was incredible, baby. Thank you for the Tesla. Oops, wrong number. So embarrassing. Delete.

How are you? Delete.

Listen, I'm totally over what happened with us, I just
wanted to tell you that I'm a big deal now and you'll
probably be seeing my poems in the near future and
REST ASSURED they're not, in any way, about you.
They're about other men, European ones, oligarchs,
and famous athletes with those sculpted Adonis belt
muscles that I said I don't like on guys, but guess
what, I actually do. I live with my new boyfriend
now, he's in the entertainment industry and we share
a dog named Churro. Things are getting pretty seri-
ous. Please don't ever contact me and if you try, I'll
be in Upstate New York writing poems about the
shape of my perfect pink asshole. Select all. Delete!

I got up and went to the bathroom, thinking a change of
scenery would be reason enough for another inbox refresh,
based on nothing other than those stories about celebrities who
seemed to always be in the shower or on the toilet when they
find out they've been nominated for some big award. I sat on
the toilet and eked out a few droplets of pee to make it real. Tug,
spin, release: nothing. I got a text from Amelia asking me to
drive her home after surgery tomorrow: *They said I can't take*
the bus if I'm heavily sedated. I tried not to engage whenever
she was being dramatic.

It was late, so I changed into my pajamas and crawled into
bed. I fell asleep, still clutching my phone in my right hand. I
had a dream where the school's paper shredder was broken and
everyone acted like it was my fault but no one said it out loud. I
tried to fix it, but I had no idea what I was doing, so I offered to
eat everyone's documents, page by page, as punishment for my
ineptitude. At first I tried crumpling them into balls, but they

were too dry to swallow, so I dipped them in water first and that helped. People would say, "Are you sure?" and I'd say, "Are you kidding? They're delicious." Then Jason appeared and handed me his birth certificate. I knew that if I ate it, he would no longer exist. There would be no record of him, and he would disappear from planet Earth. I put it in my mouth and concealed it under my tongue. I couldn't bring myself to swallow.

I woke up mid-dream; it was still night, and everything looked gauzy and blue. Without thinking, I reached for my phone. Tug, spin, release—all in one effortless motion. Two new emails appeared. The first was from my bank, asking if I had just spent forty-seven dollars on compression socks (I had, so what?), and the other had a subject line that read: "Summer Residency Application Results." I thought my eyes were playing a trick on me, so I rubbed them until blood-vessel fireworks obscured my field of vision. I stared blankly at the screen until the sparks settled and there it was again. Oh. I turned the phone facedown on the mattress. *What's the rush?* I thought. It was the middle of the night; what good would it do me to know right now? I could wait a little while longer. I could wait a lifetime.

I looked around my room, comforted by the sameness of it. It was my very own possibility fortress, a time capsule for future generations to visit my humble beginnings before everything changed for me. I looked down at my legs, which were pulsating like an exposed human nerve. I felt a soggy-paper sensation climb up my throat, and I ran to the bathroom sink to try to force it out, but there was nothing. I imagined my insides hardening like dried papier-mâché. I hurled my face into an old beach towel and let out a muffled scream. I did a little lap around my bed, then climbed in slowly as if descending into an ice bath. I fingered the cool plastic rim of my phone case, the flimsy layer protecting the metal container where my future was stored. Then I picked it up and threw it across the room, where it landed softly in a pile of dirty laundry. I stretched my arms and legs out like a starfish, rolled the covers over my head, and went back to sleep.

If I stop scrolling, I will explode like the bus from
Speed

My dream podcast is just overhearing my
boyfriend talk about me in the other room

For every new follower I get, God humbles me with
a new mole

Getting no response in the group thread is actually
very cool and character-building

For every ten-minute meditation, I treat myself to
fourteen hours of internet

When I'm afraid to read an email, I change the font
size to eight points so it looks like a little whisper

I would've picked less-terrible music had I known
my musical preferences would stop evolving after
thirty and that I'd be trapped in a nostalgic hell
loop of my own making for eternity

I feel drunk with righteous godlike power when
someone accidentally sends me a text meant for
someone else

Say it with me: Patreon Industrial Complex

Earth to Lydia

Everyone took turns sharing their most recent purchases with the group. Sinead had brought a four-piece set of wind chimes that were handmade in the Pyrenees, then packaged and shipped from an Etsy shop in Maine. Our instructor, Martin, reminded Sinead that any objects that could be used for meditation purposes were not permitted. Roger, a recovering yogi from El Sereno, said that the sound of clanging wind chimes was deeply triggering, and that he felt Sinead's behavior was problematic for the group. Martin, sensing a breakthrough, encouraged Roger to explore those feelings.

"Go on, tell her how it made you feel."

"She's not taking this seriously. It's all a big joke to her," he said, dodging her placid, benevolent stare.

"Does it make you want to punch her?"

"If I'm being honest, a little."

"Sinead, what do you think about that? Getting punched in the face."

Sinead was leaning against the wall, eating loose home-made granola from a plastic baggie. "I would accept it with grace and love, my brother."

I didn't even know why Roger was here, he seemed fine. All his impulses were intact. I thought about whether I had the guts to punch Sinead and decided that I didn't, but that I would in time. I just had to be patient. Martin explained the importance of violence as an exercise in reclaiming power. He was extremely muscular for his small frame. Whenever he spoke, the vein in his forehead bulged. He worked out almost every day; he liked telling us about what he did and for how long. He was an amateur bodybuilder and studied Krav Maga under a supposed cousin of the master, Imi Lichtenfeld. He explained that he wasn't always this way—in the ashram in India, he'd been dangerously underweight. For seven years he'd swept floors, chanted Sanskrit, and washed the feet of his guru in total devotion to his practice. When he returned to the United States, he expected to meet fellow brothers and sisters of the Buddhist persuasion. It was Los Angeles in the nineties; people were into yoga and juice fasting. Instead Martin felt disoriented and chronically ill from the constant barrage of electromagnetic waves. After a few weeks of sleeping on strangers' couches, he found himself on the streets, until a non-denominational missionary group helped him land a job mixing paints at a hardware store. He liked to joke that he was high at Lowe's. This was one of many jokes he repeated to us. He said he never intended on working but felt that transforming consciousness required him to go straight to the source of human suffering (retail) to change people's hearts from within. He believed that liberating consumers would have a ripple effect of disrupting every aspect of modern life from corporate structuring to international supply chains, Wall Street, and the global economy.

It was in the paint department where he witnessed the way capitalism erodes the human spirit firsthand. Every day, it seemed, people wanted more and more paint. Customers would buy a gallon, then come back for more, covered in it. They could never get enough paint—"Paint to cover their McMansions!" he'd say. His impromptu sermons on the nature of reality started scaring away customers. One woman couldn't decide between Alabaster White or Chantilly Lace White, so he suggested she sit under a tree until she could sense no distinction between her body and the tree, the tree and the earth, the earth and the universe, and only then would the answer reveal itself to her. His supervisor, Dan, eventually reassigned him to inventory. What's worse—Dan mistook his morning meditation for napping. Napping! Martin had had enough. He could no longer function in a dysfunctional society; he had realized that achieving total spiritual enlightenment was too premature. People in the West weren't ready for it yet.

But just as he was about to return to the ashram to count grains of rice for his beloved guru, Swami Sivananda, he fell in love. At first, it was Sharon in Appliances, then Linda, Pam, and Maureen: gorgeous women with long mermaid hair woven in braids, or sometimes permed, or pulled back in loose buns— blondes, brunettes, or some hypnotizing combination of both. In the spirit of compassion, he'd lend assistance to any female employee he noticed attempting to reach for a product on a high shelf; if the woman had already climbed up a stepladder, he would offer to spot her. It occurred to him that he had never been in such close proximity to a woman's butt and felt a primordial urge to place his hands on her backside and squeeze. Surprisingly, none of them recoiled.

Among the staff, he had a reputation for being a loner and a delinquent, which endowed him with an air of mystery. He was intriguing, misunderstood. This clerical error on his social status offered him a banquet of carnal affection from the women on the floor. Once he'd finally touched a woman's butt, explored its buoyancy, the poetry of its curvature—he could not go back to the ashram. Swami Sivananda would not receive him. Touching women's butts was against the rules, even if it was just accidental or over the clothes. But the more butts he encountered, the more the world made sense to him, as is. He soon learned that making large sums of money improves your chances of touching a woman's butt, so he became a quick study: petty online scams just to get him going, then expanding into stocks and real estate. He even took up golf to network with powerful businessmen, pulling up in luxury cars paid for with stolen credit cards to look the part. The appearance of wealth afforded him access to a certain lifestyle and elite connections; "Fake it till you make it" was a motto he claimed to have invented. He applied a similar logic to working out, grooming, and dressing fashionably. Women loved the smell of his designer cologne: a concoction of pheromones, endangered tiger semen, and vanilla extract, illegally imported from Russia. Slowly, over time, he regained his senses and a lust for life. Wanting made him feel like a human again: not just a spirit incarnating a vulnerable meat suit, but a real, full-blooded American man. For example, Martin loved documenting his physical transformation by posting shirtless photos of himself on the internet. He loved getting comments and he loved commenting back.

Nice guns! an anonymous internet user commented.

Thanks!!!! #SWEATSACRIFICESUCCESSALLDAY, he'd reply with his signature hashtag that was too long to read. He sometimes added additional hashtags like #Nike #Adidas #Reebok #WorldCup #UFC #Olympics #ESPN hoping someone would one day notice and sponsor him.

But the Universe had bigger plans. Flexing in front of the gym's full-length mirror, he finally recognized himself. His happiness quickly soured into grief for the years he lost, and he dropped into a painful one-armed plank position to keep from crying. He suddenly wondered if full-blown ego annihilation had gone too far and if there were other people out there whose enlightenment had a negative impact on their quality of life. Cultivating one's soul consciousness made more sense against the serene backdrop of lily-pad ponds and ancient ruins, but America was spiritually impotent. The ego was its crowning achievement, its means of survival, its greatest evolutionary innovation. This led him to develop a program meant to re-assimilate ego-deficient beings back into society, through a combination of exposure therapy, role play, and aerobic workouts. We were the first group.

I waited for my turn in the sharing circle and looked down at my purchase, an overpriced ceramic dish from the popular home-decor giant Crate & Barrel. It was inscribed with the word *inspire* and an image of a blue whale. After careful examination, I concluded that the dish was useless. It was too small for soap, too delicate to carry food. It was the stupidest thing I could find. Looking at it made me nauseous.

When I showed it to Martin, he beamed. "We have a winner!" he said. "Lydia, stand up. Lydia, everybody." I could hear sporadic clapping echoing throughout the mostly empty auditorium of the Glendale Community Center. He explained that wasting money on frivolous things was our birthright, and that filling our lives with material excess helped to distract from the huge bummer that was our own impermanence. Denial and distraction were the best defenses we had against death. Martin continued on, relaying the four principles of happiness: status, wealth, pleasure, and vanity. He applied a specific affectation to represent the meaning of each. Rubbing his thumb across his fingers for wealth, raising his brows comically to convey pleasure as if we could not understand most things, including English. I took no offense; I could sense that Martin needed the validation. I liked that about him, how refreshingly human he was. He was so totally himself at all times. As he spoke, I zoned out and contemplated the particularly satisfying symmetry of the tiled flooring. The geometric patterns reminded me of the ecstatic oneness of everything.

"How does it feel to be number one?" Martin asked, at the end of class.

"Great," I lied. I felt nothing. Being the best at anything brought me no joy. I feigned a smile and zipped up my coat, then helped the others stack the chairs. As we stacked, I asked Levi, the oldest member of the group, what he thought of Sinead's wind chime stunt, knowing how much Martin encourages gossip among members. "It creates a healthy us-versus-them mentality," he'd explained. Levi just shrugged; as a lifelong Buddhist who'd taken too much acid in the sixties, he was trapped in a perpetual state of present, unable to access his short-term memory, leaving him in a tormented, unrelenting now. Instead, he described in great detail the community center's indoor air quality: "Notes of cardamom and exhaust fumes, industrial cleaner," he said before trailing off.

As we filed out of the auditorium, Martin announced next week's assignment: Lust. We all looked bewildered. We had just regained our sense of greed and wanted to explore it further. Roger had bought lottery tickets with our birthdays on them and Greta, our newest member, recently purchased a vintage sports car she could not afford. Before she became a practicing Buddhist, Greta was a renowned sculptor. Her pieces were sold at auction for six figures and she'd traveled all over the world to speak at various fine-art conferences and galleries. Despite her success, she'd suffered from debilitating migraines all her life and began meditating as a way to cope with the pain. Her daily meditation practice allowed her to loosen her attachment to suffering and, with it, her desire to make sense of her suffering through art. She started giving her work away and spent most days in a blissful, catatonic state. She eventually stopped working altogether and was forced to move back in with her parents where she focused her efforts on a community garden. The life she'd worked so hard to build was over, and she simply did not care. "Capitalism degrades the sensuality of the soul," she explained. "Wake up, sheeple!" she'd say until Martin intervened by dimming the lights and saying, "No, shhh, go back to sleep." It was a miracle she'd even come this far.

Greta's sports car was electric blue and sat low to the ground. She asked if anyone wanted to sit in the driver's seat and no one did. I thought for a moment that the pain in my chest was envy, but realized it was indigestion from the leftover banana bread

Roger had brought for us earlier. We all watched Greta contort herself into the driver's seat of the compact car, scooping up the linen entrails of her pants leg before closing the door and driving off. I swore for a moment there, she looked genuinely happy.

When I got home, Nico was watching TV with Bethany on the sofa. Nico was my roommate who was still technically my husband, but I hadn't called him that in over a year. Sometimes I'd catch Bethany saying "husband" when she was calling to set up a family phone plan or when she was talking to her mother long-distance in Moldova, but Nico said they were just friends and that it didn't mean anything. I didn't mind at all. Ever since I learned how to Qigong, I no longer identified with pain and nothing ever really bothered me. Before I began practicing, I was a total mess. The old me probably would have killed Bethany by now. If she had a dog, I would've killed her dog, too. Now, every time I looked at her, it was as if I'd saved her from myself. How do you even begin to explain that to someone?

"What did you learn today?" Nico asked, his eyes fixed on the television. I walked toward the kitchen doing my Qigong in a manner that some might consider excruciating, depending on their level of attachment to how things ought to be. Breathing from the base of my spine, I slapped my limp arms from side to side to activate my chi flow.

"I learned that material objects elevate status and promote positive self-esteem," I said.

"Wow, that's great. I'm so proud of you," he said. Bethany raised the roof with her toned lifeguard arms.

Ever since my heart expanded to include all beings and not

just Nico, he's treated me like a baby. I find this to be ironic since I'm ancient energy, temporarily bound to a decaying flesh suit that will once again be released back into the Celestial Body. He knew this; he took the online Expander Course with me but gave up on it once he reached the paywall. Even though I completed the course and achieved total mind/body enlightenment in just five years, I still subscribed to the weekly newsletter to hear from various ascended masters and disembodied beings like Baba Yee, who spoke through Rebecca, a teenage girl from Sacramento, or Rami Sheen, a third-generation shaman from Queens. I liked to know where my monthly donation was going. Nico thought it was a cult and worried I'd been brainwashed. He said he liked it better when I was a shopaholic. He said he missed finding hidden receipts in the vents but now all he finds are loose prayer beads and incense dust. I don't blame him. I suppose I put him through a lot, like that time I took us to a clothing-optional meditation retreat and he got a tick bite. We still don't know if he has Lyme disease or if he's always been like this.

Bethany asked if I wanted to watch a documentary on the social organization of termites with them, because she knew that I would say no, that I'd already watched it, that I'd recommended it to them two weeks ago. She does this because she wants to have sex, and I'd told her, "If you want to do it, just go ahead. I don't care, I celebrate it. Sex is a wonderful vehicle for enlightenment." Nico could use it; he was due for some temporary ego death. He'd been dealing with some body shame lately. His favorite jeans no longer fit.

"You know, when we used to have sex—" I began.

"Lydia!" shouted Nico.

"You're right. I'm sorry, I'll get out of your hair!"

I went to the bathroom and noticed Bethany's toiletries strewn all over the sink: a travel-size toothbrush, a tube of mascara, half-empty Sudafed chewables, used yellow cotton swabs, a mound of black hair wrapped around the bristles of a hairbrush, loose gummy vitamins, an expired Macy's card. The old me would not have handled the mess well, but the new me was making room for her in one of my personal drawers. Bethany bought extra-large tampons for her extra-large vagina. The old me would've probably judged her for this, but I'd come to realize it was probably more normal-size if you consider that the blue whale's vagina is so big, six people can fit inside it at once. Everything is relative.

That night I lay awake listening to their sex sounds in an attempt to reconnect with feelings of lust. I tried imagining their naked bodies wiggling in unison, but I knew it was just consciousness dancing with itself, no different than the sound of music or the laughter of children. Eroticism and taboo required a level of separateness I had yet to reintegrate. I listened as Bethany's reliably rhythmic moans transformed into a kind of mantra, each moan directing me into the infinite now. I noticed the way it changed according to her position, beginning strong, like a coyote howl, and then, suddenly realizing she'd overdone it and unable to sustain her enthusiasm, she pivoted to a breathy sigh that finally dissolved into a soft whimper. Nico remained silent, of course, until the very end when he released a violent grunt, muffled by a soft forest of black hair in his mouth. I sat up and tried to imagine their bodies in a pretzel formation on the sofa, resting into the empty stillness that followed. I felt nothing and this made me sad, which I noted was a feeling. I told myself it still counted.

Some hours later, I got out of bed to pee. Reaching for the bathroom light, I felt an arm. It belonged to Nico, who also had to pee. I should have known this; over the years, our cycles had synced up. The arm felt smooth. The arm had been shaved. Nico and his shaved arm couldn't see me in the dark and swatted my hand away as if it were a housefly. Startled, I let out a small animal noise.

"Lydia?" he asked, still half-asleep.

"No," I responded, "you're dreaming, this is a dream."

"I can see you," he said, turning on the light. "What are you doing?"

"I have to pee."

"Go ahead, I'll wait."

As I peed, I could hear him crying on the other side of the door. Men with enlightened wives do this—they get girlfriends and take up tennis and shave their arms. They pretend it's fine, then cry suddenly in the presence of white noise of any kind: peeing, faucets, traffic, blow-dryers. They join chat rooms of other husbands who circulate a petition to legally recognize enlightenment as a psychiatric disorder but realize how difficult it is to convince the medical community of the dangers of excessive meditation. Nico nearly gave up until he saw Martin's flyer posted up on the community board at Trojan CrossFit:

NAMASTAY-AWAY: GET OUT OF THE PRESENT MOMENT!!
DO YOU OR DOES SOMEBODY YOU LOVE SUFFER FROM
EGO DEFICIENCY? I CAN HELP! SIGNS OF EGOLESSNESS:
NO LONGER ENJOYING YOUR FAVORITE BAND, GIVING

AWAY PERSONAL BELONGINGS AND/OR WEALTH, SUD-
DEN PREFERENCE FOR BREATHABLE COTTON WARES,
BRALESSNESS WHERE THERE WERE ONCE BRAS, NEW-
FOUND FASCINATION WITH THE BREATH, LOSS OF APPE-
TITE, LOSS OF LIBIDO, LOSS OF GUILTY PLEASURES,
POOR HYGIENE, BORING PERSONALITY, ACCESS TO
SPIRIT WORLD/OTHER DIMENSIONS, AND MORE!!! THERE
IS HOPE. CONTACT MARTIN TO SET UP AN APPOINTMENT.

On my way out of the bathroom, I breathed in and smelled
Nico's cologne. It smelled like tobacco and dried meats. I
remember the smell from our first date, how rancid I thought
it was. Over the years, I got used to it, loved it, and learned to
recognize it as his signature scent so that whenever I smelled it
on another man, I felt a misplaced arousal. But smelling it now
evoked no reaction. I breathed in again to be sure. I looked at
the smooth dark shape of him and said, "Good night," but what
I meant to say was "I'm trying." Because I was.

At the next meeting, everyone seemed unusually sprightly.
I chalked it up to the empty carafe of cheap coffee and the
doughnuts, but upon closer examination realized it was something else. Martin had taken the group to get spray tans over
the weekend and I'd missed the invite. "Did you check your
spam folder?" asked Roger, his tangerine face glistening under
harsh fluorescent lights. He looked healthy; they all did. "No,"
I responded, and really, I hadn't. I wouldn't have gone anyway, I have supersensitive skin. We sat around in a circle to
talk about our wins for the week: Greta got her moles removed
purely for cosmetic purposes, Roger bought a second expen-

sive watch that was identical to his first watch, and Levi got an American Airlines points card with bonus air miles. Everyone was bettering themselves. I had nothing. When I brought up Bethany's sex moans, Martin asked me to reenact them for the group. I politely declined.

Martin prodded me further: "Lydia, what excites you? What really gets you going?"

"I don't know, loving awareness? Gratitude? Overcoming my fear of death?"

"Earth to Lydia!" Martin said, knocking his knuckles against the air above my head. The forcefulness with which he would pretend to hit us suggested to me that he really wanted to but legally could not.

For the next exercise, Martin dimmed the lights and put on a sensual R&B song about a man who loves a woman so much that he can only love her for one night; otherwise, he fears he will die of a heart attack. None of us had ever encountered a love so strong that it could kill a man, but we understood that artists take certain liberties in order to convey a universal experience. *Your love's giving me a heart attack / I can't come back / Love heart attack-ack-ack.* Martin sang along. When he turned the lights back on, I caught several members of the group dabbing tears with their sleeves and the corners of their shirts. "Just beautiful," muttered Greta.

"Who here has been in love?" Martin asked the group while circling the perimeter with his hands folded behind his back. A few of us raised our hands. "So, you're all familiar with love." He nodded, using air quotes for both *familiar* and *love*.

"Guess what? Your unconditional love of all beings is naive!" he went on. "You wanna know why?" None of us did; we already knew what he was going to say. He'd recited this speech in some form or another before, with slight alterations and flair added each new time he said it. "Because real love isn't diluted. When you try to love everyone, you end up loving no one. Real love, my friends, is potent. Concentrated. Skin on skin," he said, rubbing his flat palms together to demonstrate.

"When I choose you," he said, pointing to Sinead, "I reject everyone else around you, because there is only you. You are my world." Sinead, visibly uncomfortable with being used as a prop for Martin's point, started to laugh uncontrollably.

Ignoring her, Martin continued with his hands on her shoulders. "Why is it that we love one person more than everybody else?"

Greta raised her hand. "Because we project our unhealed childhood trauma through another person who unwittingly acts as a parental surrogate, thus repeating the toxic cycle of abuse and codependency?"

"No, Greta! Pheromones!" shouted Martin. "Pheromones are nature's way of signaling us toward sexual pleasure!"

Greta nodded, writing the word *pheromones* in her spiral notebook.

"Now, I want to try something a little unorthodox. Lydia, take a look around. Do you trust us?" Before I could answer, Martin said, "Good, great. I want everyone to take a moment and write down something you don't like or find annoying about Lydia. It could be anything: her appearance, her personality, that annoying way she ends every sentence in question form. Feel free to get creative with it!"

Everyone began writing furiously; something about their group spray-tan experience had produced a tribal mentality. They seemed different, bolder somehow.

"What does this have to do with anything?" I asked.

He leaned in close. "Listen, do I come into your place of work and ask you about your business?"

I couldn't understand what he meant, so instead I tried to interpret the meaning through the girth of the vein on his forehead. It was like a silent scream. I looked away. Once everyone was finished, they took turns reciting their opinion of me:

"The only reason she's here is because she's in love with Martin. Maybe if she just admitted it, Martin would be open to it, who knows? Just sayin'."

"She was a huge bitch to me in my dream once."

"No one can pronounce her last name and I think she likes that."

"She really thinks she's pulling off that whole short-bob look."

"I get the sense that she thinks she's worse than us, which is to say she's better than us, and either way it feels presumptuous."

"If she weren't a woman, I would punch her in the tit, but I don't hit women."

It went on like this, one by one. Unprompted, the group then escorted me out of the building. What began as a slow shove soon worked itself into an aggressive tussle. We all started running toward the parking lot, or I was being chased; the lines between role play and real life blurred. I was being guided by two hands on my shoulders and little finger pokes against my back. They started chanting, *"Lyd-ia! Lyd-ia!"* Confused, I thought it sounded celebratory, like I had passed a test and maybe it was over. We would all go to the mall for haircuts and pedicures. But then I heard someone yell something in another language and the rest of the group erupted in laughter, repeating the word over and over. Since when had they all learned this language? Was it in another email I'd missed?

We made it to the end of the parking lot and the group stood, waiting for instructions, although Martin seemed to be on an important phone call, his free hand gesticulating as if conducting an orchestra. I took the opportunity to run to my car and sped off to a strip mall across the street. I parked behind a dumpster and idled in my car. From where I sat, I could still see the angry mob from a distance, exchanging high fives and stretching their calves. I watched them say their goodbyes and walk toward their respective cars. Roger and Greta lingered a while longer; I had suspected there was something between them but her hand resting on the small of his back confirmed it. I thought about plowing into both of them with my car and not stopping. The thought surprised me.

I consulted my inner landscape by closing my eyes and breathing deeply. For years, it had been a still body of water, representing my Buddha nature. Unchanged, unmoored by season or mood. This time, however, I noticed a ripple cutting through the smooth glass top as if some evil lurked beneath, swimming. Water leaked out of my field of vision into a dark space. As the tide lowered, I felt weak and hungry. I needed to eat. I looked up and saw a sign for ANYTIME DONUTS. Dizzy, I walked inside and ordered a chocolate-glazed doughnut, breaking my weeklong fast. I took a seat by the window and marveled at it: soft flaky dough bathed in a thick sheen of chocolate. When I finished, I got up and ordered another one. Then another one. Then one more. Fluffy, sugary dough slinked down my throat, filling my belly with warm, unfettered joy. Thirsty, I ordered a large vanilla iced coffee and kept going. Another powdered one. Then a cream-filled one. Then two plain ones. No matter what, it seemed, no bite was enough to fill me. Each bite con-

tained within it the violent utterance of *more*. I felt sick but kept
going anyway.

I could sense the teenager behind the counter watching me
gorge, snapping photos of me to send to his friends, my face
powdered white, my fingers bloodied with raspberry jelly. I
didn't care. My eyes half-opened in a ravenous haze, I gave
him a thumbs-up and continued. The teenager laughed unselfconsciously, like we were friends, like I was performing a trick
for him. I laughed, too. His laughter subsided and he disappeared into the kitchen. I suddenly missed him.

While I waited for him to return, I thought about his pim-
pled face, his long unwashed hair collected in a low ponytail.
I liked the way he listened to me, did as he was told, asked
if that was all, even when he knew it wasn't. I thought about
what I would say to him when he came back, something about
sports or music or what he planned to study in college. I'd ask
him for his number. I'd tell him about the social organization
of termites, how the king and queen release pheromones that
spread throughout the colony to prevent worker termites from
reproducing. I'd tell him about how the king and queen mate
in their own saliva and waste. I'd invite him over to watch the
documentary about it.

When he emerged, all I could manage to say was "Do you
have any éclairs left?" and he said, "No, we're all out," so I
asked for another of the chocolate-glazed and he said, "We're
out of those, too," and so I asked for a cup of water instead.

As my stomach settled, I could feel sugar whirring through
my blood vessels, congealing into thick clots. I felt my heart
thudding through my blouse like a death rattle. I thought about
Martin's sexy song, the one about the man who risked his life

for love. This man couldn't stay, even if he wanted to. His heart simply could not take all that love. What if he stayed? What if I stayed? I gave the boy my empty cup and walked out into the parking lot, feeling lightheaded and alive. Feeling like I could die at any moment.

It was still light out when I got home, but I went straight to bed. Nico and Bethany didn't ask, but if they had, I would have told them I had a terrible stomachache and not to worry, that I would sleep it off. I felt a twinge of sadness. Nico would sometimes ignore me on purpose to make me feel jealous, and for the first time, it bothered me. Not enough for me to do anything about it, but a little seedling of emotion had been planted. I would do my best to nurture it.

Lying in bed, I noticed an email from Martin on my phone. "Congratulations," it said. The entire class had been cc'd. It was a note to tell me what a good job I'd done, how proud they were of me for completing the exercise.

"No hard feelings, Lydia. It was for your own good," Martin said.

"Worked up an appetite, huh?" replied Greta. I must not have seen her spying on me in the doughnut shop from across the street.

"You might want to lay off the sugar, you don't want to get fat, ha ha," said Roger.

Martin reminded the group that the following week was our final session. "Lydia, you've come so far, I hope you'll join us," he said.

Of course it was a test! No one hated me or wanted me out; there was nothing wrong with my hair. The group just wanted to build up my fight-or-flight response to make sure I'd protect myself from physical harm in the real world should I ever be forced to. "I'll be there," I responded, signing off with a smiley face.

For the final class, Martin had us gather in a small conference room in the back of the community center. He handed us blindfolds and asked us to sign a waiver, claiming it was a standard photo-release form for his website. He'd used some illegible calligraphy font so no one could read it, but we signed it anyway because we had no reason not to trust him.

As I looked around, I could see that everyone's spray tans had faded except for Martin's; he'd been freshly sprayed like a bronze statue, with little white halos around his eyes. Sinead wore thick eyeliner and maroon lipstick, and her thighs were bursting out of a tight black miniskirt. I barely recognized her. Levi greeted me with a big hug and wouldn't release me until I said, "Levi, let me go," and he did, wiping tears from his eyes. The only other time I saw him cry was when he accidentally crushed an ant with his sandal and yelled, "Albert, no!" He had already named the ant and he buried it in the soil. "You're home now," he'd whispered, grief-stricken. I pretended to still be mad at him for participating in the mob exercise and flicking the air in front of my face while repeating, "I'm not touching you!" I knew it would help stoke his guilt.

"Where are the doughnuts, Lydia?" Greta teased.

"Shut up, Greta," I said, covering my mouth as soon as the words left my mouth.

"Cat fight!" Martin said, throwing a chef's kiss into the air, so pleased by our budding rivalry.

I apologized to Greta. "I ate them all, ha ha."

Martin had everyone take a seat and put on their blindfolds. "No peeking."

We all giggled nervously and waited for our instructions.

"Remove your blindfolds," he said, and when we did, we saw Martin wearing a plastic *Scream* mask and holding a gun. "Now, get down on the ground," he said calmly.

"What's with the mask? We know what you look like," said Roger, still in his seat.

"Roger, if you don't get on the ground, I'll blow your brains off."

"I think you mean *out*, blow your brains *out*," said Sinead. It was true, Martin always got popular phrases wrong. He'd say phrases like *It's a doggy-dog world!* or *One expresso please!* Sinead had a thing about correcting him.

"Sorry, but you're all going to die," he said, waving his gun around the room. Greta was already crying; it was so like her to make this all about her. Levi grasped my hand so tight I thought he was going to crush it. I could not believe this was how my life was going to end, under a conference-room table surrounded by losers.

"Why are you doing this?" I asked.

"If you can't take the heat, get out of the game," he said, doing his best mob-boss impression.

"What?"

"Knock it off, Martin," said Roger, slowly rising to stand with his hands up, calling his bluff. "Just give me the gun."

"You want it? Here!" said Martin, firing just above Roger's head to prove the weapon was real. Roger dropped to the floor and everyone screamed.

"I'll give you each five minutes to think about your stupid little lives. I really want you to think long and hard about what you'll miss most and what you'll regret never having tried because you were too scared," he said, setting the stopwatch on his phone.

Levi tugged on my shirt, trying to communicate with me, and I kicked him away. I wanted my final moments to myself. When I closed my eyes, all I could think about was Nico. I'd put him through so much, and he stuck around. He made a whole new life for himself just to make me jealous. I couldn't believe how selfish I'd been. I said a little prayer to Nico in my mind: *Nico, it's me. I'm about to die so I just want to say that I'm sorry. I love you so much and I really messed up. Also, I think Bethany is stealing from you, don't ask me how I know this. I wish we could go back to how it used to be. I'm sorry I abandoned you for the Universe, but you are the Universe, so how far could I have gone? I promise to haunt you in the afterlife, lovingly and only with your permission. Having a body was so hard anyway—this could be good for us. Anyway, I think my time is up—*

"And, stop. I said stop, Sinead, god!" said Martin. Sinead was rocking back and forth in child's pose.

"Sorry," she muttered tearfully.

"It was a pleasure knowing all of you, but now it's the end. I promise it won't hurt one bit because . . ." A long pause followed, an eerie cliffhanger.

Laughter cut through the silence. It was Martin. "I'm sorry, but the looks on all your faces." I turned over onto my back to face him and saw that he was doubled over; the gun was gone. "You really thought . . . !" he whispered. "And Levi with the . . ." Unable to finish his sentence. "You guys must think I'm a"—he fanned himself to cool off—"I'm a monster!"

Roger slowly peeled away from Greta's embrace, realizing what was happening. Sinead was still curled in a fetal position, like a bug playing dead, hoping to be spared.

"Look! You got your life back, isn't that wonderful?" Martin said. "Those five minutes will stay with you for the rest of your lives. All your desires and regrets revealed to you in an instant." He paused for a moment. "What a gift!"

It was a fireworks display of emotion. Sinead did a wolf howl, hoping it would catch on, but no one joined in. Martin was a genius, say what you will.

"I miss being objectified," sighed Greta. "I think I'll get breast implants."

"That's a great idea. I love that for you," said Roger.

"I'm going to call my kids," said Levi. "Well, they don't know they're my kids, it's a whole thing." He started crying again.

I got up and wandered out of the room without saying goodbye. I felt a new kind of clarity, like a burning hunger in my gut. I called Nico and prayed to God he would pick up. If he didn't pick up, I would drive home and stand outside and scream, *I'm still your wife and I want to come home*, like they do in the movies, and Nico would smile and out of nowhere, that Phil Collins song would start playing, the one that goes "I've been waiting for this moment for all my life," as we'd run into each other's arms, slowly and tenderly humping as we hugged. Bethany would be gone, obviously. Attacked by her new dog, who would then have to be put down, eliminating them both, exactly as I dreamed it.

Nico's phone rang and rang, no answer. I kept calling. I hadn't noticed I was in my car and my car was moving, due to my driving it. I drove down unfamiliar streets and looped back around based on pure intuition like a cat that somehow always knows its way home, but I wasn't home, I was parked in front of Anytime Donuts, I was getting out of the car, I was still calling, I was ordering a chocolate-glazed and shoving it in my mouth. *Pick up, pick up, pick up*, I mouthed, *I'm yours.*

Kind of a huge bummer that suffering is the only way to become a better, hotter, nicer person in life

Do you ever make your bed at 9 p.m. and think, *why?*

Buddhism taught me to give up my desire for material wealth, status, and success, but at what point is that also just depression?

My life goal is to embody wide-brimmed-hat confidence

My aversion to group activities has saved me from several cults

Thought I was experiencing a major depressive episode the other day but turns out it was just kinda cloudy outside

Hot fitness tip for the ladies: imagine that every man you pass on the street has turned around to chase you, then RUN FOR YOUR LIFE

Feeling judged by the spirit of my future child for postponing their existence just to relax and be online

A Free Woman

Like life, like everything, the towel rack lay on the floor waiting for me. I could have installed it the day it arrived, but it was too late now. The moment had passed. Now every time I used the bathroom, I had to look at it. Some reasons were valid: I needed a power drill. Other, less obvious reasons: my lack of enthusiasm for learning new things, my denial of reality, adrenal fatigue. Over time, it became less material, transcending into a conceptual thing, into art. Like the way it caught the light at a certain hour. I liked imagining alternative uses for it: a weapon, for example, or a measuring stick. Sometimes I'd sit on the toilet and stare at it for a long time, hoping to move it with my eyes. Really believing I could. Or I'd wonder how long it would take to decompose. My guess was a hundred years. What would life be like then?

It took months for me to see it for what it was: a towel rack. This simple task became my barometer of priorities; if I had enough time to do something as stupid as install my towel rack, then I certainly had enough time to learn a new language or make a homemade face mask—something that would better improve my body and mind.

As I daydreamed, a pile of damp, used towels accumulated in the corner by the shower. This eclipsed my original problem, due to the smell. It was a sweet, yeasty odor that lingered on my forearms. Sure, I could have just washed them, then what? Wash them again? And again? What kind of life was that? I had no one to call, and I promised myself I'd never ask for Molly's help unless I absolutely needed to. She'd find a way to make it about her; how hard it was for her to see her sister living in a studio apartment alone, and, pausing for a sigh—divorced. "What if you slipped and fell in the bathtub and no one was there to help you?" was her first question. It wasn't so much a question as it was a way for her to cosplay as Concerned Sister while still making me feel like a loser. I gently reminded her that I was an adult and that I didn't even have a bathtub, so there. Molly had never even been to my new apartment, although she told me about her dreams that are not actually dreams but astral projections where she watches me sleep and flicks my lights on and off to get my attention.

"Have you ever felt it?"

"What."

"My presence."

"No."

"Then explain how I could possibly know what your bed-sheets look like."

"What?"

"They're white."

"Close. Cream."

I didn't believe her, but I started sleeping with underwear on just in case. She claims to be more attuned to signs and messages from the Universe than most people, and she is all about the Universe because she almost died from an allergic reaction to a walnut as a toddler, so now the Universe is working to affirm her existence every chance it gets. From an early age, she learned she was allergic to almost everything: wheat, nuts, dairy, sugar. Also, certain perfumes, dust, and she swears, a specific breed of cat. Our mother prepared all manner of alternative health foods to accommodate her dietary restrictions—braised coconut curry, tempeh tacos, gluten-free pizza, tofu nuggets shaped like fish, fish nuggets shaped like dinosaurs—but all Molly ever wanted was plain chicken breast and sugar-free bubble gum. This kept her thin and starving for another source of nourishment: attention. She would say that she ate people's eyes, and, in a way, I believed her. Not only did her so-called brushes with death endow her with clairvoyant abilities, but they also made her the central figure of our family, forcing me and my parents to orbit around her and her endless whims. We never discussed the permanent damage it caused us, but sometimes I fantasized about confronting all of them on a daytime talk show that would also involve a home-makeover segment so that someone else could come over and install this towel rack for me.

Growing up, Molly used to make me do all kinds of things, like take my shirt off to show her my unformed breasts, which were just two soft nubs of uncooked pepperoni over visible ribs. "It's my dying wish," she'd plead for the hundredth time. At first I complied, terrified that she might actually die if I didn't do what she said. Year after year, she continued not dying, and I started to suspect that her wishes had no legitimate bearing on her survival. The words themselves softened into more of a catchphrase than a threat. Still she was undeterred; throughout her teens, she grew more emboldened, making bizarre demands. "Tell everyone at school I'm in a coma," she said. She wanted to see who would cry the most in order to test her friends' loyalty.

The truth is, I would have cried the most. Even though she was insufferable, she was my only friend. I loved her the way you love air or the movement of your blood: you would die without it and yet you barely feel a thing.

When I finally ran out of clean towels, I had no choice but to put the rack up myself. I took it and walked across the street to Virgil's Hardware. The interior of a hardware store was so unfamiliar to me that my instinct was to enter with aggressive force, walking purposefully up and down the aisles until I could orient myself. I often overcorrected by contorting my face to look deranged or furious as a means of fending off potential predators. I didn't want to come across as a naive and shy woman; I knew I was more prone to trickery than most. Sensing no immediate danger, I relaxed my face and scanned extension cords and batteries with a calm focus. What few products I could recognize put me at ease, like golden arches beckoning me in the middle of some crumbling European city.

I was trying on gardening gloves and sampling an air-freshener scent called *Polar Ice* when the teenage employee called over to me. He looked as if he'd just woken up, in that way teenage boys always do, wincing and tired and squinting—as if the sun were always in their eyes. His hair was neatly trimmed, as if someone had drawn a line across his forehead with a Sharpie, and he wore a gold crucifix around his neck. Besides the row of retirees sitting on the bench out front, we were the only ones there.

He smiled knowingly, and I smiled back, pretending also to know. "Do you need some help, miss?" he asked.

"I'm looking for a power drill," I said, weakly—I hadn't spoken out loud all day. He led me down an aisle where he showed me one of two power drills.

"This goes through wood and metal."

"What about the other one?"

He picked up the second drill. "This one also goes through wood and metal."

"What's the difference?"

"This one is green, and it comes with this bag so you can put it in the bag when you're done with it."

"So, green then?"

"If you want the bag, yeah."

As we walked toward the register, I watched him relax his shoulders and straighten his posture from a small jolt of confidence, which I decided meant that I was beautiful. I have always known that I am not instantly beautiful, but I am beautiful after prolonged exposure. Like the way your eyes adjust in the dark, and what you thought was a person is, in fact, a floor lamp and that is a relief. A floor lamp! Aha! Against the backdrop of copper pipes, bags of soil, and ant traps, I had become the most beautiful thing he'd seen, if not that day, then certainly in that moment. Sometimes people just need context.

From the other side of the register, I knew he saw me and not my sister. How could he? He'd never met her. Most people who looked at me in this way had never met her; that was the point. She was the pretty one. She had long brown hair that she chopped off into a pixie cut every few years just because; a risky move for anyone who didn't have her cheekbones. Only confident women and nuns relinquish their most feminine asset so easily. The rest of us have a whole litany of techniques and rituals involving medical-grade creams, powders, and brushes just to look alive—not even extraordinary. Merely acceptable for public appearance. My sister, on the other hand, had always moved through the world with the certainty that she'd be met with kindness.

The teenager and I stood in silence as we waited for the dusty card machine to complete the transaction as if it, too, had been rudely awoken from its sleep and could barely remember what its only job was: to shoot numbers into space. I caught him looking at me, then looking at the machine, then looking back at me. I started to worry that all the parts of me he liked best were in fact not mine, but hers. We had the same eyes and lips, but our noses were different. Our bodies were different shapes, too. Mine was softer due to a lifetime of being given what she couldn't have as some kind of penance for my body's digestive good fortune. She would often ask me to eat something just to describe it to her. What was it like? How was the texture? Was it salty? Tart? Did it make me feel sick? She liked to watch me eat and fed me treats like I was her little pet. I ate for her even when she wasn't around. I know it sounds strange, but it felt virtuous and I was happy to do it.

As he handed me my receipt, he looked down and noticed

my hands. They were swollen and covered in veins that pro-truded like soft noodles under my skin. His eyes wandered up my face, as if struggling to see hers in mine: some likeness that he remembered from a dream he had. Somehow, somewhere, she had seduced him from afar, on a plane of consciousness I couldn't access, on account of my hideous noodle veins. I took the receipt and said "Cheers" for maybe the first time in my life, and somehow, he also knew this.

When I got home, I took the drill out of its packaging, remembering how easy it was to just do something so that it could be done. I wanted to bask in the victory of taking the first step toward completing the task, stretching it out for as long as possible before the next step, which was installing the rack. I called my mother and asked her how she was doing, but instead of answering, she told me how other people were doing because she'd never asked herself the question her whole life, so why start now? Dad was fine, she told me. He was in his office working on a puzzle, alone.

"He says hi!" She was lying; I could hear him talking to Uncle Keith on speakerphone in the background.

"Oh," I said, and she yelled out, "Angela says hi!

"You won't believe it," she said. "Guess who died."

"Who?"

"Joey."

"Who's that?" I asked.

"Joey Torres? He was in your sister's class, his mother was an alcoholic, you remember." My mother loved to tell me who had died, who had gone to jail, who had got out of rehab, and I could always hear her smiling with some sick joy about it, as if she were doing me a service, telling me. Much like my sister, tragedy imbued her with a sense of smug superiority.

"His poor mother," she added, feigning sympathy to conceal her gleeful dispatch. "Heartbreaking!"

I knew what she really meant. In the summer before my junior year, I got into an argument with Molly over a missing lip gloss and she blurted out, "Twin eater!" then quickly covered her mouth, pantomiming shock and regret. Confused, I asked what she meant by it. She took a dramatic breath like they do in soap operas, and told me that before I was born, I had a twin, but I ate her in utero.

"It's called vanishing twin," she said matter-of-factly. "Don't tell Mom I told you," she warned me. "You're not supposed to know."

I was blindsided by the news, but it confirmed my suspicions that I was an unlovable monster. I wept in secret for days, in the shower mostly, until I taught myself how to cry internally without any tears. It involved painful swallows: like pushing marbles down, all the way into my guts, until I peed them out. I ached for Molly's approval after that: knowing she was the only sister I had and the only one I hadn't eaten. I'd done so much harm before ever coming into this world, so I vowed to protect her. Now, whenever my mother told me something terrible, I knew what she was really saying: Remember what you did.

It was true that in the last few years, Molly and I had grown apart. After she married Tomás, an unvaccinated Ayurvedic practitioner from Santa Fe, she dove deep into the healing arts and started dressing like an amateur cult member. But after I left Paul and moved out on my own, she started calling me every night. It took us a few minutes at the start of each call to get acquainted, but then she'd grow tired of trading niceties and say something cruel like how ugly some famous child actor was now. It was a relief to hear her abandon her artificial namaste decorum and reveal her true self. It gave me a familiar sensation, like a stomachache. I was moved by her attempts to reconnect but had to receive cautiously. Mostly the calls went like this:

"What are you making for dinner?"

"I don't know, it's so hard to cook for one p—"

"I just emailed you a recipe, it's for a cherry-and-port-glazed ham."

"Don't."

"I'm sending another one for parmesan potato cakes."

"I'm really not in the mood f—"

"Do you trust me?"

"Not really."

"C'mon! Pwease, Angewa!"

I started cooking meals from recipes she sent me every night, reporting back with photos and notes on how it tasted. "The ham tasted rubbery; I think I undercooked it. The potatoes were burned and oily but tasted better with scrambled eggs the next morning." It pleased me to see how happy it made her, how comforted she was by our special bond. Eating for her was a small reprieve from the grief I carried around, not so much for my failed marriage, but for the dark shape where my twin used to be. Whenever I looked in the mirror, I saw her face.

After three weeks of making home-cooked meals for one from complicated email recipes, I'd gained thirteen pounds and still hadn't installed my towel rack. I was staying in most nights and watching porn, fully clothed (not for pleasure, just to remind myself that the desire to consume and be consumed was our shared human predicament), and generally feeling like my life was over. Paul was it for me, even though he was an out-of-work comedian who'd been spectacularly canceled on the internet for trying to start his own child beauty pageant, as a joke? I don't know. He covered my face with a T-shirt whenever we had sex. I'd had only one brief fling since we got divorced and it barely counted.

"Whatever happened with Ron, anyway?" Molly asked, dragging his name out melodically.

Ron was in charge of landscaping at my apartment complex, and every Friday he would come to my door to see if I needed any help with my garden. I made the mistake of telling her about him.

"Your *secret* garden," she said.

When I met Ron, I had only been single for a few weeks, and I was a wreck. I wasn't sure when I would once again take a painless, human breath despite having done it my entire life. Ron was a quiet man whose wife had died on a cruise in a manner that he was not yet ready to tell me about. We cried together, sometimes during home-insurance commercials, other times with his hand wrapped gently around my throat. I didn't love him and his dry, leathery skin reminded me of beef jerky, but he steadied my breath with a simple yet effective maneuver: he'd press his palm firmly against my chest until my heart rate slowed and my shoulders slumped and my whole body turned to Jell-O. I was grateful for his company, and on our last encounter, I said, "Thank you for your service," and to that he nodded and lowered his baseball cap like a sheriff, or a cowboy, and went about his work. Maybe love is not love, it's something else: it's Ron's hand on my chest, and I never deserved it.

"No, not Ron," I sighed while I steamed my face over boiling pasta water.

Molly, sensing I'd gained some weight from the timbre of my voice or from her astral spying, suggested I join her water-aerobics class at the YMCA. I hesitated at first, mortified by the idea of wearing a swimsuit in public, but she'd already signed me up, knowing that I hated disappointing her. She had a strange power over me, and I couldn't tell if she was doing it because she felt sorry for me or if she was jealous of who I'd become: a free woman. She didn't believe me when I told her I was getting used to being alone, that I preferred it now. To her, being alone must've seemed like a kind of hell. She always needed someone to behold her, a witness to her beauty. Her husband was the kind of guy who jerked off to photos of his own wife. It seemed like a violation. She said she thought it was romantic.

The first class was in two weeks, so I was determined to shed some weight before then. I didn't even own a bathing suit so Molly suggested I borrow one of hers. "Ha ha, imagine?" I said, eking out a labored laugh. To curb my appetite, I put ghost pepper hot sauce on top of everything I ate so that I could only manage a few bites before I felt like I was dying. I wasn't sure if it was working, but I began to associate eating with pain and my appetite eventually waned. If I really had to eat, I would only do it while watching videos of rat fights and maggots squirming in garbage and reconstructive surgeries until I couldn't eat without thinking about blood and guts and vermin. Crunching potato chips in my mouth was the only thing that relaxed me; I would just chew a whole bag and spit out the mush. I felt light and sick all the time. I told myself this was what success feels like.

The YMCA was a crumbling government-looking building that was nothing special, but inside, the bright blue Olympic-size indoor pool revealed itself to be a complex ecosystem. I sat on the bleachers, watching prepubescent girls with broad shoulders and slicked ponytails somersault into the deep end, creating a whirlpool like their limbs were made of cement. There were babies in water wings excitedly blinking the chlorine from their eyes, snot running from their noses, and their worried mothers who wrapped their shivering bodies in old bath towels, pulling them in tightly. I imagined that to be what heaven was like: not a place or a state of being, but the feeling of being gently smothered by old bath towels, in the arms of your mother.

The class had already begun, so I sat and watched so as not to interrupt. I was still participating on a mental level, which was basically the same as the real thing, except dry and less obvious. There were about a dozen people submerged up to their chests, splashing their arms from side to side. I watched the back of Molly's head as she swung it around dramatically to the beat of some inaudible generic pop song. No one else did this. Everyone else in the class was old, and possibly disabled; their only goal was to keep up and try not to drown. But my sister would always add her own flair to every move, even if it was not called for or endangered those around her. She seemed to think it made her look sexy in the same way everyone thinks they're really good at doing an English accent.

At the end of class, she climbed out of the pool leaving behind a shimmery film of what looked like self-tanner. I approached her, waving, and she went in for a hug and pushed me into the deep end, fully clothed. Instead of drowning, my weightless body floated up to the surface and I emerged gasping and coughing. I didn't know I needed that; it was like a baptism. I was never late again.

After several classes, I surprisingly transformed into a full-fledged devotee of water aerobics. Being in the water felt invigorating. Plus, the hot-sauce diet was really working. I'd lost a noticeable amount of weight. Chronic fatigue aside, I felt euphoric. Molly never mentioned the weight loss, but I knew she could tell. During one class, the instructor, Jean, confused me for Molly. "You two look so much alike," she said, "practically twins." Molly made a face like she'd just farted. I kicked her underwater, but she couldn't feel it because of the resistance.

I waited for Molly after class, but she was busy talking to Jean—a muscular woman with a tight bun secured by bronze bobby pins and at the right angle, a protruding Adam's apple. The room's acoustics amplified Jean's screaming laughter, as if anything Molly said was ever remotely funny. Jean loved my sister, which is saying almost nothing. On some level, everyone loved her, even those who'd never met her. To them, she was a warm breeze, a quiet knowing in one's heart that God is good. I loved her, too, but I also knew better. I knew that beauty is too often confused with goodness and human eyes are faulty, prone to mistake. Some people might go their whole lives without being able to see a certain color, and others might see the face of God in my sister's cheekbones instead of a woman who didn't pay taxes and believed she was a Native American medicine woman in a past life.

After Molly finished telling Jean about how her dog "was actually the one that rescued me," they exchanged a wet hug and we made our way to the women's changing room, where stagnant pools of water and strands of hair covered the pink-tiled floor. Molly rolled down her damp bathing suit and kicked it to the side. Her naked breasts stood commandingly upward like two eager sunflowers. Her thighs never touched. Onlookers studied her from their peripheral view, sucking in their guts out of respect. Somewhere, a teenage employee felt a tightness in his jeans. I felt a tightness, too: not in my jeans but in my throat, like the beginning of a sob. I swallowed it down.

It only took a few moments for reality to settle in and for her beauty to become commonplace, the way the Grand Canyon loses its grandness once it has been photographed and someone has to pee and someone else looks down at their phone to check their email. I looked toward another woman's backside, her folds of skin lapping into one another in a doughy pattern, and observed the way droplets of water curved and fell, curved and fell, into the drain below, and this too was beautiful.

"Did you see the way Jean looked at me?" my sister asked.

"Yeah."

"Like a"—she put her mouth to my ear and whispered loudly—"*lesbian.*"

"She is a lesbian. Her partner, Sylvia, is in our class."

"You're only proving my point."

"What's your point?"

She raised her eyebrows as if I were an idiot and squirted a palmful of shampoo into her hand and smoothed it over her scalp. I tried reaching for the shampoo, but she was bent over all the way with her legs spread, blocking it. She liked to make me feel uncomfortable.

"What!" she said. "Stop looking."

"I'm not looking," I said, my neck craned toward the ceiling as I rinsed my armpits.

She turned the water off and stood, wringing out her hair, which she'd grown out to butt-length to annoy me.

"Look at us, we're so old," she said, lifting and releasing her perfect water-balloon breasts.

"You're not old. I'm old," I reassured her. I was fourteen months older, but she always rounded it up to two years because she's bad at math.

"How old would you think I was if you didn't know me?" she asked.

"I don't know, twenty-five? Maybe younger if you got bangs again."

I never asked her what she thought of me. I already knew. I was a cautionary tale, a reminder of a body type she narrowly escaped. She smiled and wrapped her wet hair up in a turban, and as she did this, I could see wrinkles fanning from the sides of her eyes. I didn't mention it.

I quickly changed and waited for her to put on her clothes. I watched her violently stuffing her breasts into place with her eyes fixed on her own reflection. In my periphery, the accordion-shaped woman sat half-draped in a towel like a Renaissance painting, with her fat finger choking the flesh around a thick gold ring. She was married. I liked to believe that someone loved her, worshipped her even. I imagined her husband divulging to his poker buddies, in grotesque detail, all the sexual things he'd done to her. The shape of her curves. Her breasts. Her gigantic ass. The way she wrapped her mouth around his cock. He probably said things like, "Now *that's* a real woman," and it wouldn't even be a lie, it would be the truth—his truth. His effortless love. His hand on her chest. I relaxed my stomach at the thought of it.

My sister handed me her used towel and I threw it in the bin next to her. I wrapped my still-wet hair in a tangled bun and felt it drip down my neck. We packed our things and before we left, my sister stopped at the vending machine in the lobby, pressing her face up against the glass and fogging it up. She fed it a coin and pulled out a king-size candy bar, smelling it like a prized cigar before handing it to me.

"Here," she said, like it was a gift, something rare and expensive.

"I don't want it," I said.

"Just keep it," she said, stuffing it into my bag.

Maybe she'd noticed something different about me: my body, in its early stages of becoming something that resembled hers. I knew this gesture wasn't love, it was probably the opposite, but to me it still felt like it. Sometimes you do something long enough and it can feel like love—like a bad habit or a religious belief.

We parted ways, and I got into my car and waited for her to exit the parking lot. Sitting there, I turned on the radio and listened to the DJ inform callers they were sadly not the fortieth caller and would not be getting the two-thousand-dollar cash prize. *Sorry, you are the fifth caller, try again! Uh-oh, hey there, eleventh caller! Too bad.* I watched Molly get in her car and idle for a little while. What was she doing? Whatever it was, it felt like it was being done to me on purpose. I slunk down in my seat and eyed her reverse lights, willing them to light up with my stare. *Ma'am, you are the sixteenth caller, try again.* The DJ had a playfully smug affect and I could tell he was enjoying himself. *Thirty-two, too bad, so sad!* Finally, Molly's car began to move. I watched as she cautiously backed her white oversize SUV out of its spot. I leafed through my bag as she drove past me, reciting everything I touched without looking: wallet, makeup brush, cell phone, crumbs, a knot of hair wound around an elastic band, a jumbo candy bar. I gave the bar a knowing squeeze as I watched her turn left at the intersection. Spit pooled inside my mouth. I never took my eyes off her as she sped off into the distance and out of view.

Once she was gone, I pulled the candy bar out of the bag. I waited an extra minute to be sure.

My grocery store self and my 1 a.m. refrigerator self do not share the same goals and dreams

Sprouts are the pubic hair of vegetables

Meloncholia: eating a whole watermelon in one sitting, alone

The naive optimism of buying bagged lettuce and thinking to yourself, *This week it'll be different, this week I* will *eat this bag and I will not shove it in the back of my fridge and forget about it until it rots*

I want to go back in time to when I thought Caesar salads were good for me

Watch Me

I'm expanding outward: splayed out on the bed, doing laps in the living room. The house is so big that I'm trying to fill it up with my whole body to make up for Eric's absence. No one taught me to do this, so I wonder if it's biological—like sleep or giving birth or the way animals urinate to mark their territory. I turn the TV up all the way to let the ghosts know I'm not afraid, that I come in peace. I shower and use more towels than necessary, which is three. I attempt a fourth and feel ridiculous. I scoop my wet hair out of the neck of a giant T-shirt. I feel the labored breeze against my thighs and bare butt as I circle the couch and climb aboard, pressing the full weight of my body into it until there is no distinction between me and it. *I am couch woman! Sit on me!* I'm slightly high.

I run my hands inside the couch's leather folds and feel tortilla chip crumbs and something cool and plastic: a tortoiseshell guitar pick. My boyfriend, Eric, left this morning to go on tour with his band for three weeks, and before he left, he said, "Keep an eye out for my iPad," which was supposed to have arrived already, and "Water the plants." Whatever else I should do was to be determined by me alone. It felt like a dare. I wanted to cry with relief, not because I was unhappy, but because I was tired of impersonating myself. The difference is negligible but over the span of a year, it gets harder to maintain. I'm always a few degrees off from the real me, but with more smiling and feigned enthusiasm for topics like gear and sync rights and things being derivative.

It's not him, by the way, it's me. I have this disease where I forget who I am in the presence of another person. I sometimes find myself mispronouncing my own name to strangers, like a barista or a bank teller. My name is Anya, but I'll say Anna because most people say Anna and I'm tired of making people feel dumb when they first meet me. It takes up so much time—the explaining, the repetition, and for what? It makes me seem pretentious, which I am incapable of being because I'm so broke. The bank teller already knows this. At this point, I lack the confidence to say Anya with authority because I'm like, is it? Like I'm asking the bank teller what she thinks my name should be.

Before I met Eric, I rented a little studio apartment overlooking the blue Scientology building in Hollywood for nearly four years. Whenever I felt sorry for myself, I'd look out my window and see aspiring actors in little vests handing out pamphlets to tourists and homeless veterans, occasionally arguing with Jehovah's Witnesses who were there first and refused to

move, and I'd remember: it could always be worse. At least
I had my freedom. I loved my dumpy apartment and how it
made me feel both very young and old at the same time. I was
like a college student eating day-old supermarket sushi over the
sink and artfully arranging magazine collages on my wall, but
also, a lowly widow hanging threadbare towels on a clothesline
in the yard, screaming at rats. I worked at a bookstore during
the day and sold handmade ceramics in my free time. Mugs,
mostly, and also little miniature sculptures of faces and breasts.
You could call it my passion since that's what you call something that doesn't make you any money.

Being broke and alone isn't so bad; it requires discipline
and resourcefulness, and it keeps you a little bit hungry all the
time, so that you have something to work toward, like a stupid
little hamster on a wheel. But after I met Eric, I found myself
as in love as I was in debt (extremely), and I could no longer
justify spending most of my money on an apartment that I only
occasionally slept in. So, when he asked me to move in after
six months, I said a little prayer to myself, sucked in my gut,
and swan-dove into my new life, shedding any extraneous frills
that might've compromised our arrangement: my used canopy-
bed frame from Anthropologie, for example, and my period
underwear.

By the time Eric reached cruising altitude, I was already rear-
ranging the bedroom and promising myself I would put it back
by the time he comes home. I pushed the bed into the center
of the room, arranging a lagoon of pillows around it. None of
the furniture is mine so I have to work extra hard to create
my own unique relationship to each piece: not of owner, but

of property manager. I took everything else out of the bedroom except for the dresser, which was too heavy, so I draped a white linen sheet over it for some ambiance. Eric bought the house himself, can you believe it? He doesn't even come from money, he's just good at saving and his parents love him, which makes everything seem possible, such as a music career and home ownership. He doesn't think of it as his home because once you buy something, you get to stop thinking about it. Half the pleasure of buying something comes from having this particular relief. It's why I'll never stop thinking about designer sunglasses. I have a pair of knockoff Céline glasses, but I can't bring myself to wear them in public. It feels like I'm lying with my face; in my mind I'm thinking, *Everyone can tell.* I can always spot fakes myself: flimsy plastic frames, loose hinges. The logo is off. I get secondhand embarrassment at how smug a person looks wearing them; the way they expect us to accept their reality with such little effort to conceal the truth. It's the problem with everything: a crisis of authenticity.

I dangle my legs over the couch's soft armrest and my chest pounds with exhilaration or the feeling of getting away with something. In a matter of weeks, I went from a crumbling studio apartment with a STATE OF CALIFORNIA CARCINOGEN WARNING sticker over my door to having a claw-foot bathtub, central air-conditioning, and a yard teeming with hummingbirds and oversize mutant lemons. Any other woman in my position would know exactly what to do with all these lemons; so far I've only thrown them at overly confident raccoons. If I were less anxious—scuttling around the house like a little bug, making my home in dark corners—I might actually collect all the fruit from the trees and make something with them. Like jam or pie. Some women are natural homemakers, laboring over desserts for hours, just because. They never stop to ask if there's anything else they should be doing with their lives. Or if anyone even wants pie. I secretly envy these childless mothers, mothering anyone or anything they can: lovers, friends, neighbors, pets. "Here, I baked this! I just whipped this up this morning!" The women I know who are like this all have giant breasts, so maybe there's some biological imperative to bake, some correlation between milking and feeding and loving. I can barely remember to buy the basics. Whenever I get home from the grocery store I look inside my bags bewildered; it's like I blacked out and returned with a jar of olives, popcorn, instant coffee, Wheat Thins, and ketchup.

In my clearer moments I'm able to remember it's an act, like how we all pretend that we're not dying, like life is this completely ordinary thing we've all done before. La-di-da, big deal. I've never been good at pretending. Whenever we have friends over for dinner, someone will inevitably say, "Your house is beautiful!" and I'll say, "Oh it's not mine, it's Eric's, I could never afford it myself, I can barely afford these pants, I found them in a garage-sale pile, huge stains on them, you can still sort of see them if you look hard enough. Gross, right? Ha ha ha! Anyway, can I get you a drink?" Whenever there's a knock at the door, I'm half expecting it to be a man wearing a uniform, requesting that I vacate the premises, that they've made a clerical error and that I'll need to return to my old life. I won't even fight it, I'll just grab my things and tell him I'd been waiting for him to come. I don't want Eric to think my love for him has anything to do with this house. I never asked for it. If anything, it's a burden. It asks so much of us, to fill it up with furniture, to tend to its unstoppable weeds, to patch its endless leaking holes. It's like a baby, but worse, because I'm expected to love it, but I don't and it doesn't resemble me at all.

Despite my domestic deficiencies, I've unwittingly managed to hypnotize Eric into falling in love with me by merely having interests of my own: art history, music, books, a few cool card tricks. His past girlfriends were all models or former child actors. Girls with trust funds. He told me the last girl was a photographer, but she only took artful photos of herself partially nude or in a tub filled with milk or wearing a homemade flower crown and a loose sarong on the beach, doing a peace sign. She enjoyed playing into her ethnic ambiguity, despite just being a very tan Italian. As such, he treats me like some kind of anthropological discovery, or some great oracle of wisdom, but really, I'm nothing special. I think he's beginning to catch on, now that we live together. I'm not as driven as I used to be, as evidenced by my habit of lying down a lot. To compensate for this, I clean constantly. I scrub the bathroom, clear out the globs of wet hair from the drain, wash the dishes, kill bugs, and vacuum. When Arnold the gardener comes by, I wave through the window as if we're old friends. I want him to know I'm no better than him. That I helped my mother clean hotel rooms when I was a kid and I don't know how I ended up here either, but I do feel bad about it. I try to communicate all of this with my eyes, but I don't think he notices.

This is Eric's first time leaving me alone with the house, and I wanted to prove I could handle it, so in preparation, I demonstrated my competency whenever I could: disarming the security system, unplugging and replugging the wireless router, etc.

These were the seeds I planted that would bloom inside him at a later time—at a layover or at the rental car pickup, or at the hotel bar. He will think of me, untangling the garden hose, and it will move him to think of me like that. The idea of being loved from afar comforts me, and I know that distance and time can do more than I ever could to transform me into something more desirable. I won't have to shave or wear outside clothes or watch reality TV on mute and pretend I'm working. I won't have to do anything. His mind softened by jet lag, he'll remember me as somehow more beautiful than I really am, or the exact kind of beautiful I am, something proximity and routine made him forget. All I have to do is wait.

On my first official day alone, I sleep in later than usual. I give into my old ways easily, opting not to leave the bed unless I have to. After a few minutes of staring at a lizard doing push-ups through the window, I get hungry and roll out of bed. On my way to the kitchen, I'm spooked by my own reflection; my hair is knotted in sweat and sunken, ghoulish gray eyes look back at me. Something in me has unfurled overnight: my butt-hole relaxed, and I along with it. I shudder and look away the way one might when someone changes clothes in front of them and they accidentally see something they wish they hadn't: a tuft of hair, a nipple.

I open the kitchen windows and see a neighbor standing in my driveway, holding a leash attached to a dog in our bushes. *This is my house*, I think. *You're on my property. I own it. Go away. Be gone.* He walks away and I feel proud of myself. I feel powerful.

I prepare my usual: almond butter on toast topped with raw almonds. I eat in bed and scroll through my phone until I'm interrupted by a coughing fit brought on by a mild nut allergy.

I wheeze and choke and my nose runs, but in a few minutes, I recover and move on. It's not that I love almonds; I don't. I'm building up my pain tolerance every day by inflicting it in small doses; that way when the real pain of life hits, I'll be ready for it. Comfort breeds entitlement, so I have to remain vigilant and remember that everything can be taken from me at any moment. The trick to life is to always anticipate chaos. I'm like an athlete, playing out every possible worst-case scenario, that way nothing can hurt me.

My phone lights up with a text from Eric telling me he's arrived in Berlin and he's exhausted after the eighteen-hour journey. He types: *loveyo1* accidentally and says he'll call when he wakes up. *Love you!!!!* I write back, but not before deleting two exclamation marks.

The first days fly by and I let them. Eric checks on me when he can, but the time difference makes it difficult. He sends me photos from his day: terrazzo tiles of a hotel lobby, a thin pro-sciutto sandwich wrapped in meat paper, some phallic-looking historical monument. *Wow*, I say. *Wow. Wow.* But by the time I respond, he's already in the future, asleep. There are things to do at home, general maintenance. I take out the trash and say hello to the neighbors and passersby, straining to see them through my smudgy eyeglasses. Our next-door neighbor, Irene, runs a day care out of her house. She's a big fan of Eric's band and happens to always be in her front yard, making loud phone calls, yelling at her geriatric dog, telling a toddler to *get that shit out of your mouth*, then doing some dramatic countdown where nothing ever happens.

"What's Eric up to?" she shouts.

"Working," I say. I don't want to tell her anything else about our lives; she already knows too much.

"Rock-star life!" she says. I hate the thought of her sitting at her computer in the dark, researching him. She probably memorized his tour schedule. I bet she tells everyone about him, and when his song comes on the radio, she feels a pang of recognition so strong, it almost feels like it's about her. Eric only humors her because he's friendly to a fault. Unlike me, he never has to assess the probability of danger with every encounter he has on planet Earth, because he does not live in a rape and murder world. I can visit this safety and goodwill world when I am with him, but the moment he leaves me, I'm exiled back to the land of rape and murder. *Say hi to all the neighbors*, he will plead. As a lifelong renter, I've trained myself not to engage. Once contact is made, you can never return to anonymity. You must always engage, losing hours of your life to pointless banter, like long-winded monologues about lawn maintenance, retaining walls and missing pets. Neighbors belonged to a class of people who, by their nature, will never advance beyond their lot and cross over into the interiority of our living room, our lives. Socializing with them is endless intellectual foreplay with no reward. It's rude to expect everyone to play along: *Oh beautiful day, fellow property owner! Absolutely gorgeous, have a freshly plucked orange! Let us rejoice in the bounty of our rising property values and low-interest-rate investments!* I have nothing to offer; as his girlfriend, I'm basically a ghost. Irene has never once asked about me, although to be fair, I've never asked about her either. From what I can see, her life is miserable. It's all tantrums and Legos and soiled diapers. I find it in my heart to feel bad for her, and smile.

I go back inside and try to work on redesigning my website but instead I look at other, more successful ceramicists online, for inspiration. I click on photos of their husbands and their perfect babies who somehow remain chubby infants and never grow past the age of two. I have a theory that they stockpile photos and stagger them over years. I have no proof of this. One ceramicist is married to a famous actor and doesn't even need this, but says it gives her a creative outlet. *How fun for her.* I zoom in on a recent photo of the ceramicist's face and something is off about it. Her jaw appears narrower and the bump on her nose has been smoothed out. The comments suggest she's had some work done and a shock of heat pulses in my ears. I click around to find a side-by-side comparison of her face before and after, posted by a Turkish surgeon, with little arrows pointing to various reconstructed zones. I soon find a whole world of before-and-after photos, and I can't stop clicking and zooming in. My eyes bathe in images of grotesque noses reshaped and slimmed, fat engorged lips, and bruised, broken jaws shaved down and sculpted. I imagine what it must be like to kiss a face like that, how gentle you would have to be not to puncture or deflate it, the artificial hardness of it, the clear ooze that might leak out with enough pressure. I look in the mirror and with my newly calibrated perception, my face now looks like thousand-year-old salami, discolored and sweating, uneven looking.

I look until the sun goes down and my phone rings. It's Eric calling from his hotel room in Copenhagen. He asks to see my face, and I panic and quickly change and brush out my hair, then walk purposefully around the house with the front-facing camera on my phone, trying to find a decent angle and lighting to conceal my undoctored human face. I take a seat on the floor, in the dark.

"Why is it so dark over there?"

"What? Oh. I think my phone's being weird."

"Turn on the light, I want to see you."

Reluctantly, I get up and turn on the light, but keep my face partially out of frame to conceal the glowing pimple above my right eyebrow. I fix my gaze on my reflected image and forget to look at him. I watch myself smile and laugh, embarrassed by all of it. He is talking, but I'm barely listening.

"We played so bad, the sound was awful. I don't know what happened."

"I bet no one noticed," I tell him. I never do. I'm always too moved by the sound of live music to pick up on minor technical flubs. Crowds are so forgiving, anyway. Sometimes I think, do they even need to be onstage? The audience seems thrilled simply to be an audience—a collective unit instead of their individual selves. Applause spreads like a contagion. They'd cheer for anything, even the idea of cheering itself. It sounds so nice to be entertained without reciprocation.

"What are you doing right now?"

"Working. Might go for a run soon," I say, unconvincingly.

"At night?"

"No, I mean in the morning."

I momentarily leave my face unattended to steal a glance at him. He looks tired, but still very handsome. His stubble has grown in, and the dark circles under his eyes make him look worn out and submissive. Like he's been crying. Wait, has he? The thought of it almost makes me cry. I prefer him this way. He needs me and only I can comfort him. I remember when we first started dating, I liked him too much to conjure his face on command. I don't know if there's a psychological term for that, but whenever I tried, it always came up blank, or instead I saw a celebrity who resembled him, or him but with a deformity. Over time, I calmed down and his face materialized. I can now visualize what he will look like as an old man, and also as a baby. I can also see him as a woman, a cloud formation, certain rocks.

"I miss you," he says.

"I miss you, too," I say, followed by a prolonged pause.

"Hello? Are you still there?" he asks.

"Yeah, I'm here."

"Well," he says.

"Yeah," I say, "okay." Empty words ping-pong across oceans, war zones, and farmlands, dissolving on contact. When I hang up the phone, my upper-lip hair is slick with sweat and my pits are drenched. I hate the phone: it's like suddenly my short-term memory gets erased and I'm only interested in topics like food and time zones and the weather. I make a note to come up with some anecdotes and jokes for our next call. Maybe something about our neighbor, Debra. We both hate her. She refers to her dogs as "my babies" and lets them take huge dumps on our front lawn. I type *Debra* into my phone so I won't forget.

The next day, I don't hear from him at all. This gives me time to construct entire fantasies about what he's doing and then ruminate over them. First, I look up his tour schedule and see that he's in Vienna. I truly do not know what country it's in because I've never been outside the United States. I google "current time in Vienna" and imagine him, wandering off from a guided tour, enchanted by some ancient religious building, then stumbling into a café and being recognized by some locals who teach him simple phrases and giggle when he gets them wrong. Maybe from there they take him to a secret sex club located inside an abandoned castle where he discovers parts of himself that can only be coaxed out by new kinds of people, people with less baggage. Tale as old as time. I get a little jealous, but I've ruled out the possibility of any cheating in our relationship since we're both taking antidepressants that soften our libidinal desires in exchange for the ability to be functionally alive. Besides, he's a hypochondriac and too afraid of sexually transmitted diseases, which he fears are so pervasive, they must be airborne.

I could've joined him, but I'm not cut out for it. The one time I went on tour with him was hell. It was only a weeklong trip up the coast, but I was chronically constipated and could barely sleep. The tour bus could only accommodate the band and crew and the bunks were like child coffins, so I slept on the floor in the back room among the equipment and luggage, my body rolling violently at the slightest bump. I tried to force a deep meditation using the hum of the engine, where I could contemplate and then come to terms with my own untimely death but was repeatedly interrupted by a crew member with a cell-phone flashlight in search of their contact solution or an extra phone charger. No one tells you how boring it is: how every city looks the same and if it doesn't, who cares, and there is only ever one bathroom within earshot of twenty people and a lone shower located in the basement of a haunted hundred-year-old theater and everything smells bad and everyone's in a bad mood. Or that your boyfriend and only ally is only half-available to you and your needs because he is *working* and this is his *job* so you better not even *look* at him before he goes onstage (a sacred time for the men to huddle and shout affirmations at each other). Or how the front of the bus is filled with grown men playing video games on full volume and there is always a lone TV in the back playing movies like *Eyes Wide Shut* on mute for some reason, and no one socializes and there are no drugs (anymore) because someone took it too far that one time and ruined it for everyone, and the only other woman has been time-stamped by tattoos and hardened by years of this, so she makes silent bets on how long you'll be in rotation before the next one appears as predictably as her seasonal depression. And just as predictably, you get your period even if you're not supposed to, it appears somehow darker and angrier than usual and you tell no one, not even your boyfriend, for fear of messing with the vibe and "making it all about you," so you take your seat and watch them soundcheck, wishing you could astral-project back into your childhood bed, before you ever encountered a male musician with swoopy hair, where you experienced your last recorded restful sleep.

It wasn't even the physical discomfort so much as it was the feeling of being a tourist in someone else's life. The only thing that makes up for such a grueling lifestyle is the rush of performing in front of thousands of people each night. I liked watching Eric from side stage and seeing the way teenage girls and their stepmoms fawned over him, or the way men studied the architecture of his pedal board as a way to relate. I tried redirecting some of their energy onto myself, but none of it was for me, besides the leftover bruised apples and trail mix in the green room. I was so inconsequential to the entire operation, I actually didn't matter at all. When the show ended, Eric would always emerge from stage wide-eyed from mainlining adrenaline for two hours, as if an electric current were running up his spine. He was on an island of euphoric mania I could never reach. I could only wave halfheartedly from the shore, rubbing his back while saying, "Good show!" because what else do you say? "This experience reminds me that I'm wasting my life"? "No amount of Metamucil will help me overcome my fear of public restrooms"? "Everywhere I stand is the wrong place to stand"? I was always being asked to move, but I wouldn't know where to go, so I would just walk around aimlessly, studying expired show flyers for local bands with horrible names like Cassandra and the Bleep Bloops, Gay Jesus, and The Old Crow Down by the River. Radio DJs would often find me wandering the halls during sound check and call security; promoters would assume I was a fan on the loose, and I had no accreditation to prove I wasn't. I remember a bald man wearing a laminated pass shouting, "What are you doing here?" and for a moment I couldn't answer him. I didn't know.

At home I'm safe. I don't need a special pass to move from the living room to the kitchen. I can go outside or stay inside; I can ship orders or not. Given all my options, I choose to do nothing. I tell myself it's a virtuous thing, an act of resistance. I read a horoscope app on my phone that says, "Stasis is needed to allow for something big to happen, something so big it will require all your energy, but for now just rest and wait." I screenshot it as proof, disregarding the part where it tells me to accessorize with turquoise and lie naked facedown in the sun.

On day ten, I stop checking the calendar and my email. I no longer see a point to it. The only emails I get are shipping notifications for things I order online when I can't fall asleep: bath salts and socks and self-help books on cultivating good habits. I forget about them until they arrive, and it feels like a surprise gift. I learn that Wednesdays have the same shape as Sundays, both with their usual fanfare: the sky moving from blue to orange to purple, ending predictably each night with a black sheet of stars above the San Gabriel Mountains. It used to make me cry, but I got used to it and now I feel nothing, so I make myself stand and watch the sun and say, *This is the last time I'll ever see the sun, so I must see it with all my heart.* Sometimes it works. I watch videos featuring animals as unlikely friends, until I come across a video featuring a rabbit and a snake in a heartwarming embrace until the snake eats the rabbit in the end, like the disturbing title "Snake Eats Rabbit Friend" warns. As a palate cleanser, I search for a workout video by typing *workout video* and click on the one with the most views. It's called "20-MINUTE HIIT CALORIE KILLER" and features a trainer named Haley with muscular arms who keeps telling me to smile through the pain and to keep smiling and breathing, but also smiling. I'm doing neither, and somewhere around my thirtieth pop squat I realize it's too hard, but I don't want to stop, out of spite, and every time she tells me to smile, I think about how much I hate her and want to murder her or murder her then kill myself, and I wonder how many of the twenty million other viewers also hate her and if she worries about this part of her job, the way it unleashes an unwieldy animal hatred in people or if animal hatred is the number one, most-effective calorie killer, so being the most annoying person is just her long con to trick us into killing more calories. I finish the workout and collapse on the floor, feeling all the hatred leak out of my body while vowing to never, ever do that again, and letting the next video play, because I physically cannot get up to change it. It's a playlist of inspirational videos on Becoming Unstoppable and Awakening to Reality set to nature photography slideshows and massage music, and I decide, there on the floor, that this is my new religion.

I rise, against all odds, and feel moved to write out a list of life goals and wishes for my future. With the right attitude, I believe my future self will emerge from a lifetime of pain, false starts, and several expensive surgical procedures as victorious. Finally at peace with herself. Extremely wealthy, etc.

My future self won't even remember any of this anyway; she will be too busy doing something important, probably for others, because she's going to care about social welfare and the environment. Future me won't ever have to remind herself to cancel trial subscriptions to the *New Yorker* and YouTube Premium before they start charging, then resubscribe with a new email address, because she'll be a successful artist with disposable income so she won't have time to keep refreshing her bank account. All her enemies will feel shame and regret for doubting her, and they'll write long apology emails that will go unanswered. Future me will be content and filled with gratitude for very mundane, quotidian things, which will seem novel to her against the backdrop of her exciting life. She'll say things like, "God, I *wish* I were bored!" or, "I love airplanes; it's the only time I get to be fully alone!" Most important, Eric will still love her not because of these things, but in spite of them, because he was there at the very beginning, back when she was a nobody. A girl with a dream.

The following day, I don't feel like cooking so I alternate between various snacks. Olives, croutons, popsicles, cubes of cheese, followed by cereal. At night, I get panicky and overly preoccupied with swatting flies. I have the urge to sweep the leaves outside, and once I'm done I notice there are more leaves on the road, so I continue, sweeping all the way down the street. I imagine myself sweeping the entire neighborhood, sweeping the whole world. I could never sweep it all. By the time I'd finish, fall would begin again and I'd have to start over. I pretend this time is a test to see if I could live without Eric, sparing the grief of any real loss, but practicing what it would be like to function alone again. I run the empty dishwasher just to have the company, some sign of life. The mechanical whooshing calms me and drowns out the loneliness. With him gone, the idea of us stretches and thins to encompass several time zones. I begin to worry that I've done too good a cleaning job. That I've washed away any trace of him. All his chest hairs, his dirty socks, a royalty check from his publisher I accidentally tossed because I thought it was junk mail. I try remembering our old life here: the way we ate dinner in front of the TV and how he sang theme songs off-key on purpose and not with his real singing voice, the way I pretended not to notice when he farted in his sleep. It seems impossible that it ever happened at all, never mind every night for a whole year. How easy it is to lose it all, a shared life. An entire person. I thought solitude would nourish me, make me whole, remind me of myself before him—instead it has revealed the top layer of what appeared to be a submerged, ordinary sadness.

He calls me in his afternoon to show me the view from his balcony overlooking some gloomy Eastern European city. From there he's on his way to a radio interview before the show, and I can hear the ambient chatter of his bandmates in the background. His life sounds so big and important while my life is contained and measured by square footage. I try speaking in a lower range to seem sexy and cool and I can't believe how boring I sound: "There's a family of pigeons in our yard, or maybe they're doves," or "Our neighbor's car alarm went off yesterday. I thought it was my car at first, but it wasn't." He forces a laugh, and I worry he can tell that I hadn't showered and that showering now seems like an impossible feat that requires more energy than I'm capable of. I spend the rest of the day in a starfish position on the living-room rug, watching movies upside down. I do six sit-ups and give up, then think about how sit-ups are the most depressing of the exercises. Each strained, random sit-up a reminder of your boredom, your lack of follow-through. Always done on a whim, and rarely repeated, with some vague fitness goal that will never be realized, usually ending in a defeated nap. I want to blame YouTube Haley for it somehow.

It's not until later that evening when I'm carrying a laundry basket to the living room that I spot a tiny red light flashing from a security camera. Eric installed it when I moved in and showed me how the camera feed linked to an app on his phone so he could monitor the living room remotely. He placed it there strategically so that it would capture both the front and side door if ever someone tried to break in. After he set it up, we spent the afternoon watching ourselves move around with a three-second delay. We both behaved differently in front of the camera; I froze like a bug and he flailed in slow motion as if underwater. I forgot about it after that. It's mostly hidden behind a snake plant and the red light is only visible at night. Noticing it now spooks me and I drop the laundry basket and backward-walk out of frame. I crawl into bed, fully clothed and wide-awake. I can't stop thinking about the camera, and how I spent days completely oblivious to it. It reminds me of the time I accidentally sent Eric a text meant for my mom, which was a press photo of him I found on Google Images with the caption, *This is him.* He wrote back, saying, *did u mean to send this to me?* and I proceeded to have my very first panic attack in the cereal aisle of Vons. I'm suddenly self-conscious and try to remember what I did in there, what he could have seen. Would it disturb him to know how much time I spent sleeping? Would he care that I ate my meals on the floor while watching videos on my laptop? It's very likely he wasn't watching; he was obviously busy. But the option to watch was there, and that was enough to stir something in me.

The next morning, I rise early to a new reality and dutifully wash my face and clean the backs of my ears and the dirt under my fingernails. I make the bed and punch the life back into each pillow. Living under surveillance is what I imagine performing for an audience must be like: it's both terrifying and thrilling to feel so exposed. I decide not to bring it up the next time he calls for fear of ruining it. I prefer not to know yet. I shower and put on some real clothes—butt-sculpting leggings and a tight white tank top—and I wander into the living room and pace around slowly, pretending I'm on an important phone call. I act casual, gesturing with my free hand, pausing for an imagined response, nodding in agreement, but when my gaze accidentally catches the camera, I fear the jig is up.

I keep going. From that point on, everything is a performance. A love letter. A record of a woman luxuriating in her solitude: self-assured, goal-oriented, effortlessly beautiful. I try communicating all this from a seated position on the couch. My movements feel loose and improvised, and I let my body guide me. I roll back on the couch and kick my legs up in a deep stretch. Imagining him watching me gives me a surge of confidence. I pull myself up like a gymnast and think about how my actual gymnastics career ended prematurely when another girl's coach complained that my pronounced camel toe was inappropriate, but there was nothing I could do about it. I'd just gone through a growth spurt, and my body had yet to distribute itself evenly. I was too embarrassed to ask why he was looking. I let it go. None of it matters anymore under the forgiving black-and-white filter of the security camera.

Lost in the flow, I notice a strap from my tank top fall loose, leaving my shoulder exposed. I take what I remember from my college improv team and go with it, flicking the other side off in a reveal, like *oops . . . what do we have here?* I lift my shirt to reveal my loose, tiny breasts, and slowly shimmy them from side to side. I imagine where he is at that moment, in a bathroom stall or an elevator, a place both private and public, smiling to himself. Unsure of where to go from there, I cover myself with my arm and step out of frame for a quick break. Does this performance call for role play? Maybe a sexy camgirl or a shy, but horny, housekeeper? We've never done this kind of thing before and maybe we aren't even doing it now, but I want to get it right, just in case. My breaths are short and I'm light-headed and buzzing as if I've just stumbled on a new power source coming from inside me, activated by a flashing red light reminding me that I'm not alone and never was.

That night, I call him to see how the show went and also to listen for any unusual tone in his voice that could suggest he might have tuned in to my performance. I read an article somewhere about committing to a fantasy as a way to avoid humiliating your partner. I play it cool so as not to let on.

"Where are you?" I whisper.

"Singapore," he says. "Taipei tomorrow."

"What's it like there?" I ask.

"Honestly, I don't know, I only left the hotel to go to the venue. The hotel is nice though."

His voice sounds different, a little distracted or bored. Tired, more likely. I decide not to read into it. "That's good," I say. I hate small talk with people I already love. It never made sense to me, why we act out these formalities only to eventually get to the heart of things: souls, the meaning of life, how fears and desires are the result of unexpressed childhood trauma, the impossible task of reconciling self-objectification with self-respect, and how the body often does not represent the mind, if anything it betrays it. How the internet siphons energy from both, making me constantly tired. I want to ask him if he feels it, too, that strange distance between us.

"This is weird, right?"

"What? Sorry I can't hear you."

"It's like our signal is weak."

"Yeah, the signal is weak. It's better in the lobby."

As phone people, we are getting nowhere.

I find myself being pulled toward the red light, to better express myself nonverbally. Through body movements, I can more effectively convey abstract concepts and ineffable emotions. He tells me he has to soundcheck, which means I'm safe for at least another hour to practice. I stand in plain view of the camera, my feet firmly planted on the hardwood floor. I carefully walk my feet out into a splits position. Halfway down, I change my mind and cartwheel myself to a more comfortable squat. *What am I doing?* I suddenly hate him for watching. *What a creep. Why is he watching? Does he not trust me?* I make an ugly face, open my mouth wide and drool. "You like this?" I say. I consider covering the camera with a towel, unplugging it, burying it in the yard. Instead, I decide to be myself for the first time in my life. I defiantly rise to a standing position and begin my improvised one-woman show: the story of my life, from birth to childhood, to early adulthood. I make sure to spend extra time on the events that shaped me most, like the time my high school boyfriend performed a surprise baptism on me in his parents' pool while they watched and did nothing, or the time I learned I was allergic to tree nuts and found out you could die at any time and not just when you are very old.

By hour two, I tire myself out and sit cross-legged on the floor to address the camera directly. I tell it all about my loneliness and my feelings of inadequacy and the oblong mark on my back that I'm convinced has grown. I confess to it every fear I've ever had: that I lack the discipline to become someone great and will soon be found out. That I love him some days but other days am less sure and that no one can be sure of anything. Or that I withhold my admiration for him, for fear of seeming clingy and obsessive. I tell the camera that I accidentally broke the espresso machine and that I killed a lizard (in self-defense—I was being chased). At no point am I ever judged or interrupted, just listened to. I scooch up close, so close that my nose almost hits the camera lens, so he can get a good look at me and see inside my soul and know that it is good.

He never mentions it when he calls. I have a feeling he isn't watching, but it doesn't stop me. All that matters is that at any point, he could. I no longer need to know anything for sure. The red light comforts me. I tell it all my secrets. I relax my shoulders, stretch, rest. I unwrap one of my tiny handmade ceramic butts and place it on the fireplace mantel to make it my own. I hear a knock and a man in a uniform is standing at the door. He hands me a package. Eric's iPad. "Package," he says, "sign here." I thank him and watch him get into his truck and drive away.

Remembering the unique horror of a crush texting,
your so pretty

You can be in a deeply committed one-sided
relationship with many people without them
knowing

Them knowing would only complicate things

Keeping it one-sided does not discount its
legitimacy

During my last breakup, I watched a six-hour BBC
documentary called *The Death of Yugoslavia* to
calm myself

Can't believe I used to subject myself to the saddest
music on planet Earth for yeeeears and was also
like, "Why am I so sad?"

My biggest fear is finding out my boyfriend is just
a ghost with unfinished business

The Contestants

You might assume that once the cameras stop rolling, all the women in the mansion unzip their gowns and swim naked in the pool or drink those oversize margarita slushies until they pass out, but most of us just want to take out our hair extensions and go to bed. Everyone has their own reasons for being here, and very few of them have to do with falling in love. We're not idiots. I mean, yes, some of us are, but you don't sign up for something like this unless you want to change your life. We belong to a long lineage of women willing to risk public humiliation for a chance at a better life for ourselves and our children. What do we have to lose? We had nothing to begin with. Phoebe hasn't seen or spoken to her three-year-old son in weeks, and I think she's losing it. Sometimes I'll find her cradling a swan-shaped hotel towel in her arms just to have something delicate to hold. Elena's work visa lapsed so she's taken to memorizing scripture to impress Brad's Presbyterian parents for hometowns. Every night, I can hear her crying in another language. She says she'd rather die than get sent home.

I'm only here to locate my biological father on the off chance he's tuning in. It's not impossible; millions of people do every week. I've looked for him my entire life, but has he looked for me? Would he even know where to begin? He left my mother before I was born. They'd only been dating a few months before he moved to British Columbia (or just regular Colombia?) to do missionary work after graduating college. It'd been so long, my mother couldn't remember. She never told him about me—she didn't want him to resent us for ruining his life. His parents were extremely Catholic in that they were judgmental. Also abusive. I don't blame her for keeping me to herself. But don't you think he can sense some part of him out there, floating around? A phantom limb, weird dreams, mysterious chest pains, some vague, misplaced longing? People know. I like to imagine him flipping through channels and pausing at the sight of me on horseback, a mirror image of Pauline from Des Moines, his first love. There she is on national television, wearing a crop top, straddling a stallion. What if he's a cowboy? What if he lives on a ranch somewhere in Montana? I have no contact with the outside world, so I cling to the possibility of it like a life raft.

Just in case, I carry myself as if he were always watching. Whenever the producers ask me if I could see myself spending the rest of my life with Brad, I always say, "Not without my father's blessing," and look straight into the camera until they yell, "Cut!" None of it is usable. They beg me to just follow the script. Oh, and there's a script, by the way. You probably thought I actually hated Hannah for telling Brad not to make out with me because I had HPV, but none of that was true. I don't hate Hannah. The producers choreographed the whole thing—the champagne-flute toss, the hair pulling. They had to shoot it several times because I took my role very seriously; I would overdo it, throwing her into the pool, biting her arm, breaking skin. I wasn't afraid to give them a real show. She was a good sport; she could tell how much I needed it.

Out of the twelve women left, Hannah is my favorite. I'm not sure I would have ever noticed her in regular life, but with my scope of human interaction limited to this particular group of women, I've been forced to adjust my standards. I do my best to get along, but I'm a loner by nature. I was surprised to learn that I could do this: love people out of sheer will. I'm proud of how much I've grown. I remember my first day at the mansion: I was standing by the pool with something in my eye, lodged somewhere between my iris and tear duct, and every time I blinked, I could see it dart upward then float down in slow motion. I rubbed my eyelid, trying carefully not to smear any makeup off, but it was still there. It was shaped like a crescent moon, this thing, which was funny because Christine K. started telling me about the moon, and astrology, and how unseen forces dictate everything from our menstrual cycles to allergic reactions and if I could somehow call my mother to find out the exact time of my birth, she could email me a natal chart based on this information. I wanted to excuse myself, but I didn't know how. Once I moved into the mansion, everything, even very small things took enormous effort. Like knowing how to leave a conversation. Or going to the bathroom in front of other people. My body is too shy, I can always hear someone putzing around, right outside the door. I just sit there and pray for ambient noise, a blow dryer or a running faucet. It's becoming a real medical issue. My stomach hurts all the time. Some women leave the door wide-open while they do it; they seem to want a constant audience.

A lot can change in a matter of weeks. Accelerated by our forced intimacy and the producers' brainwashing tactics, we've grown to be like sisters. Or I guess, sister-wives. We've survived the psychological obstacle course designed to wear us down and make us complicit: isolation, sleep deprivation, calorie restriction, listening to pop music on an infinite loop. Our strong mental fortitude was rewarded with more screen time. Everyone brought their own flair to it: Mackenzie could cry on command, Yessica was a certified hypnotherapist, and Shelly could pole dance. Hannah had accomplished more than any of us, despite being considered "mature" at thirty-two. She had already made a fortune with the success of *Hello, My Name Is*, an app for people who have trouble remembering names. She developed technology that used vocal recognition to recall the name of the person you forgot and discreetly remind you via text message. The app had millions of downloads, because as it turns out, no one can remember anyone's name. She hoped to leverage the show as a platform to bring awareness to her humanitarian efforts. I admired her for her willingness to go topless at the first rose ceremony for victims of human trafficking. I told her I would've joined her if my dad wasn't watching. The fact that we had been cast as rivals on the show only made us closer in real life.

Most nights, Hannah and I like to meet in the hot tub to unwind from the day. None of the other women ever use the hot tub; they perform like method actors, often sleeping in their makeup to stay in character. They fear what might happen if it smeared off: what they would see, who they'd become. Our hot-tub conversations almost always start by sharing what we missed most about the world outside. Bread. The internet. Access to legal counsel. Freedom. Privacy. Full-coverage underwear.

"I miss the hum of freeway traffic, just the sound of life happening nearby," Hannah says. It's eerily quiet where we are, which is still unknown to us since we were blindfolded on the flight over. My guess is somewhere in Florida, considering the humidity and the size of the bugs.

"I miss wearing pants," I say. The strict dress code doesn't allow for them, unless they're cutoff jean shorts, which are not pants at all. Does it matter to us that we are active participants in the reinforcing of patriarchal systems that treat women like property, sold as infantilized, decorative props competing publicly for male validation to gain temporary status in the eyes of the fickle public who would no sooner destroy us should we ever, at any point, fail to titillate them? Of course. But I try not to think about it too much.

"Sure, I'm conflicted," she says, pushing her hands against the whirring jet to create a fountain. "But I would rather it be me here than someone else, someone more susceptible to abusing their power."

"Someone like Tonya," I say. Tonya was kicked off the show following the third episode after she failed to get a rose and had a full tantrum on the front lawn, forcing security to carry her into the SUV. She later claimed to be a victim of abuse in an incoherent long-form tell-all in some women's lifestyle blog, citing Brad's predatory behavior that made her feel self-conscious and "scared for her life" at times, despite never having interacted with him directly. Her accusations didn't square with that time she locked herself in the bathroom and refused to emerge until Brad gave her a date card. "I'm Mrs. Brad!" she wailed drunkenly into her mic. Brad wasn't even there; he was up in a hot-air balloon one-on-one date with Kelsea. Tonya was just a jilted fan taking her last gasps of fame before returning to obscurity, which, for her, was Sacramento. We all have our own versions of obscurity waiting for us.

"I hope she gets the help she needs," Hannah says.

"I heard that was all an act."

"What?"

"One of the producers told Shelly, who told me. Apparently it was just a media stunt to promote the launch of her new cruelty-free sunscreen line."

"I thought she was a flight attendant."

"She *was*."

"Oh. Good for her, I guess."

"I hate flying. Fear of heights," I say.

"Have you ever done ayahuasca?" she asks, pushing her legs out to float horizontally.

"No," I say, cupping my hand against the force of a warm jet.

"You should, it totally changed my life. I used to have a stutter."

"I have psoriasis," I say, in the spirit of sharing.

"What do you think is going to happen when you meet your dad?"

"God, I don't know. I guess I'll tell him how I spent my whole life looking for him and he'll apologize and offer me cash for all the birthdays he missed. At first, I'll hesitate, but then I'll accept."

"Have you ever considered that he might be dead?"

"No, never."

"I know when I'm going to die."

"What?"

"Yeah, do you want to know? Let me see your palm."

"No thanks," I say, crossing my arms. "He's definitely still alive."

"I believe you."

"Sometimes I feel like I'm already dead and no one told me."

"Like, *The Sixth Sense*?"

"I haven't seen it."

"Oh, whoops."

"I want to die alone," I say.

"Alone?"

"Yes, physically alone. It's such a private act, I don't want an audience."

"This show is like a big rehearsal for death," she says. "Think about it. It requires us to surrender ourselves fully, not only our valuables, our medication, our credit card numbers for incidentals. It asks us to give up our dignity, our bodies, our time."

"We're here for Brad," I say, quoting the script to the hidden surveillance cameras in the trees.

"Right. Brad."

"I love Brad," I say.

"Me too. He's so tall."

"And strong," I add.

"From all the . . . sports?" she says.

"Yes! Professional sports." I nod, cluelessly.

"I know I'm not here to make friends, but I'm glad we're friends," she says.

"Me too." We laugh at our futures, at how big and bright

they would be. A sudden garbled animal sound escapes from inside me.

"Wait, was that you?" she asks.

"It's my stomach." I give her a look that means I have to poop. The heat has cooked my insides. I am relaxed and calm and ready.

"Go, go, go," she says.

I hoist myself out and speed walk cautiously toward the nearest bathroom, barefoot and dripping wet. My guts moan and whistle with regret as motion-sensor lights from security cameras illuminate my path. It's time.

"You got this," Hannah whisper-yells in the distance.

I press my warm palm against my stomach, and pray.

I like to break the ice with a new friend by telling
them every traumatic thing that's ever happened
to me

When someone says "that's hilarious" instead of
just laughing . . .

All adult friendships are bound by a mutual
exchange of incriminating photos and text-message
collateral

An Anthropology is when you say sorry with a
tiny, expensive candle

Thinking about how I ended all my childhood
friendships with my signature curse, "Have a nice
life!!!"

I am no longer tolerating the "coy and secretive
about my birthday" type, either tell me or don't, I
refuse to play your little game!!!

Ghost Baby

I was in the room, hovering in the corner, unseen. The man, Carl, was under the covers next to the woman, Emma, who was sitting up with her legs covered by a top quilt. Lying down meant giving up, but she was still awake and upright—her face awash in the glow of her phone. Carl was also on his phone, playing a game. Look at him, a grown man. Winning points, then losing them. Most nights were like this. I already knew it wasn't going to happen, but when he grabbed her hand and placed it on his neck for a massage, I felt a jolt of something resembling hope. Her hand just needed to slide down and rest on his crotch, which would activate blood flow, stimulating arousal. Unlike the rest of him, Carl's penis was ready at a moment's notice, stirred by only a brush, a small gust of air, or an erotically shaped fruit. Although I couldn't speak directly to his genitals, I felt an alliance with them; we had the same ambitions, the same end goal. *Touch it!* I commanded in an undetectably high frequency. Dogs barked in the distance. Emma couldn't hear me, of course.

She gave his neck a few weak rubs, barely trying, then gave up and returned to her phone. What was on her phone, anyway? From what I could read, it was a news article about a decades-old cold case involving the gruesome murder of a babysitter. The case had new evidence: an anonymous tip and a DNA match that led to an arrest. *Get a life, Emma. By that I mean, get a life inside you. Tonight!* I found her morbid obsession with death ironic, since I'm basically dead, or rather prebirth, and it's not fun. Being disembodied severely limits what you're capable of doing on the earthly realm. Sure, you can fly around to remote islands and exotic locales, but then you're stuck watching people jump off waterfalls and swim with dolphins while you try to remember the feeling of being submerged in Mother Earth's giant saltwater womb. Must be nice. Or, if you prefer, you can wander around gated communities and enter any home you want: mansions and country homes and cliffside villas where celebrities hide out while their surgeries heal. But once you've done it all, you're mostly stuck waiting until you can take another birth. Try waiting outside time—it's agonizing. You're constantly like, *Wait, was that ten minutes or ten years? How long have I been here? What is* here*, anyway?* There are no longer edges to my days, just a lonely swirling expanse of eternity.

This particular couple wouldn't have been my first choice, but that part wasn't up to me. A governing celestial counsel assigns you a couple based on a number of factors that have to do with your karmic order, astrology, and available human inventory. Likewise, they consider what kind of effect your integration will have on your host parents. Given the precarity of modern relationships, you may find yourself attached to one partner specifically. In my case, Emma. I began visiting her sometime after her first period. It took me a while to realize that not every boy she liked would become my father. Her hot older cousin Aiden, for example, or her fourth-grade science teacher who rode a Vespa and said, "Call me Paul," or one of the Jonas Brothers (not Kevin). It was only when I saw Carl at a party years later that I knew. There he was: *Dada*. He was wearing a backward cap and khakis, unironically, but my judgments were muted by the sound of what I could only describe as celestial church bells clanging victoriously. It took him a while to notice Emma's dead stare from across the room, but once he looked up from his phone, he smiled. They didn't meet that night, but their vibrational soul cord had been established; it was a matter of time. I was told to "trust the process" because the higher-ups have been doing this since before time, which is a concept that is inconceivable to you, so don't even bother trying. Carl watched one YouTube video on quantum physics and thinks he's an expert now. Sure, Carl. Whatever.

As instructed, I'd been waiting in the corner of the room for months (I was guessing) for Carl and Emma to have sex so that I could swoop in and assume human form as their child. As a spirit, I'm weightless and formless—I'm barely anything at all. Consciousness without a container. But I am teeming with potential: I'm almost a baby, which is almost a person. I'm told I will forget about all this once it happens. I'm told that life is mostly painful and tedious, deficient in meaning.

But I'm also told there are drugs for that. And if I'm lucky, I might find my soul mate, become famous, or come into a large sum of money. Had I ever been so fortunate in a past life? Did anything cool happen to me? Did my life matter at all? I'm told that I will never know, as my mind has been wiped and restored to its original factory settings. But what about the people I left behind, loved ones, children? I grieve these faceless, nameless people. Or were they enemies? In that case, I curse them with what little power I have, which is practically nothing. Demons are the ones moving furniture around and turning appliances on and off, not us. I don't know when that rumor started. Besides my omnipotent knowledge of all human thought and events, past and present, I can't interfere in the material world at all. The most I can do is occasionally enter a person's dream state and freak them out a little. Not well enough to do any damage, just enough for them to wake up and say, "I had the weirdest dream! I saw a being, but I wasn't afraid, strangely, I felt at peace," something like that. Meanwhile I'm assuming grotesque hybrid animal shapes, like a horse-shark type thing or a beautiful mermaid who shape-shifts into your mother, but it never does much. People see what they want to see, I guess.

Around midnight, Emma put her phone on the nightstand and turned off the light. Carl saved his place in the game, then rolled over to her to say good night. Finally! Contact. He wrapped his long, spidery arms around her and swept her hair aside. Sensing what was coming, she fought to break loose, but he maintained his grip. He put his mouth to her ear and jammed his tongue into her earhole. She screamed and laughed, kicking him away.

"What?" he said. "I thought you liked it?"

"Ew, no," she squealed. "Leave me alone!"

It'd been six months with this tongue thing, sometimes alternating with a toenail graze or an armpit tickle, real child's play stuff. Sometimes she'd fart in retaliation and I could almost hear his member soften with platonic affection. They used to have sex more often before they moved in together, but Emma had an IUD in then. It was unbearable for me, like watching thousands of babies get annihilated, entire civilizations wiped out and flushed down the toilet, swallowed, or led astray down the indistinguishable darkness of Emma's butthole. Yes, I can see everything in high definition. (If you find yourself getting hung up on the laws governing my omnipotence and what I can and can't do, you're missing the point entirely and it might benefit you to surrender to the paradox of consciousness instead of attempting to demystify it through logic. You've got the perspective of a pinhole. Just embrace the mystery.)

For years, my nemesis, birth control, safeguarded them against an existential threat (me), giving them the freedom to experiment: doing it in public parks, hotel hot tubs, and once in the presence of Carl's roommate, Ian, who they only realized was watching halfway through and let him stay after he promised not to be weird about it. Things changed once they signed the lease on their own apartment. Overnight, their shared space became a museum of fungal creams, antidepressants, stained underwear, morning breath, Carl's dog-eared copy of *Atlas Shrugged*, and the mystifying migration of pubic tumbleweeds from the bathroom floor to every corner of the apartment. Little hairs appeared everywhere from kitchen countertops to ice-cube trays. Every piece of their corporeal selves had been laid out on display under harsh track lighting, becoming mutual collateral, bonding them like siblings. They'd never been this exposed and this comfortable with another person. This, they thought, must be real love.

Emma finally decided to get her IUD removed before her health insurance expired, so that she could "feel" herself again. I couldn't agree more. Afterward, she said her hormones were all out of whack, making her chronically bloated and depressed. Her teenage acne angrily resurfaced, which led to a regrettable decision to get bangs. She said she didn't feel "in her body" anymore. All I could think was *Ha! Just you wait.* Carl presented as patient and understanding, but his compulsive masturbation suggested a deeper frustration with Emma's erratic moods. He placated his unwieldy animal want with a routine, almost-medical act every morning, like brushing his teeth. Whenever I witnessed him in the shower, tugging violently at himself, his stare vacant and mouth half-opened watching muted porn on his phone, I thought, *Thank God, I won't remember any of this when I'm incarnated.* I felt flush with embarrassment just for being in the room, like he could sense the potency of his own offspring looming in the ether and that alone aroused him.

On more than one occasion it appeared as though we briefly locked eyes, as if he were looking right at me. I know that's impossible—no one can see me except for a few mediums who've accidentally summoned me during seances, mistaking me for a beloved relative, someone's late husband or great-grandmother. If I'm bored enough, I'll play along and say something vague like "It's buried in the yard!" and then watch them spend months digging up their property in search of treasure. Anyone can summon a spirit, but almost no one can summon the right spirit at the right time. It's actually a little presumptuous to assume your deceased relatives are always on call, with nothing better to do than wait around to talk to you about the results of your recent job interview. Whatever happened to rest in peace? Leave them be.

It was a Friday night, and I was feeling unusually hopeful. There was something in the air, which I later discovered to be the smell of weed wafting in through the vents from the German exchange students who lived below. Carl and Emma lived on the second floor of an old pencil-factory-turned-loft building with concrete floors, exposed brick, and a lobby furnished with gray modular furniture resembling life-size Lego pieces. The sparse industrial architecture reflected a kind of stoicism, lacking in sentimentality. Their generation had become utilitarian, efficient, machinelike. In the hallways, none of the tenants made eye contact. They only ever spoke when a dog was present, usually to the dog, only engaging with the owner about dog-related matters without acknowledging the owner's full humanity. Otherwise, tenants kept to themselves, living alone in overly air-conditioned pods of one or two.

Carl and Emma had recently instituted "date-night Fridays," which I thought was only something you did once the spark was gone, as instructed by your couples' therapist, along with "do one thing every day that scares you." Scheduled romance didn't have the same thrill to it, but Carl and Emma compensated for its absence with heavy drinking, which gave the evening a warm glow and allowed them to temporarily disassociate long enough to forget this and most other problems. When they returned home from dinner, Emma, visibly drunk, pulled Carl in for an embrace, then began thrusting her hips against his thigh in a humping motion: slowly at first, then faster and more labored, panting like a horny dog. Carl laughed as he tried to peel her off, pretending to be creeped out by her performance.

This kind of silly foreplay was the only way for either of them to initiate real sex, and if the gesture proved to be unsuccessful, the initiator could always claim to be only kidding, then start play-wrestling to avoid the sting of rejection.

Carl placed Emma's hand on his visible erection, and she said something like, "Oh, hello there, sir!" He ignored her as he started kissing her neck. I could suddenly relate to those nature photographers who wait for months to capture a rare sighting of an endangered mountain lion as she finally emerges from her cave. It's a mixture of elation and disbelief, and a feeling that any sudden movement could ruin it entirely. I imagined having breath, then holding it. Carl carefully removed Emma's shirt, catching a strap between the teeth of her hair clip as he lifted, accidentally pulling her hair. Emma helped Carl untangle her, while Carl whispered, "Sawwy, are you okay?" in a baby voice. Carl, the eager feminist, began undoing Emma's pants, then paused to ask if he could go down on her.

"Wait, I haven't showered, I might smell," she said unselfconsciously, and stuck her hand down her jeans to check. "Yeah, I do a little bit," she said. "I kind of like it, though, is that weird?" Her green fox eyes and baby face cursed her with a misleading kind of attractiveness that failed to represent her complex inner world. It was a kind of false advertising that confused men and annoyed most women. She found any excuse to reject it, usually through neglecting her appearance and describing her bodily secretions in great detail. She believed that being somewhat gross all the time would make her less appealing to prospective rapists and murderers, while signaling to women that she was nonthreatening, but eventually it became her entire personality. "Let me go wash it quick," she said, which just meant splashing cold water on herself and then drying her vagina with a hand towel that went unwashed for weeks. They'd talked about designating one towel for sex but kept forgetting which one it was.

Carl had a weird thing about towels, but knew to pick his battles, having recently broken their cardinal rule of never shitting in front of each other. He'd barged in on her while she was in the shower and ran to the toilet. "Don't look at me!" he'd said. "Stop! I'm in here! No!" she yelled. "I can't, I'm sorry! It's an emergency!" She made the mistake of looking. The image of him on the toilet imprinted itself into the dark folds of her brain. From then on, she could never unsee it. She recalled it again as she patted herself dry, as if to blot the memory away.

Carl, left briefly unattended and thus instantly bored, grabbed for his phone to check Twitter while he waited. Emma returned, completely naked. She did a nervous twirl and lay down on the stiff, gray sectional they'd bought together because it looked nice, and for no other reason. "Sorry I didn't shave," she said, opening her legs as he dutifully got on his knees and used both hands as if parting the seas. I watched intently, like a gymnastics coach, praying for Carl to land the dismount. *Focus, Carl. Eyes on the prize.*

He buried his head between her legs while she played a slideshow of sexy vignettes in her mind to steady her focus. These images were private to her and exempt from any moral scrutiny so long as they were confined to the psyche and never uttered aloud to anyone. They were all fairly benign, other than a situation involving a horse and a few others that concerned the very young and the very old. The slideshow worked reliably as long as she stayed on course. But during the girl-on-girl bathtub scene, she noticed her mother standing in the corner of the room with her arms crossed. Startled, she quickly became distracted, detouring into childhood memories: the softness of her grandmother's speckled, blue hands; the strange pride she felt for holding in her pee on long family road trips; her dead cat, Petunia. This led to unrelated thoughts about a recent subscription she'd forgotten to cancel that'd been on autopay for months now, and that gnawing feeling that someone, somewhere was mad at her. Panic bloomed inside her. She could never return to the lesbian bathtub knowing that her entire family would be there by now, asking her why she still hadn't accepted their friend requests online, or why she no longer believed in God.

Emma finally gave up and said, "Actually, wanna just do me?" Carl wiped his mouth and obliged. I'd heard whispers that romance had died and there was no longer a need for it. Everything had been optimized, streamlined, and abbreviated. "P in my V," she'd say, without a hint of sexiness in her voice. In doing away with the ceremony of lovemaking, something had been lost. But it wasn't my job to restore it, all I needed was successful insemination.

They relocated from the sofa to the bedroom, agreeing that it was better not to ruin the couch in case they ever wanted to sell it. *Why would we ever want to sell a perfectly good couch? Not unless we broke up,* Emma thought. It seemed the worst thing that could ever happen to her, yet the thought of impermanence suddenly turned her on. She pretended this would be the last time they'd ever have sex and her performance alone would determine their fate.

Emma rolled back on the edge of the bed, while Carl stood over her. Carl's butt clenched with each thrust, revealing a hideous constellation of butt-cheek dimples, graciously hidden from Emma's view. He struggled at first but soon found his rhythm while Emma bent her knees up and over her shoulders. She always amazed herself with her own flexibility, like some hidden talent she'd never cultivated but was always available whenever the situation called for it. It was a natural gift, like a high metabolism or thick hair. This acrobatic legwork did most of the heavy lifting for her while the rest of her body lay limp like a dead person. Occasionally, she would moan in support. She considered this her signature move. She had no other moves.

A few silent minutes later, Carl had that look on his face, that helpless, pained expression that I'd come to recognize as Shower Face. He kept his eyes shut as he readied himself for the big release. Emma, sensing completion, started chanting, "Yes, harder! Harder! HARDER, CARL!" This threw him off a little because he was going as hard as humanly possible. He'd harbored an inferiority complex since childhood and had only recently discovered that he enjoyed being humiliated. He'd never mentioned this to Emma for fear of being judged, which you would think he'd be into, but the secrecy preserved the necessary element of shame. Explaining it would ruin it, as I have just done. He began convulsing to the tune of, "oh, oh, oh, uh, oh," until he collapsed next to her in bed, burying his face in a pillow. Emma's satisfaction came not from her own physical release, but from basking in the brief flicker of total control she had over Carl. This is how she preferred him: a submissive little boy, whimpering with pleasure.

I was too distracted to notice that he'd pulled out and finished on her stomach. *Are you kidding me?* I looked down at the aftermath: my life, my future left out to dry. I watched as Carl cleaned the crime scene off Emma's stomach with their unwashed, multipurpose hand towel. What a waste. I felt duped, once again. At thirty-four, Emma wanted a child in the ambient sort of way you want to be the kind of person who wakes up early and exercises without making any substantive changes to your lifestyle or behavior. She spent her twenties avoiding me and her early thirties half dreading my arrival and half worrying about whether I was still possible. Some days, she'd even go so far as to joke about baby names with Carl. *We'll name him Carl Junior. If it's a girl: Carly Junior. Wendy? No, Dairy Queen.* They had no real plans, just vague theories about what mental illnesses and personality defects their off-spring might inherit.

What a cruel joke. I suppose it was my fault for getting my hopes up. I had to find a way to accept my current reality as a pre-corporeal entity. I would need to start acting like I preferred it, as if it were a kind of pleasant purgatory, everything in its own time, what's the rush, etc. I didn't want to come into the world with the stink of resentment, I needed to be pure of heart.

"Do you want to watch something together?" Carl asked, breaking their usual routine of separately staring at their phones until their eyes burned.

"Sure," said Emma, "like what?"

"I don't know, something light, maybe a comedy," said Carl. "You pick," he added. His face was flush with a stupid kind of happiness. She scrolled the menu screen in silence for forty-five minutes, unable to find anything to watch despite the infinite options available to them. They'd either already watched it or something like it.

"There's nothing," Emma sighed, "I give up."

"Okay, can we watch a YouTube clip then?" said Carl. He

couldn't end the night defeated when everything else had been so perfect.

"Yeah, pick whatever," said Emma, reaching for her phone out of habit.

Carl found a video of a chimp that acts like a dog. "Chimp Thinks It's a Dog" was the title. They watched more videos about animals doing funny things, which eventually led them to a video featuring an intelligent octopus being subjected to a battery of psychological tests. After several attempts, the octopus miraculously opened a sealed jar like a magic trick. Carl and Emma were impressed by the octopus's problem-solving skills and agreed to stop eating octopus, then debated whether calamari were still okay, since they'd yet to find a video featuring an intelligent squid.

I watched the weeks pass, forced to endure long stretches of wasted time. Emma binged all six seasons of *The Sopranos*, read supplement reviews online, and worked on a Pinterest board called "Dream Home," populated by images of designer furniture she could never afford. Carl argued with strangers on the internet, refreshed his cryptocurrency investment app, and watched a documentary on Leonard Cohen that inspired him to write a poem and publish it online, then delete it hours later after no one seemed wowed by it. They acted like they had all the time in the world and there was no way for me to warn them: Death comes for all!

"Mama! Dada! Ball!" I practiced saying, really imagining my grabby little baby hand wrapped around Emma's finger, her hair in my mouth. I longed to be a tiny, blameless creature in her arms. I thought that by repeating the words over and over, they'd lose their awkwardness and start sounding like meaningless vibrations. Like a band name. But it all came out forced and unnatural. I wondered if it'd become easier with vocal cords. I wondered about other things, too, like: *Has there been a mix-up? Is there another Carl and Emma out there for me?* I kept quiet, not wanting my harmless speculation to offend the "all-powerful gods." Perhaps this was my punishment for past transgressions and Carl and Emma were simply a part of my lawful, karmic comeuppance. For starters, there was nothing parent-y about them. They seemed like the type to dress me up and post photos of me on the internet against my will, recording my every move and exploiting me for content. How else were they going to pay for my living expenses? Carl didn't even have a real job; he was a freelance journalist writing about topics like climate change and technology, devolving into personal essays on cancel culture and autofiction because it tended to pay more. He spent his free time making skateboarding videos with his friends. Emma was finishing up her last semester as an intern at an architecture firm but had recently decided that she hated it. Despite her student loan debt and utter lack of professional experience, she was considering a career change. Something more rewarding; something in the healing arts. Still, I believed their love would provide a protective shield around us all, inoculating us from their poor judgment and generally irresponsible lifestyle.

But was it enough? Carl had recently "liked" another woman's photo on social media. The caption was a lengthy and spirited call to register to vote, featuring a photo of her pronounced cleavage. "Now that I have your attention," it began. Her name was Remi and her bio described her as a *writer, model and activist*. A triple threat (to my existence). I told myself the like was an innocent gesture of his support for the democratic process. But the act itself proved slippery. The *like* became a *comment*, which became a *direct message*, and so forth. Harmless banter at first, mutual frustration with "the system," links to progressive political websites and Twitter threads reinforcing their shared worldview. They soon traded war stories from Thanksgivings with hostile relatives and dystopian predictions of impending civil war and economic collapse. There was never any mention of Emma. She had no idea, not even when she practiced her energy-clearing sessions on him, hovering her hands above him to absorb any excess ancestral grief blockages he might be carrying. All she could feel was a simmering rage over his belly.

"Are you mad at me?" she asked.

"No, why?" He was on his back with his eyes closed.

"I'm picking up on some anger," she said.

"I ate a burrito an hour ago," he joked, releasing a stinky, soundless fart on command.

"I honestly think there's something wrong with you, medically." Emma knew Carl was distracted by something but assumed it had to do with work. *Work* was a catchall phrase Carl used to describe all his online activity. He considered it more of a lifestyle.

"Want to see a magic trick?" Emma asked.

"Not really in the mood, sorry," he said, turning over.

"Pweeease, it's real magic I promise. I have special powers."

"Okay," he conceded.

"Okay, watch, I'm going to move this pen with my mind," she said. She stared at the pen intently for two minutes.

"I'm pretty tired, Em."

"Can I kiss you over your underwear?" she asked, trying to redeem herself.

"What?" Her need for constant validation annoyed Carl, but he didn't have the energy to explain why.

"That's all, I swear. Then I'll never bother you again," she said.

"Okay, fine."

Emma unzipped Carl's jeans and pressed her mouth against his cotton boxers. "Mwah!" she said, smacking her lips.

"Thanks," he said, zipping his pants back up.

"I'm pretty tired, too," she said, pivoting her approach to seem aloof. She got into bed, fully clothed, hoping he'd notice the bit and laugh. He sat up in bed looking at his phone. She started playing footsies to get his attention, but he wouldn't budge.

"What?" he said.

"You're being weird," she whispered. Arguing reminded her too much of her parents; she did her best to avoid it. She preferred the slowness of a thoughtfully worded long-form email.

"You're being weird, actually," he said.

"How am I being weird?" she asked.

"With all your Reiki and magic stuff," he said.

"Fine, I won't bother you with it anymore," she said.

"Are you getting your period or something?" This was low-hanging fruit, even for Carl.

"No, are you?"

"Yeah, actually. I'm bleeding out of my butthole. That's how it works, right?" Phew okay, we were back. Carl with the *yes and.*

"It might be hemorrhoids," she said, playfully trying to worm her finger up his butt.

"No, stop, it hurts!" He laughed, betraying his serious affect.

"Can I at least look at them? I'm a healer. I can shrink them."

"No, don't! I've already named them."

"What are their names?"

"The Hemsworths."

"More like Holesworths . . ." she said, dragging the joke a beat past its natural expiration.

If I had no skin in the game, I would tell Emma to dump this loser and find someone new, preferably with health insurance and some upper-body strength. But I felt a connection with Emma, in that we both felt we had no other choice and that this relationship had to be salvaged or we would die of a broken heart. I wouldn't die, but I would continue not living, which is more or less the same as dying, likely worse.

Emma would've understood Carl's infatuation with Remi; she had crushes of her own. But instead of indulging in them, she did the opposite. Whenever she felt a crush coming on, she constructed elaborate fictional narratives about the crush that provoked rage and disgust in her. She convinced herself that her yoga teacher, Forest, had fathered thousands of children in a decades-long sperm-donor scam. Her coworker Jesse? Human trafficker. Her optometrist, Richard? Near death. She imagined his body riddled with sores and all manner of contagious diseases. Preemptively squashing crushes before they flourished was the key to long-term relationship success. She could've taught Carl her techniques had he simply come to her. Instead, cowardly, he retreated inward, and by inward I mean, his phone.

I abandoned my post and rested briefly on Emma's chest, the way a dog would, hoping she might sense me and take comfort in my presence without knowing why. When a person feels joy for no reason, it's usually because of a nearby benevolent spirit wishing them well. The opposite is true, too, but try not to think about it too much.

Emma woke up early the next morning to jog. Never a good

sign. Jogging was for people who want to improve themselves in an unspecified way, whereas activities such as kickboxing or ballroom dancing are for people who know what they want. These activities also happen to require a willing partner, unlike jogging, which is a solitary pursuit, by design. Jogging in pairs is just two individuals who happen to be jogging together, one slowing the other down, causing distraction and mutual resentment. Jogging was also something Carl hated, which was the point. Emma was making all sorts of points, mostly subtle ones that were a little too abstract for Carl to pick up on. Her active withholding of sex looked too much like her indifference to it in that no sex was being had either way, so the added sprinkle of hostility went unnoticed. I began to wonder if anyone in the world was having sex. I checked their downstairs neighbors. I crossed the street into a cul-de-sac, college dorms—nothing. I later overheard Emma on the phone saying that a national day of mourning had been declared after a bomb went off at a nearby mall. Tragedy: the ultimate libido killer.

Carl ended up leaving town for a week to cover a protest over armed mall cops. His absence grew into its own familiar shape that Emma eventually preferred to the sound of him sighing loudly at his computer, waiting for Emma to ask what was wrong. The answer was always some version of "everything." He continued following the trail of civil unrest from city to city and upon his brief return for clean underwear and supplies, he appeared different, like a stranger. He grew his hair out long and got one ear pierced for some reason. Each incremental change helped Emma forget what she ever liked about him anyway.

As far as I could tell, the Remi thing was over before it had begun. She left him "on read" for a few days, causing him to compulsively check in on her online activity, wondering what he'd said to offend her or, worse, to bore her. He reviewed their correspondence and confirmed that he was perfectly charming, almost mentor-like and therefore blameless. Her silence had nothing to do with him, personally. Reflecting on it, he even found her to be a little immature. This made sense, given that she was nine years younger than him. He wondered aloud to his friends if he should continue reaching out or protect his dignity and preemptively block her. They all agreed that blocking was the best and clearest message to send, then they all touched the tips of their surfboards together as a gesture of homoerotic affection safely buried under layers of irony and alcohol.

Emma existed only peripherally to Carl now; she reminded him too much of his old self, the one he'd shed as he became radicalized into an activist. He resented her for this reminder. There was never a formal discussion about breaking up; it happened so excruciatingly slowly that it was merely implied. Articulating it was too painful and direct, and they no longer spoke in painful and direct ways.

Emma moved out. She left the gray sofa behind, believing it to be "haunted" now. I did my best not to take offense to that. After that, Carl's texts shortened until all vowels were eliminated and what was left remained lowercase: *thx! np! ttyl!* A month went by with no texts exchanged. I don't know the exact details because I too left town and went on a cruise to get my mind off things. Out at sea, I watched aging couples dance to old-timey music, with their tan lines and dentures glowing in the dark. I watched lonely old men gamble away their life savings and console themselves by gorging on unlimited buffet shrimp and fat-free frozen yogurt, telling themselves it's healthy. I witnessed several crimes including a murder that

would later be deemed an accident, citing lack of evidence—
namely, a body. I also saw a humpback whale. Emma would've
enjoyed it.

After a stout British woman bonked her head on the pool
diving board, her head injury opened a portal to the spirit world
and allowed her to communicate with me. No one believed her,
but it was nice to have some company for once. At first, she just
kept asking for her three wishes, and I kept telling her that's
not what I do, and anyway, did she really think I'd be hanging out with her if I had that kind of power? I'd be sprouting
eyeballs inside a womb right now, no offense. Then she said
something I'll never forget; she said, "You're more powerful
than you think." Something about her British accent gave her
an air of authority, and so, I let myself believe her.

When I returned, I found Emma sulking with her old friend
and new roommate Mandy, who gave an impassioned speech
on how she'd never liked Carl anyway, citing a list of times he
was rude to her. Emma nodded in agreement even though she
thought Mandy was kind of a bitch and probably deserved it.
Mandy's comments were meant to comfort Emma and validate
her decision, but they stirred an unexpected defensiveness in
her. Her mind was suddenly awash in memories of the good
times she and Carl had shared together. The everyday acts of
heroism he displayed by catching a mouse in the kitchen and
disposing of the body in a shoebox burial service out of respect,
or his impressive ability to assemble IKEA furniture without
consulting instructions, or the way he really listened when she
complained about anyone other than him; the way he always
agreed. She recalled false memories, too, ones I'd implanted
after weeks of concentration: Carl catching her moments
before she peered over the edge of a rocky seaside cliff, nearly

falling to her death, the annual birthday card he'd written her listing all her best qualities. "You're a strong woman" one of them read, "so flexible." I guess I *was* more powerful than I thought. Emma blew her nose with her shirt, patiently waiting for Mandy to finish her thoughts on why Carl was definitely gay. She'd spent most of the evening waiting.

Carl was waiting, too, for his dad to finish up in the bathroom so he could go. He'd moved back in with his parents after making big bets on crypto called MegaKoinz and losing it all. He spent most of his nights flanked between his snoring parents on the couch, watching old Jim Carrey movies, the ones where he hits rock bottom and learns some big life lessons, like being honest or saying yes to life, or how hard it was to be God. Carl especially liked the part where Jim Carrey redeems himself, despite the years of pain he'd caused himself and everyone around him. He could relate, as a fellow protagonist. It made him miss his old life, especially Emma.

Meanwhile, Mandy suggested to Emma that they make nachos. "Let's be bad," she said. Emma agreed, having no other choice; the living room was her bedroom now. At that moment, her phone lit up. She glanced down and nearly choked. It was a text from Carl. All it said was *Sup?* The brevity of the message contained a whole universe of unsaid words inside it. It was a question just for her. An invitation. An appeal. Emma stared at the text, beaming.

I rested against her shoulder, leaned into her ear and whispered, "Let's be bad."

I think about the love of a future baby like a drug I haven't tried yet

Giving Up

I hated Jesper. I barely knew him, but I hated him as if he'd wronged me over the course of several lifetimes; as if he'd done something so unforgivable, we both forgot what it was entirely. Only in the forgetting could we sit in the same room together, day in and day out. We shared a small room on the second floor of an office building, overlooking the noisy outdoor patio of a restaurant I couldn't afford to eat at. Jesper was Danish, which wasn't the problem, but it was the only thing he'd ever told me about himself. I could have asked him other questions, but I didn't want to reveal how little I knew about the geography of that region. Did that mean he was from Denmark or the Netherlands? Was he also then Dutch—like, are those two interchangeable? Or is Dutch the language and Danish the people? Is Holland involved somehow? I just said something like "Very cool" out of self-hatred and returned to my screen.

He was the first to arrive each morning, so when I came in the ceiling fan would already be set to maximum speed. Have you ever been subjected to light wind for eight hours a day? It's a kind of hell. No matter what I did, wisps of hair softly whipped against my forehead like tiny invisible bugs. The pile of papers on my desk blew wildly, threatening to leave, then changing its mind. It was a subtle attack, like the frequency of ultrasonic waves.

He was always playing dubstep on full volume with cheap headphones, forcing me to listen to an isolated synth for a twenty-minute-long song. The obnoxious melodies wormed themselves into my brain so that I sometimes found myself humming along involuntarily. He added his own percussion by pounding away at his keyboard with impressive speed, as if he were being controlled by a high-functioning parasite or possessed by the spirit of an artist with unfinished business. The steady thrum of his keys irritated me so much that I some-times took to tapping randomly, not even forming words or sentences but a torrent of nonsensical letters, symbols, and numbers—*AsVV95Js//blafRIL!!!!*—just to make a sound, to prove I existed.

As a new tenant, I said nothing, and he took my silence as an agreeableness or a lack of preference due to my being a cool, low-maintenance artist type. Anyone willing to work in this little dump had to have low standards. Some days I pictured him getting hit by a car—not badly enough to die, but enough to transform him into a new person. I'd waited too long to speak up, and when I finally did politely ask him to turn the fan

off, he obliged, then returned from lunch and absentmindedly
turned it back on out of habit or as a means of reasserting dominance. Maybe I wanted to kill him, or myself, although he was
more of the problem, so yes, him. Until I was ready to kill him
on the physical plane, I was killing him psychically, through
telepathic signals meant to trigger feelings of worthlessness.
I couldn't tell if it was working, but he stopped wearing that
wool hipster cowboy hat around me, so I remained hopeful.

Whenever I found myself trembling with rage over his
offenses, I'd close my eyes and try to come up with reasons to
like him. Number one: he had never tried to rape me. He technically could, but he hadn't and most likely wouldn't. Sometimes I would pretend he knew he could rape me and chose
not to every day, and I was thankful for that. Number two:
he'd never once asked about my art. He truly didn't care if I
made art or if I sat here all day doing nothing besides stare
out the window or cyberbully people from my old high school.
The only thing he expected me to do was pay rent, empty the
trash can, and lock the door when I left. Everyone else in my
life seemed overly preoccupied with my artistic career, which
required me to constantly defend myself and reassure them that
I'm fine, fine, fine, great, so grateful, so blessed to get to do
what I do. But if they seemed like the type to give me money,
I'd tell them the truth: I was barely scraping by and I couldn't
work hard or fast enough to keep up and I hadn't created any
personal work since my solo show three years ago because I
never had any time and was always mysteriously tired (maybe
some autoimmune thing? thyroid-related?) but I couldn't afford
health insurance, so I just took vitamin C chewables and tur-
meric pills and hoped for the best. This confessional approach
only ever worked once, when I sat next to a lonely middle-aged

businessman on a flight and he ended up giving me fifty dollars and his phone number, out of pity. I'd since lost his number, but I would think of him every time I overdrafted and wonder what he was up to.

Naively, I had anticipated a seamless upward trajectory toward a thriving art career, propelled solely by the intensity of my wanting it. I clung to premature signs of my potential, my early work: brooding sunflower watercolor paintings, complicated zoo-animal napkin origami, and my Matisse-inspired macaroni art, all featured prominently in my fourth-grade student newsletter, published by my teacher Ms. Baker—an early fan who mistook my unbrushed hair, forgotten snacks, and occasional stutter as signs of neglect. I was fine, but the one time I accidentally called her "Mom," she burst into tears with maternal recognition. She really believed in me.

Another sign came just after I graduated with an MFA and negative eighty thousand dollars, when I landed on an indie art magazine's list of "emerging female illustrators to watch," which I coasted on for far too long, considering the magazine folded a year later. Seven years was more than enough time to finish emerging and establish myself as a serious artist. Instead, I started freelancing and ended up spending most of my time drawing zodiac animals to represent what type of life insurance you should buy. I never told anyone about the corporate art I made, because it wasn't real art. Real art was meaningful and honest: a person's soul—materialized. But making real art required focus, time, and energy, and I was too dopamine deficient from years of staring at screens to finish anything substantive. I didn't have a choice; being online was crucial to any artist's success. A well-curated social presence had the power to elevate mediocre art and create a vague impression that you were someone important, or successful, or at the very least, you existed. As such, I wasted huge chunks of my day reposting art memes to maintain my algorithmic relevancy until I had real work to share, but finding the right meme took hours, and the act of posting always left me icky and depleted, as if my soul had temporarily left my body, out of embarrassment.

On a Tuesday morning, Jesper was sitting at his desk peeling a hard-boiled egg for breakfast. The fan whirred rotten, sulfuric smells into my face. I looked at him, then looked down at the brunch patrons through the window, like a hostage, with one hand pressed against the glass, hoping that someone would look up and see me: a person in distress. Oversize sun hats covered the patio like lily pads. No one looked up. I breathed through my mouth and went back to working on a logo for a food-truck company that couldn't afford to pay me but promised me free tacos for life. It was an empty gesture, but I had already screenshot and printed the offer as proof. After a few minutes, Jesper turned the fan up a notch and a lone strand of hair slapped against my temple like a soft, unwanted kiss. I tucked it behind my ear and it swung back harder, in retaliation. Then again. I wanted to scream. I had no other option but to rise slowly from my seat.

Standing up gave me instant relief, the kind you only get when you've made a big life decision. I collected my few papers, my pencils, and my drawing tablet and stuffed them in my backpack. Jesper continued his trancelike tapping; he didn't look up once. I threw up a peace sign and instantly regretted it. I walked out of there for the last time. From the hallway I could hear him cough and hoped it was the beginning of a choke.

———

People always ask when you first knew you really made it, but nobody asks when you knew you didn't and maybe never would. My parents hated each other, but they never gave up, and look what happened to them! Cancer. You know what's better than sticking it out? Knowing when it's time to go. I walked out into the parking lot, toward the dumpster where my bike was locked, and added another reason to like Jesper: he changed my life. I wasn't only giving up on the studio, I was giving up on being an artist. I'd never considered it before, but it made so much sense. I liked the cleanness of it: there would be no need for ceremony, just a quiet, dignified exit out of this life and into a new one entirely. People do it all the time. Saying the words "I give up" out loud to myself immediately filled my body with adrenaline. I ran all the stop signs riding home.

As soon as I got home, I told Mark the news. He gave me a confused look and joked that if I stopped working he'd be forced to take up the family business. "Your dad's an optometrist," I said.

It was hard to explain to him why I had decided to change my life on a whim. But there are no whims, not really. Whims are the result of an accumulation of signs: some blatantly obvious, some so microscopic that they only register on a vibrational level. A whim can only materialize under the exact right conditions: the love of your life could be standing right in front of you; a book you once thought was incomprehensible now makes perfect sense; the thing you thought you'd never do, you are now doing. Looking at things cosmologically always reassured me that every move was the exact right move, that there were no mistakes.

Mark didn't believe in all that. I stood on the other side of the kitchen island, watching as he poured a glass of seltzer and took pained little sips like it was alcohol. We'd been engaged for three years and something about it immobilized me. I preferred the feeling of being on the verge of something, which was my problem with everything—I never arrive.

"I'm done," I said.

"Because of the wind?"

"Yeah, eggy wind. Like one long, continuous fart."

"Just find a new studio. Giving up is not the answer. Look at me," he began.

Mark had his own perspective on things. He survived a car crash in his early twenties that left him with a big scar on the side of this face, so mostly, he just felt grateful to be alive. After three days in a coma, no one believed he would make it, but he claimed to have willed himself awake using the power of his mind. Self-mastery had become a religion to him. He was no longer a victim of forces larger than himself, but rather, an architect of his own fate. Also, people were nicer to him in general, because of the scar. They don't ask, they just know enough to know it was bad. I want to tell them that it looks worse than it is, but I don't. Before the scar, Mark was just an average guy, but now he's been marked by suffering. Having a scar has its perks; for example, no one can ever fire you for it. It'd be discrimination, against the law. I was jealous of the scar and how much attention it got. It reminded me of that time I stared at the sun for hours as a kid just so I could wear glasses, but everyone wears glasses now, so who cares?

"It's not about the studio. You don't know what it's like," I said.

"Trust me, I do," he said, turning his head to display the pink scar tissue that snaked from his left ear to his nostril. Surviving a car crash, it seems, bestows upon you a kind of all-knowing omnipotence that can be applied to almost anything. No one can argue with you because you almost died once.

"I'm tired of being an artist," I said to the normal side of his face, hoping to reason with it. What I really wanted to say was that I still loved making art, I was just tired of asking myself the same question every day: "Is it good? Am I good?" Most people go their whole lives never having to ask themselves that; they already know the answer: it doesn't matter.

I stayed up late that night tending to my affairs the way the dying do. I unsubscribed from several art publications and notified all but one of my remaining clients, a real estate agent who kept me on retainer and had forgotten about me. I edited my website bio, removing any trace of my work from it. The last seven years, deleted. It took very little effort for my life to completely unravel; I was surprised at how easy it was. It occurred to me that being an artist was more an idea in my mind than a real thing, and you'd think this would make me sad, but instead I was relieved. The timing could not be better: I was supposed to be a part of a group show at a gallery that I would have to cancel. I hadn't even started on my piece yet and I had a feeling that Ilana, the curator, had only chosen me because another artist dropped out. I had no proof of this, but I could tell because my name on the flyer was so tiny compared to everyone else's that it looked like an addendum. I notified Ilana in a thoughtfully worded apology email. She never responded, but by the following day, I had been replaced by the

teen daughter of a famous actor who had become famous in her
own right for artfully photographing her nosebleeds on Insta-
gram. She had three hundred thousand followers and embar-
rassingly, I was one of them.

I came into not being an artist with relative ease and was now
free to spend my days however I liked. I finally had time to do
the things that brought me joy. Sleeping, for one. I could sleep
forever, and I did—skipping whole days swaddled in too many
blankets, concerned only with flipping over to the cold side of
the pillow and getting up to pee. If I ever caught myself rumi-
nating over what I'd done, or failed to do, or what my "plan"
was, I would calm myself by browsing luxury items online and
putting them in my cart; it was the closest I'd ever get to own-
ing them. I was a few clicks away from buying an emerald pen-
dant worn by Princess Diana and a yacht named *Andiamo*. My
inbox filled up with abandoned cart notices and the occasional
subscription renewal, an email from Jesper requesting rent
money, credit fraud alerts and emails I sent to myself, which
were just links to healthy recipes I wanted to try.

One day, I received an email from an alumnus about an offer
for a part-time teaching job and I turned it down. I could've
used the money and health insurance, but I no longer wanted
to perpetuate the myth of the artist's life. I could offer no con-
solation. Lesson one: Are you rich? Are your parents rich? No?
Have you considered the exciting world of software engineer-
ing! Dentistry! Joining a cult! Literally anything else!

I understood the appeal. All my friends shared the same
romantic notions about being an artist. I barely knew anyone
who wasn't a painter or an illustrator or a writer or a musician.

None of us questioned it because we couldn't conceive of another way to be in this world. I once went out on a date with a butcher and asked him if he saw his work as a creative expression, considering how close he was to the marrow of life and the circle of life and death that connects all living things. He said he didn't think about it too much, although he felt extremely passionate about the bullshit parking ticket he just got for blocking a driveway, which technically wasn't even a driveway, and at that point I spaced out and tried to remember the lyrics of a song from my dream and if it was a real song or not. Other than minor assaults on his civic freedom, my date genuinely wasn't burdened by existential anguish nor did he feel compelled to use his mind as an instrument of truth. I told myself his indifference was actually humility when I let him go down on me and then told him I'd moved to Russia when he asked to see me again.

Maybe the butcher was onto something. He made the best of his lot in life, and it was a fine lot, it was respectable. Being an artist was almost impossible unless you had money. Rich artists often hid in plain sight by electively renting shitty apartments and wearing thrift-store clothes to appropriate the poor, but sometimes they'd slip up and mention something about their parents' beach house in Malibu or disappear for the summer to some idyllic Mediterranean estate where they were photographed hanging out with a Kylie or a Kendall or a Timothée. Finding out an artist friend was secretly rich was like finding out God wasn't real. Devastating, yet it explained so much. You kind of always suspected it. A private smugness formed inside you. The smugness was maybe all you had, but at least it was yours. You would have, of course, abandoned your smugness for their friendship should it at any point be offered to you.

The rest of us artists were forced to hustle and seek out the few meager opportunities left. This meant constantly subjecting yourself to the whims of institutional opinion by applying for grants, residencies, and contests. Even if you did win, it sucked. I remember being shortlisted among five other illustrators for a big prize: ten thousand dollars and a feature in some flashy art journal. We all lost out to this anemic professor-type named Tim who had already published two graphic novels. I was depressed for about a day until I started getting messages from strangers on the internet telling me I should have won and that I was robbed. I'd never considered the unexpected fame that came from being a loser. No one really likes a winner, and I would know because I happened to see Tim on the street through a café window the next day looking so pretentious, with a cigarette behind his ear and a film-festival tote bag over his shoulder. He was visibly blushing and looking around, sort of half expecting someone to come up to him and say something, but no one knew he'd won except a handful of people on the internet. You could tell it was a big deal for him. It was the biggest deal of his life. I wondered if he was now walking a different kind of way, the way a genius would: a little aloof, but deliberate. Like someone with somewhere to be. I worried for Tim, poor Tim, whose life would likely be ruined by this award because no one was actually happy for him and getting it didn't feel as good as he thought it would, and now nothing would ever come close, which meant the rest of his life would be a disappointment. I let smugness wash over me like a warm shower. Like a mother's hug.

I could have tried a little harder. I'd always avoided flying too close to the sun, but I'd seen the way the art world can destroy a person: hoist them into public favor then hurl them back down, leaving them with the stink of a moment that only depreciates over time, becoming less and less relevant. It was a psychically violent thing to do to an already sensitive, depressed person. Maintaining smallness and mediocrity was a form of self-preservation. Disappearing altogether was self-care.

As a part of my rehabilitation, I decided to get offline and into the real world. I went to the mall to reacquaint myself with the general public: a group I'd largely avoided to preserve my out-sider identity. Now I wanted to be like everyone else. I wanted to buy novelty glasses from a Sunglass Hut kiosk. I wanted to sample lotions from Bath & Body Works. I wanted to sit in a massage chair and eat a giant soft pretzel while mechanical knobs punched my spine. For two weeks straight I'd sit and people-watch and pretend I was a ghost who roamed the earth alone, without a body or a name or a Squarespace website. One afternoon mid–chair massage, I wondered: Could this be art? Doing nothing as performance art? I was performing an act of political resistance against the problematic art world! Failure was subversive in a culture of winners and losers! Something, something, capitalism? As I workshopped a manifesto in my mind, the shrill sound of a toddler's tantrum returned me to the present moment. The entire food court fell silent. Everyone stared as the mother tried to lift the toddler's fat wiggly body off the floor. I studied the baby's screams for apt metaphors and the look of horror and pity on the faces of nearby strangers, but soon the screaming drowned out all thought. What was I thinking? How quickly I reduced any human experience to art! I had so much to unlearn. I mouthed *Thank you* to the baby and walked out.

———

Meanwhile, Mark kept asking me the same questions: "Are you okay?" and "Do you want to talk about it?" He was seriously worried about me. I could hear him on the phone saying, "She'll get over it" or "I've been reading about it, something to do with low estrogen." My new way of being rubbed up against his growing obsession with self-optimization. He'd used his personal-injury settlement money to start a podcast on biohacking and unlocking human potential through methods like cold plunges, sun gazing, and self-hypnosis. He was always trying to motivate me. Over breakfast the next morning, he showed me a YouTube video of gymnast Nadia Comăneci performing a perfect ten at the 1976 Montreal Olympics. He loved watching inspirational sports videos to psych himself up to work out. In the video, she soars acrobatically across bars with elegance and athleticism. Her movements look effortless but are basically humanly impossible. From afar, she's an optical illusion, but up close, she's a child. There's a red bow in her hair. Her contoured face disturbed me; she looked clownish, almost trashy, but she had the composure of a soldier. When I looked over at Mark, he was teary-eyed.

"She reminds me of you," he said.

"Why?"

"You both have a gift."

I hated it when he talked about me like that; it made him seem untrustworthy. His understanding of the art world was too limited. Whenever I showed him a painting I was working on, he'd say, "Cool colors!" and pat me on the head like a dog.

"I can't do this," I said, referring to us.

"You could if you tried; it's never too late," he said.

"I'm leaving," I said.

"Where to?" he asked.

Realizing I had no place to go, I panicked and said, "The store. I'll be back." I'd gotten ahead of myself. Leaving everything seemed so easy now. Shedding parts of my identity had become so addictive, I fought the urge to shave my head.

Walking out of my house was disorienting: The world was new or I was new inside it. Everything was bright and vivid now. Before, the world was background noise, that blurry space of unreality between my home and the studio. Now I behaved like a tourist, noticing everything about our suburban sprawl: how the trees looked like old men, drooped over, barely able to hold themselves up; the year-round Halloween decorations on my neighbor's lawn; the fragrant jacaranda trees shedding purple confetti piles onto the sidewalk. I could've stayed there forever, but I really did have to go to the pharmacy to pick up my birth control. I no longer wanted to create anything, including other people.

The pharmacy line was long and mostly made up of elderly people with nowhere else to be. I watched the pharmacist fill each prescription in an unhurried manner, taking great care with each customer as she described which pills to take and when, and which ones go with food or water. She prepared insulin and sedatives and antibiotics and heart medication, listing their side effects and telling patients to call her if they had any questions. They'd probably call her with unrelated queries about their last bowel movement or about an alarming new disease they'd heard about on the news. She was doing the real work. Not me. I felt embarrassed by what I'd spent my time doing, all in service to my own glory. Was this what was happening while I was in the studio? People were pointing other people in the direction of compression socks and multivitamins. Others swept the aisles for debris, clearing a path for customers to get home. Elsewhere, people in lab coats were inventing new ways to keep people alive. I must've looked emotional when I finally reached the counter, because the pharmacist reassured me not to worry, that this brand had the lowest dose with hardly any side effects. She told me to take them at the same time every day and I promised her I would; it was the least I could do for her.

In the parking lot, I ran into my friend Kelly, whom I hadn't spoken to since I quit being an artist. She barely recognized me with my hair pulled back in a low bun, wearing a plain white T-shirt and gray sweatpants. I was careful not to take any artistic liberties with my personal style. Fashion was a slippery slope. Kelly and I did a group show together years ago, and she still owed me money for a painting, but I didn't mention it. She cocked her head to the side with concern—the adult equivalent to kneeling before a child to establish trust. She asked how I was doing and I told her the truth, I was the happiest I'd ever been.

"Really? You don't miss it?"

"No. I'm relieved."

"Is it drugs?"

"What?"

"People were saying it could be drugs."

I tried to conceal the smile on my face from the thought of being the subject of gossip, which imbued me with a certain celebrity status. I didn't think anyone would notice, or care. I felt sorry for her; she was still hustling as a photographer's assistant and spent her weekends at the farmer's market selling prints. I wanted to tell her that no one buys photographs any-more, but I think she already knew.

"Listen, if you ever want to talk—" I said, clasping my hands behind my back like a wise old man. I felt as if I embod-ied some unknowable truth about the meaning of life and I wanted to share my message. We said our goodbyes, and she said, "Good luck with everything," and I said, "You too," and I knew we both meant it.

On a Sunday afternoon, Mark suggested we go to an art mu-seum downtown in an effort to cheer me up and reignite my passion for the arts. He didn't believe me when I said I was fine. "Happy people don't take that many baths," he said. I don't know where he got that idea from. I would've said no, but he'd been putting up with me for weeks while I did very little besides pick up trash in the park by the basketball courts. I'd seen an elderly man wearing a reflective safety vest doing it and asked if he wanted some company, but he had no inter-est in talking to me. If anything, I think he was a little jealous of how much trash I could pick up. I'd be on my third full bag while he worked steadily on his first, bending over slowly and cautiously. As soon as I sensed it was getting competitive, I moved to a different part of the park and continued on my own. Sometimes I would dump out the contents of my bags on his side, just so he could have a fresh crop of trash to pick up the next day. I don't think he appreciated it.

Mark held my hand as we wandered around the museum, and although I tried in earnest to get into it, I felt an empti-ness, like the feeling of returning to your childhood bedroom as an adult. In each room hung hundred-year-old paintings and sculptures made by people who'd long since died. What was the point? No one understood what any of it meant—portraits of ugly aristocrats and their children, the occasional bowl of fruit, some religious scene. Life-size nude men with small penises. How would any of it make my life any better? Did anyone leave this place changed? I stood in front of a Jackson Pollock piece trying to feel something about its chaotic squiggles, besides annoyed, then decided to play a little game in my mind with the woman standing next to me to see who would give up first. I vowed to stand there for as long as it took, counting each squiggle like grains of rice until she eventually moved on and I won. After that, I watched a bored security guard rocking back and forth, a couple making out in front of the restroom, and hot girls taking selfies in front of a gruesome civil war battle scene. I tried imagining one of my pieces on display a hundred years from now: Would a hot girl ever take a photo in front of it? Would anyone stop and look, if only briefly, before looking at something better on their phones? There probably won't even be phones in a hundred years, or museums, or art, or people at all. After an hour, Mark said he had to pee, and I was bored, so we peeled the stickers off our shirts and left.

"What did you think?" I asked.

"It was okay. That big orange one was kinda cool, did you see it?"

"Yeah, I saw that one."

"That one was probably my favorite."

"Yeah."

The sun was blinding when we walked out and it took a moment for my eyes to adjust. I'd forgotten my jacket, but the wind felt nice against my bare arms. On the way home, I was hungry so we stopped to get pizza and I ate half of mine while

Mark used the restroom. I finished the rest of my pizza on our walk home while Mark ate a protein bar he'd packed because he was "off carbs" now. As we walked, I asked Mark, without a hint of sarcasm, if he ever thought he'd be fully optimized one day.

"That's not how it works; it's a process," he said.

"So, you just keep working on yourself forever?" I asked.

"It's about pushing yourself beyond your own limitations," he said, a little defensively. He looked away from me and up at the sky.

"For what?"

"So you can be better than you were."

"Why?"

"To be happy. To inspire others. I don't know." He looked like he was going to cry. I squeezed his hand.

"That makes sense," I said.

When we passed the basketball courts, I took my used napkin and paper plate and laid them out along the fence as an offering to the old man. He didn't look up. I waited for him to acknowledge us, the way you might when the barista turns her back the very moment you place a tip in the tip jar.

"Let's go," said Mark.

I stood there, waiting. The old man kept his head down, toeing an empty bag of Sun Chips. He didn't seem to concern himself with the question of how to spend his time here on Earth; he was here and wasn't that enough? He already understood that trash would never be treasure; it contained no meaning or metaphor. Picking it up didn't make you special or happy or get you closer to God, but you did it anyway.

Later that evening, Mark and I role-played "Footprints in the Sand," where he picked me up, fully nude, and carried me around the room for a while pretending to be God. Like most things, it began as a joke and now it's the only way we feel truly connected. When his arms tired, he put me down and we had sex in that desperate way that you sometimes do when you feel that life is precious and terrifying and the only thing keeping you from refracting into millions of pieces is the warm body of someone who loves you. Afterward we clung to each other like twins in a womb. He whispered inspirational quotes in my ear and I let some of his ambient optimism rub off on me.

"I'm going to wake up early tomorrow," I told him. "I'm serious," I added. He was already asleep.

At dawn, I peeled my heavy, sleep-drunk body from bed, awake at an hour I'd only ever seen a few times in college after going out all night, but otherwise never intentionally sought out by choice. Mark was already standing barefoot in the yard, waiting for the sun, waiting to harness its power, as he did every morning. I stood next to him, mimicking his stance with my palms outstretched and my eyes closed. Then it began: a wall of light hit our faces; my eyelids burned orange and started to water. A light breeze blew in my face and wisps of hair caressed my forehead. I let it all happen. I wanted to lie down on the wet grass, I wanted to throw up, but I didn't. I kept standing and that was something. That was the least I could do.

Eventually I wandered back inside, feeling dizzy and light. All I could see were blue fireworks in my eyeballs, like a show just for me. Something in me was changing. I felt proud. I tied my hair up in a clean bun, washed my face, and boiled water in a kettle to make coffee. As I waited, I scanned my emails, out of habit. I noticed a new email from someone named Aleks, who was asking if I was interested in illustrating a series of children's books on body positivity. He said he was a friend of Jesper's, who had recommended me for the job. He said the publisher was willing to make it work for me and included a proposed base fee that had so many zeros I had to say it out loud to make sure. He said other words like *royalties* and *negotiate* and *perfect fit*.

Mark was still outside; I could see him stretching through the window. I closed my eyes. My mind raced. I imagined the pharmacist, the butcher, and the garbageman, all shaking their heads in disappointment. Then I imagined Mark, Jesper, and thousands of body-positive children, cheering me on, chanting my name in unison.

Thank you for your email, I typed. *Jesper is a close friend.* My fingers hovered over the keyboard; I watched them move about like a planchette across a Ouija board, asking the question, *Are you free to chat this afternoon?*

Writing a book is just a part of my long con . . . to be liked!

I wish I had a long-distance, no-strings-attached benefactor who's just glad to know I'm trying my best

Sometimes I worry Jenny Holzer quotes are only good because she capitalizes them, she'll be all like THE FUTURE IS THE PAST IN REVERSE and I'll be like, *wow, so true*

Going to call my book a long poem so it doesn't have to "make sense"

Moved to tears by the manufactured authenticity of pop-star propaganda documentaries

Hot girls love to post photos of themselves with the caption *live by the sun, love by the moon*, and everyone's like, *a poet!*

Nothing good happens between the cursed hours of 3 p.m. and 5 p.m.
From now on, 3 p.m.–5 p.m. will be called "Long 2 p.m."

I heard a siren in the background of a porn video
and I couldn't stop wondering who called for it and
if they were okay

No one wants to admit that some birdsongs are
really annoying and derivative

The Party

The luxury-bedding brand's online personality quiz told us to get the Super Luxe Hardcore Bundle and we believed it. So did the thousands of couples who came before us. When the sheets arrived, I knew I would die in them. Not now, but forty years from now. They came with a warranty. "We still have ninety days to decide," said Eli. "Don't worry."

Eli didn't have to worry about anything, he was two years younger than me and still looked like a boy. A tall thirty-year-old boy. I was ahead of him, in the future, where aging had become less of an abstract concept and more of an event happening on my face. It started with that slow rot around my mouth: the way the skin slopes like melted wax. My friend Leslie says she's "aged out of gallery lighting" and won't even come to art shows with me anymore. The last time I went to a gallery alone, a teen goth asked me where my pants were from and I said, "Urban Outfitters," and she said, "What's that?" and I dissolved into a pile of dust, right in front of her.

One way to justify aging was to have a baby. Suddenly every woman I knew was expanding and multiplying, as if there had been a meeting about it. Babies once the size of almonds soon became kumquats and papayas. Naomi gave birth last week. She said her vagina looked bruised and puffy the next day, like it'd been badly beaten. Why did she look? I couldn't stop thinking about it. Maybe I wasn't sad, but my body was. Could a body feel betrayal? I bled more each month. My abdomen ached. I wasn't ready for a baby; I needed more time. If I'm being honest, I needed lifetimes. I'd been working on a novel for the last three years that kept changing course every time I thought I had it. The more I tried, the more confused and meandering it sounded: all of my half-baked philosophies on womanhood and "the truth." The worst part was that I wasn't even consistent in my desire to be great; most days I just wanted to read articles online until my vision blurred and a soft halo formed around my screen, signifying it was time to sleep. Still, there was something virtuous in committing to art and not giving in to the seductive forces of nature ready to upend your life at a flick of the genitals.

Eli opened the window and inhaled. "Smells like burnt marshmallows," he said. Less than thirty miles away, the Santa Ana winds were kicking up wildfires that had already violently decimated public parks and beachfront properties in gated communities, making the air thick with toxins. Every year it gets worse: thousands of acres, gone. Air-quality advisories told us to stay indoors, warning of poisonous particles in the atmosphere that could lead to long-term respiratory issues. But the smoke made for psychedelic, blood-orange sunsets, beckoning us all to go outside and take the same photo from different angles. Seeing the beauty in everything, even horror, was a virtue, we told ourselves. The fires hadn't reached the east side and probably wouldn't, so we were spared. Friends sent links to articles about celebrity homes engulfed in flames, and we filed those images in the unreality of our brains reserved for whatever was happening in the Middle East or another mass shooting in a city we'd never visit: all of it happening elsewhere. No one thinks it'll happen to them, not really. Sometimes I'd find Eli eating protein bars out of our earthquake survival kit, promising to replace them later. When it does come, whatever it is, we'll deserve it.

Our friend Malcolm was turning forty next week. I couldn't believe I was friends with a forty-year-old man. Time had a way of moving fast and slow in Los Angeles. The weather had a hallucinatory effect; with no discernable seasons to punctuate the passing of time, my memory was unreliable. I'd lived here for nearly a decade, but it felt like one long summer to me. Weren't we still twentysomething? Hadn't I just thrown up on my shoes? Lost my phone and cried to the bus driver to let me ride for free, pleading with him until a homeless man in a front seat gave me change? Were those days up?

"We used to live!" I cried.

"Did we?" Eli teased.

Maybe I dreamt it. I could've been sitting here on the couch this whole time. I looked at our life, at the bag of wet baby carrots and the half-eaten tub of hummus on the coffee table with a pube stuck to the lid. It wasn't mine, I had none. It didn't belong to Eli either; his were finer, like baby eyelashes. It was just a rogue pube that must've blown in from outside, and who knows how, but I've noticed that if you look hard enough, you'll find them everywhere.

I watched all the color drain from the sky until there was only a black sheet of night catching the city in its net for the billionth time. I used to think it was beautiful, but now all it does is remind me that I'd wasted another day putzing around the internet instead of writing. I turned on every light in a small protest, as if to say, *There's still time.* I sat at the kitchen table and opened up my Word document but I was distracted by the filmy buildup in the back of my throat. Carcinogens from outside wafted up my nose and coated my lungs. I googled *how long to die from smoke inhalation* and wondered aloud if we should get an air purifier.

"They're like two hundred bucks," said Eli.

"Oh. We're probably fine?"

"I don't know."

Eli knew how hard it was to finish something; he was working on something unfinishable himself. He was making a documentary in fits and starts on the long-term health risks of glyphosate exposure in migrant farmers, but he kept getting threatened with cease-and-desist letters from pesticide manufacturers. Part of me thought it was just his idiot brother Steve pranking him because so far all he'd done was internet research, which is totally legal. I once looked up how to dispose of a dead body just out of curiosity and nothing happened to me.

"This came for you," Eli said, handing me a letter.

I noticed it earlier, but thought if I never opened it, I wouldn't have to respond and I could go on with my life as if it never existed. I tore the envelope and a pile of loose glitter sprinkled everywhere. "Another gender-reveal party," I sighed. I couldn't think of anything more boring than spending the afternoon at Rhiannon's newly purchased million-dollar Craftsman that she could only afford by illegally subletting four different rental units on Airbnb. The whole thing seemed so precarious. One call to her landlord and it would be over for her—I'd fantasized about it more than once.

Our phones pinged in unison. It was Malcolm texting our group thread about his birthday, telling us he wanted to go big and "party," which could've just meant staying up late and re-enacting some hazing ritual from his fraternity days—forming a human pyramid or petty theft, whatever he did. But I took it to mean doing drugs. I'm not a drug expert or anything, but I've done them enough times to know how it works, which is to say, three times. I acted quickly before he could change his mind. "I'll handle it! I know some people," I said. I wondered if this was what it felt like in an emergency when someone yells out, "Is there a doctor here?" and you are that doctor. I'd prepared for this moment my whole life without ever knowing it would come. Malcolm gave me his blessing with a prayer-hands and a fire emoji.

I'll admit, I presented as confident over text, but I had never directly engaged in a drug deal. After a few failed attempts at friending high school acquaintances on Facebook—teen mothers with their now-adult children, and rich kids with learning disabilities—I remembered my old neighbor, Reese, who'd offered me Ecstasy in exchange for borrowing my plunger. I sheepishly texted, *idk if u remember me . . .* and he responded within minutes, *plunger girl!* as if no time had passed between us. He texted me a phone number along with a complicated set of instructions with code words ascribed to different types of drugs. I ended up requesting "4 Alanis Morrissette CDs" (Molly, or Ecstasy, for the olds) and was given an address.

Later that night, I embarked on my mission. I pulled up to an apartment complex in Koreatown, held my breath and ran up to the second floor where a baggy containing eight pills was concealed inside a ceramic mushroom, next to what appeared to be an outdoor shrine to Neem Karoli Baba. The spiritual decor reassured me, as though the drug would get us all closer to God. Unfamiliar with any other religious gestures, I made the sign of the cross before I left.

On the night of the party, I sat on my bed waiting for the drugs to kick in, which was easy because I am a professional at waiting. I'd waited all my life for it to begin; my real life, not whatever this was. I had decided to take the drugs first to make sure they were safe. I couldn't have Malcolm die in front of all his friends. Imagine? They'd blame me. The only child of divorce. *If it is my final act, let it be generous,* I thought, before emptying the pill's contents into a shot glass of water and gulping down the gritty elixir, then licking off the remains. After twenty minutes, I heard blood whooshing in my ears and felt my heart thudding through my shirt. I lay down on my bed and waited for the wave to pass. I tried to think about anything else, about regular things, nondrug things. I thought about birthdays, then I tried to think of other celebratory words like *special occasion.* I tried spelling *occasion,* but I couldn't remember

if it had a double *C* or a double *S. O-C-C-A-S-I-O-N*. No.
O-C-A-S-S-I-O-N. Whatever. It was strange to have such regular thoughts and pretend that reality hadn't become a porous,
pulsing dream.

Once the rush of anxiety settled, I could feel my skin sitting
heavy on my bones. The mortal heft of it. I dragged my tongue
across the slimy coating of spit on my teeth. Black pooled out
from my pupils. I'd never paid this much attention to my body
before; it was both somehow overly complex and dangerously
primitive. It could summon consciousness from matter, and it
could die from a peanut. I preferred to live inside my head; it
wasn't the most ideal place to be, but imagine being a vari-
cose vein or an asshole, god. If you asked me to describe the
protrusion of my belly button or the shape of my labia, I honestly couldn't tell you, I'd have to check. Even in the shower, I
took to memorizing the Dr. Bronner's soap label to keep from
looking down at myself. *The intensity of man's emotions is a
greater driving force and more decisive than the sum total of
his education, his money, plus the size of his brain! Proof: Ein-
stein!* When you spend all day on your laptop, everything from
the neck down seems extraneous.

Eli was in the kitchen half listening to a podcast but not
really listening because anytime I would pass by he would ask
how I was doing and laugh, and I would laugh, too, the way
a laugh betrays you when you are being tickled and you're in
pain but no one can tell, and worse they think it means you
like it.

"You okay?" asked Eli.

I was just okay, and that was the problem. I was supposed to
feel euphoric and in love with the world. The veneer had been
lifted, but what was underneath was not some naked awareness,

but instead, something icky and sinister. I felt all the disorienting symptoms of a drug trip without any of the pleasurable effects. Everything was too much. Too loud, too bright, too close. I couldn't, in good faith, let the others join me at the bottom of this well. If one of them freaked out, I wouldn't be able to help them. I panicked and flushed the remaining pills down the toilet to be safe. The captain must go down with the ship.

"I don't think it works," I said.

"Give it time," Eli said.

The party was within walking distance, and I thought the fresh air might help coax the supposed tingly, good feelings to emerge. *Maybe it'll still happen,* I thought. I swayed my arms exaggeratedly from side to side, hoping to catch a breeze.

Eli grabbed my hand and said, "Don't worry, I'll take care of you."

"No, don't," I said, yanking my hand away.

When we arrived, Malcolm greeted us in the hallway with a knowing grin. "How are you?" he sang. I rolled my eyes and walked ahead, leaving Eli and him to whisper about me to each other. I wanted someone to blame for my plans not working out, but I wouldn't know where to begin. I imagined a chain of command that spanned several time zones, involving not just the drug dealer, but a broader, unregulated international criminal enterprise and corrupt government officials. It was pointless, there was already blood on my hands.

"Poor girl," said Malcolm.

"She'll be fine," said Eli.

I walked slowly down the stairs without breathing too loud or throwing up or crying, convinced that with the right attitude,

I could still salvage this and have the night I intended. When I reached the living room, I let out a sigh of world-weariness, partially due to the drugs, but mostly due to the fact that everyone seemed to be dressed in formalwear and I was dressed in jeans and a white turtleneck with a faint concealer stain on the neck, because I never got the memo. It would be so like Malcolm to forget to mention a dress code just because we were neighbors and he no longer felt the need to roll out a red carpet for us. Eli and I had been relegated to a status typically reserved for lesser blood relatives, like cousins or half-siblings, just because we shared a zip code.

I looked up and saw a gold HAPPY BIRTHDAY sign and was reminded of the occasion. *O-C-C-A-S-I-O-N.* I should've worn something nicer. I thought about walking back home before anyone saw me, but it was too late because I accidentally made eye contact with Chloe, who was standing by the bar next to Jess. They both motioned me over as if we were close friends, but we only ever saw each other at parties. Their performative friendliness always confused me, like they were both in on a joke and I was the joke. Their voices made shrill, inhuman sounds as they took turns wrapping their thin, hairless arms around me. I did my best to energetically mirror them so as to come across as normal and not debilitatingly high.

"Oh my god," said Jess, her bra pressing firmly against mine. "You smell so good."

"Thanks," I said, genuinely confused since I wasn't wearing perfume and I'd been silently blowing out a burp from a fish oil supplement I'd taken earlier.

"How's writing going?" asked Chloe, which wasn't even a question I felt emotionally capable of answering with a sober mind. I'd always considered it one of the rudest questions you

could ask a person, like asking how much money they made
and if you could have some. Her voice, which normally had
a passive-aggressive "we just want the best for you" quality,
took on an accusatory tone in my more penetrable state. Chloe
was a social media strategist for some girlboss corporate skin-
care brand and her contempt for my unemployed, laissez-faire
writing life was so obvious I often resorted to forced self-
deprecation to appease her. Conversation with her was a test I
could never pass.

"I'm barely writing," I said, hoping to satisfy her.

Jess interrupted and asked Chloe where she got her cropped
mohair sweater and Chloe said she got it at the Eckhaus Latta
sample sale. A Cow's Latte? Eckhart Tolle? I had nothing to
offer the conversation; I was too poor to know the names of
designer brands. The sweater was a way of not talking about
the fires and all I could think about was how flammable her
shirt looked, how irresponsible it was for her to wear it. I bit the
inside of my cheek, hoping that one of them might sigh and tell
me it was good to see me, which usually meant it was no longer
good to see me so they had to mosey on to some other person
in the world's most boring game of musical chairs.

Miraculously, Chloe kept talking and asked if I'd ever had a
vampire facial, a procedure that involves removing blood from
your arm and painting your own plasma on your face. I wanted
to offer some cool beauty tip in return, but all I could manage
to say was that I didn't think there was any discernible difference between body wash and shampoo and admitted that I'd
been shampooing my body my entire life.

I was impressed by my capacity to keep it together despite
feeling somehow both dissociated and agitated by my proximity to other people, especially Chloe's sweater that shed fluff

into the air every time she moved. The fluffs seeped into my
nostrils and expanded like a sponge inside my throat. I could no
longer breathe comfortably without making a whistling sound.
How long had I been standing there? Ten minutes? Eternity? I
decided to leave, feeling that our conversation had reached its
natural conclusion. Walking away, I could almost hear them
squeal over my poor performance. Joke's on them; whatever
they said about me, I probably agreed.

"Fresh air feels nice!" I laughed to myself on the balcony,
hoping to trick my mind into feeling joy. In my periphery, I
noticed Charlotte rolling a joint by herself. She had bleached-
blond eyebrows and tiny bangs and wore an oversize tie-dyed
T-shirt, which was to say, she was twenty-three. It dawned on
me that Charlotte was basically my dream girl. Not in a romantic way, more like a muse. A like soul. I walked over to her and
confessed that I was high, but I felt weird and gooey and was
possibly choking on wool fibers. I knew she wouldn't judge
me. She was a new friend, and her newness made us closer
than my old friends who could barely see me as I am, stub-
bornly clinging to some younger, crueler version of myself. No
matter what I did, I would remain a static image, a caricature.
I wish I'd known when they decided who I was, I would've
tried more. Who ever really knows what sticks to a person and
what sheds? Charlotte's opinion of me was unblemished and
therefore, more accurate. She blew smoke out of her nostrils,
and we wordlessly agreed to be allies against the normies, who
only ever wanted to talk about historical podcasts on obscure
topics you should "definitely know, but never thought to ask,"
or how their neighborhood was getting a Whole Foods, signal-

ing it was "up and coming." No one wanted to talk about the end of the world. When anyone brought up the Anthropocene it was only ever in reference to Grimes's last album. Dystopian predictions were reduced to zombie-apocalypse fantasies and hypothetical "would you rather" games. My friends would take turns over dinner asking, *Would you rather die instantly or stay and fight? What skills do you have? Where should we go? New Zealand? I keep hearing about New Zealand. Should we take a private plane? Do you know anyone with a private plane?* I always opted for a quick death, citing that I only ever had six months' worth of contacts before I ran out. I was useless without them. I didn't mention any of this to Charlotte, for fear of bumming her out. She had the rest of her life for that.

"Stay here, I'll go get you some water," she said, and walked back into the party. I followed behind not wanting to be alone, but I lost her in the crowd. I headed for the kitchen hoping to meet her there, but instead I found a group of women congregating around Malcolm's sister, Lacey, who had just given birth two months ago to a chubby baby named Harlowe. I had watched her stomach bloom over months without pain or nausea. Her work had hardly suffered, either. She hosted a podcast about serial killers and rapists, but when she got pregnant, she made a natural pivot to motherhood and career and her fan base exploded. Big deal. I shuffled around the huddled group to get a glass of water from the sink, listening to her talk in great detail about her labor; about the hours of agony and tearing and how incredible and sacred women's bodies are. I tried not to laugh, thinking about how I was clenching my butt to hold in a fart.

"It changes you," she said, in a soft tone that seemed to utter only platitudes. I briefly imagined punching her in the stomach and, immediately ashamed, lightly punched myself as karmic retribution. I didn't really believe in karma, but I did in the way you pray to Jesus when you're prostrate before the toilet with the stomach flu.

I studied every pregnant friend with a mixture of horror and fascination: the way they abandoned their solitude for a stranger, the way it made them strangers, too. The more my friends got married and had children, the more I wanted to sit back and watch, leaving my own life unattended. Leaning against the refrigerator, I could see it all: the way Harlowe would grow and walk and eventually speak. His first wet dream and his love of skateboarding and anime. Every milestone laid out before me as if it had already happened, while I just stood there, doing nothing. It was like staring at the sun until my eyes burned. I covered my face with my hair, careful not to draw attention to myself as I slithered by without paying my respects. I couldn't reach Lacey even if I wanted to; an entire galaxy separated us now.

I abandoned my search for Charlotte and wandered into Malcolm's bedroom to use his private bathroom. I felt safe knowing no one would enter such a personal space, but as a neighbor, I considered it one of my privileges. Waves of nausea pummeled through me and up my throat. I searched the medicine cabinet hoping to find something to settle my stomach, but instead I found rows of pharmaceutical drugs for sleep and wakefulness, beta blockers for nerves and antidepressants for a more general malaise. There was something for acid reflux and some expired painkillers from a dental surgery. It occurred to me that everyone was medicated for some reason or another. I gave up looking and sat on the cool marble floor. My heart kept beating speedily even though hours had passed. What was it that I took? Was it cut with something else? Was I having an allergic reaction? I took my phone out of my purse and called the number for the telehealth doctor that came free with my insurance. I'd called the hotline before to get antibiotics for a cold sore that ended up just being an infected ingrown hair above my lip. The doctor on the line had been so thorough and patient with me as I listed all the unnecessary details of my medical history, my diagnosis of HPV and astigmatism, unrelated allergies and surgical procedures that might be helpful for him to create a comprehensive health profile. I often found myself making up symptoms just to have a reason to call. The doctor was always there for me. It was his job.

I gave my personal information and answered every question of my identity trivia correctly. I did it quickly so there would be no doubt it was me.

"What can I help you with this evening?"

"Sorry to call so late, I just don't know if this is an emergency or maybe life-threatening. I ingested a substance a few hours ago and I want to be sure I haven't poisoned myself."

"What did you ingest?"

"I took Ecstasy, you know, Molly. But who really knows? I know you're not a cop, but I just want to be honest with you: it was my idea. I took the pill first, to test it out before my friends. I'm pretty sure it was a bad batch, so I flushed the rest down the toilet. I guess that makes me like a designated driver but in reverse."

"What are your symptoms?"

"I feel dizzy, a little light-headed, and speedy. I'm supposed to feel euphoric, but instead I'm agitated, like maybe I should have a baby and stop judging everyone."

"And can you rate your pain for me on a scale from one to ten? Ten being agony, one being normal."

"I'm not in any physical pain, but emotionally I'm a wreck. I'm off the charts."

"Have you thought about harming yourself?"

"No, never. I love my life, and I still have this vague sense that I'm meant for greatness, like I'm on the cusp of something really big."

"Just make sure you're staying hydrated. Magnesium might help, too. Otherwise I think you'll be fine. It should be out of your system by morning. Although, legally I am supposed to tell you to go to a hospital. If anything bad happens to you, I'm liable. So that's also an option."

"Got it. Where are you right now?"

"I'm in Los Angeles."

"No way! Me too. Maybe you can come over here and make sure I'm okay? Do you do that?"

"I can't do that, but if you really feel unwell, you can go to a hospital, like I said."

"That's okay."

"All right, well, do you have any other questions for me?"

"Are you mad about the drugs?"

"I would advise against it."

"Why, because of Lacey?"

"Who?"

"Nothing. Do you have kids?"

"I don't know what that has to do with—"

"Do you think this is it? The end of the world."

"I don't know."

"Kinda sounds like you do know, though. Did the fires reach you? Eli says he likes it because it smells like camping."

"Who's Eli?"

"My boyfriend."

"Where is he now? Can he help you?"

"I was feeling weird, so I told him to leave me alone. I don't know why. He's the best person in the world."

"Well, go find him to take you home and try to get some rest, you'll be fine. Or go to a hospital, which, for the record, I mentioned earlier."

"Okay. Thank you, Doctor."

"Oh, and please stay on the line to rate this call. I'd really appreciate it."

"Of course."

I hung up the phone and went in search of Eli to take me home. Time was a conga line of disappointments: of course the drugs didn't work as intended, of course I was getting less young and more old at the same time, of course eating one coconut-fried shrimp made me gassy and bloated, of course. I followed the sound of a nineties-pop playlist someone had ironically put on downstairs. A few people were shuffling back and forth in the darkness as if they wanted to dance but didn't want to fully commit. When a Missy Elliott song started playing, I felt a primal urge to dance. I rocked from side to side, warming up a rhythm and rounding my hips in a clockwise motion. I looked around the room to see if my performance was moving anyone to join in. Two shadowy figures sat on the floor, watching, and a girl stood against the wall taking photos of herself. I closed my eyes and began swinging my arms, hoping that my dance moves might thrust these bystanders into the present moment, forcing them to question their misguided allegiance to some prescriptive social role that forced them to stand idly with their arms crossed, already bored to death. Didn't they know this was it? This was our prime? It was happening right now! Hadn't they heard that the ancient ritual of ecstatic dance had been practiced throughout history as a way to unlock altered states of consciousness and open a portal to the divine? Couldn't they feel Missy's buttery voice vibrating against their skin? I spun around faster and faster, hoping to freeze time itself.

When I opened my eyes, the room had mostly cleared out and someone had turned on the lights. I found a floor pillow and dragged it to the middle of the dance floor, then pressed myself against the shape of it, gently humping it with what strength I had left. Bystanders did not circle me, nor did my performance arouse or inspire them. No one cared, no one even noticed. I put my hands on my stomach and felt air pockets moving around—at one point I swore I felt a kick. Whatever it was, it did kick.

Should I Go Out and Wish I Were Home, or Should
I Stay Home and Wish I Were Out?: A Memoir

Setting my documents folder to "view as icons" to
make them feel better

A butt dial is a mysterious form of somatic
communication that we should regard with
symbolic meaning

Wonder if con artists love being referred to as
artists

I don't want to be on social media, but I still want
to know what everyone is doing all the time

I keep refreshing my Gmail waiting for someone to
tell me what to do

Hate-watched a YouTube video and now it has
grown like a fungus over my home page as
punishment

Resent how it takes more effort to begin typing
a sentence with lowercase, defying its original
purpose to convey a lack of effort

Going offline for twenty-four hours so I can return
as a thought leader on the dangers of tech

Edging

Paige sat in the passenger seat, singing along to a pop ballad on the radio. I knew every word of the song, too, and felt a secret pride in how I kept it to myself and wasn't all show-y about it. I'd never once earnestly tried to sing out loud, and part of me was terrified that I might be the best in the world and would die having wasted my gifts. I was holding it all in—my gifts and my problems: sloshing around in my guts, soggy and probably atrophied from neglect. Anytime I tried to let them out, at home in front of the mirror or into a pillow, I could only manage to release a strange *hugck* sound. Like a dry heave. I couldn't make the sound on command. Paige and I had only been friends for a few weeks, but she was the only person who knew about my *hugck* and seemed totally unfazed by it. For this, I forgave her for her young breasts and her wild and unearned confidence. I was very lonely and would tolerate almost anything for her company.

We arrived at her apartment in an undisclosed location that only a few people knew about; all I can say is that it's above a Korean barbeque restaurant and even that's saying too much. The nature of her work required a certain level of anonymity to protect all parties involved. She described herself as a consultant because "sugar baby" sounded too amateur to her; it failed to illustrate the degree of nuance and skill required in her line of work. I'd never met a sugar baby before, so when she explained it to me, I made sure to act cool and calm, out of fear that she would stop talking if she sensed any judgment. I would often overdo it and pretend to be bored, periodically looking down to check my phone, muttering, "Totally," just so she knew how okay I was with it.

"No sex stuff," she said. "He just likes the company."

It seemed odd that a corporate executive from Marina del Rey would pay eight thousand dollars in cash every month for the platonic company of a nineteen-year-old. The absence of sex somehow made the whole thing worse. Everyone knew that life was designed exclusively for the pleasure of powerful white men and whatever the rest of us got was a bonus—a clerical error, a happy accident. I wondered if this man felt duped, like he'd come all this way in life just to find himself alone in a hotel room nervously texting a teenager who was being paid to respond. I imagined a middle-aged man sitting on the edge of a hotel bed typing *sup* then *wassup* then finally *hey* and doubting all of it.

Paige assured me that it was totally safe, which is something people say about things that are not safe at all. She told me she kept a separate address and phone number and even had a separate name: Darla. I told her that was the fakest fake name I'd ever heard. She said it was her grandmother's.

All I wanted to do was ask her about her brother, Seth, whom I recently started dating after several weeks of intense eye contact. It was a trick my mother taught me from an online course she took in kinesics, the study of body language. She explained that eye contact was a universal sign of attraction and could be felt from as far as forty yards away. "Use it wisely," she'd say, with the confidence of someone with much larger breasts than me.

I'd begun by using Seth's head as a centering device during the half-moon pose in yoga class. Steadying my gaze, I imagined an invisible string anchoring me to the mole on the back of his neck. It took him a while to turn around, but when he did, he said, "Did you say something?" and I said, "No, did you?" and we both laughed from our diaphragms, as instructed.

If *hugck* is the sound of uncertainty, then *ahh* is the sound of love. *Ahh* is short for *ahh ha ha*, because it's funny when you're in on the joke, and life's a joke. You just open your mouth and all that comes out is that "Ahh ha ha ha."

I waited for the exact right moment to ask about Seth. I didn't want Paige to think that her brother was the only reason we were friends. There were other reasons, I was sure of it.

"How's Robert?" I asked. Robert owned a rental car company in Brentwood and was recently divorced. He was her main client.

"He wants to bring me to his nephew's First Communion."

"So his family knows about you?"

"No, he told them I'm an intern shadowing him to get a sense of how an executive conducts themselves in a social setting."

"Right," I said, peeking through the blinds. I was careful not to retain too much knowledge about Paige's work in the event that I got a phone call from a detective or a reporter asking about it. Instead, I ran through a list of things I wish I could ask her but never would because of the sibling thing:

Have you ever seen your brother naked?

How many girls has he been with, if you had to guess?

Is he cut? Actually, never mind, I don't have a preference. I know most girls do, but not me.

Seth and I hadn't done it yet, and it occurred to me that perhaps withholding sex ran in the family. On our first date, he told me all about the pleasure principle and how he was building up his immunity by deferring gratification, or "edging," in order to harness his sexual energy toward more meaningful pursuits. When I asked him what pursuits, he said creativity and bodybuilding. He said he'd only been doing the energy work for three weeks but already felt the effects.

"Feel that," he said, rubbing his abdomen.

I put my hand over his shirt. His stomach felt like a mannequin torso.

"I've gained seven pounds since last week," he said. Then he looked me up and down, adding, "Besides, it's for your own good. Trust me."

"What do you mean?"

"The things I'd do to you—" He cut himself off and paused for dramatic effect.

"Oh yeah?" I said.

He took his finger and started rubbing the back of my knee in a circular motion until I felt it inside my belly button. I slumped over the edge of my seat; various parts of my body wept. I learned about all the things that were allowed later that night, which included making out and something that resembled Reiki, where I just hovered my palms a few inches above his jeans while I concentrated on the happiest moment of my life until he told me to stop.

"Was it on a boat? 2004?" he guessed with strange specificity.

Now, I thought. *Right now.* That old vibration wormed itself through my body and I clenched, hoping it would go away. He burrowed his head in my lap and inhaled deeply. I stroked his thick brown hair and thought, *Good boy.* Whenever I saw him after that, I thought the same thing: *Good boy.* This was always easier than goodbye, which was maybe what I should have said.

"How's your brother?" I finally asked. And by that I meant, "Where's your brother?" He would often disappear for days without telling me. This was long enough for me to complete the five stages of grief, and as soon as I reached acceptance, he would text me a photo of a baby monkey wearing pants. I would immediately forget what I was upset about and reply *noo worries, lol* to let him know that I was chill and easygoing. I was a self-sustaining amoeba, totally void of human needs. Nothing could ever hurt me. He could run me over with his car and I would peel myself off the pavement and apologize for my body being in the way. *Ahh ha ha ha,* etc.

"I think he's still in Portland on that bike trip," Paige said, pouring almond milk into a cup of instant coffee. She lived so efficiently, like a camper. I wondered what it would feel like to be so light on your feet, so unencumbered. I carried three tote bags for some reason, extra sweaters and my laptop, blank journals, each one lacking purpose, weighing me down. I had no idea what she was talking about. I didn't even know Seth owned a bike. There was so much I didn't know about him, come to think of it. Whenever I asked him questions about his life, he'd repeat the question back to me, knowing how much I loved answering questions about myself.

"With whom?" I asked.

"I don't know, Max? Daniel? You know those guys," she said, and I didn't. I sat on her couch, too afraid to ask any follow-up questions. I pictured Max and Daniel, both natural blonds with lean builds and vacant eyes. They must've been brothers. Biological or fraternity. I pictured them recklessly leading Seth through dangerous terrains—the edge of a cliff, a poorly lit country road, a busy freeway—prodding him toward certain death.

Why would he hang out with these losers? He wasn't a jock; he was an artist. He was self-possessed, a loner. He painted self-portraits on large canvases, laboring over unseen details for months: tiny flecks and shadows, things the untrained eye couldn't see, and that was the point. He kept parts of himself hidden in plain sight; only the most observant and dedicated viewer could ever truly see him. Some pieces took him years to complete, but it was worth it. His work received critical praise, and although he'd never sold a painting, they were featured in galleries in New York and London, as well as in obscure outsider art blogs and podcasts. He felt he was on the verge of greatness and believed spiritual mastery would give him a competitive edge. A dense accumulation of quantum energy swelled from his sacral chakra, just above his crotch, priming itself to burst.

If he'd been a graphic designer, I could've walked away, but the hope of becoming a muse was too strong. Being a muse was less practical than being a sugar baby, but it was more romantic and required less work beyond maintaining a near-constant level of intrigue. For example, when he invited me to a friend's birthday party, I didn't respond, then showed up later in the evening unannounced in my tightest shirt, bleeding. I spotted him leaning against a refrigerator talking to a frizzy-haired woman wearing a blazer with lopsided shoulder pads. He looked surprised when I approached him, as if he'd forgotten he invited me. Panicked, I presented him with a fresh wound on my palm, wrapped in toilet paper. I'd accidentally sliced it with a knife, and that's all I said, hoping it would make me sound dangerous. In reality, I had been mindlessly stabbing the Bubble Wrap that came with my ergonomic pillow and missed.

"Aw, you dummy!" he said, pressing into the slit to make it gush. A little bit came out but not enough to hold his attention. "You're fine, it's not deep," he said. Before I could formulate a witty response, someone called for him from the living room. I stayed back as a matter of intrigue maintenance, but from afar I could see a procession of people form around him. They seemed to be congratulating him on some good news. I had no idea what they were talking about. How could I? He barely told me anything. I relied instead on body language and secondary sources, like his tagged photos and intel from Paige. I tried to get a better look, but a tide of people kept pushing me farther out. I suddenly felt like I was in a foreign country where no one spoke English. These people hadn't even heard of English. *"In-gleesh?"* they would say, shaking their heads, laughing. I left the party and walked home alone with my shoulders hunched over and my arms crossed. At one point I kicked a rock and missed. *Goodbye, goodbye, goodbye.*

The next morning he texted me, *I wish you woulda stayed!* And even though it wasn't true, I felt a smile grow across my face until it spilled into laughter. *Ahh ha ha ha.* I stopped by his studio later that afternoon, due to being "randomly in the neighborhood." He grabbed my hand and held it up to his face to monitor the wound's progress.

"Does it hurt?" he asked.

"Not really," I said.

He guided my injured palm into his back pocket and pulled me in for a kiss. I almost choked. It was an angry kiss; angry, as if he couldn't kiss hard enough, like my teeth and gums were in the way. Angry, as if there were years of things unsaid to so many people, people who were now gone, lodged inside his throat. He didn't know how to coax them out or what to call them. But the kissing, the muscular rhythm of it, the slippery texture—that made it feel better, like he could almost begin to sound it out. I took his hand and slid it underneath my bra; he rested it there limply and kept kissing me. I put my hand on top of his hand and squeezed. He did nothing.

"C'mon," I said, "it's been long enough!"

"Babe, I can't. You know that." His hand was still cupping my breast.

"So never?" I asked.

"Maybe you can't handle this," he said.

"I can. I want to," I said.

I watched his face contort. "What if—" he began, pausing to think.

"What?"

"Okay, picture this." He held up his fingers to create a box shape, as a visual aid. "What if you slept with someone else and then told me all about it. Would you do that for me?" He stood and waited for me to finish laughing.

"Babe . . ." He lowered his chin until there was no distinction between chin and neck. "It'd be so hot. It's a win-win."

"No."

He lowered his chin even farther, obstructing his vocal cords. "Babe."

"You're nuts," I said, gently pushing him away, hoping for levity to return us to a shared reality. He'd really got me there for a second, what a clown, etc. He relaxed his chin and put his hoodie over his head, pulling the drawstrings as far as they could go until his face disappeared completely and all you could see was a tiny mouth hole. He did this whenever he felt embarrassed, or cold.

"Whatever. Forget I mentioned it," he muttered through his mouth hole. "I'm outta here."

I tried leaving him. Not *leaving* leaving, I just went on a little solo trip for a week. I told him that I needed to clear my head and work on my novel. I said it just like that, "my novel!" with gusto. All he said was "Good for you, babe!" Never mind that I wasn't a writer and now I'd have to write an entire novel just to prove a point. Maybe that's how all great novels start, out of spite. I hoped that my absence would reveal a profound longing in him; life would suddenly seem unbearable without me. Radio love songs would start to make sense to him, their lyrics poignantly capturing his unique state of agitation. *Nothing compares . . . to you!* He'd mouth it tearfully to himself.

My uncle had a little cabin in Topanga. He'd recently moved in with his new girlfriend and told me I could stay in the cabin whenever I wanted as long as I fed the cats, but there were no cats. I promised I would. The day I arrived, I was already bored but knew that I had to stick it out, if not for Seth, then for myself. I needed to learn how to be alone. I took out a piece of paper and decided to write whatever came to mind. I began:

It was a beautiful day, the mountains were . . .

In a sleepy mountain town, the mountains . . .

Seth Seth Seth Seth

I love you, Seth.

I love you, too.

Let's make love.

But your art career.

You're my world, babe.

Wow, writing sucks. Why would anyone want to do this?

Seth, can you hear me? If you can hear me, send me a sign. I'll be waiting . . .

I looked at what I wrote and read it out loud, amused with myself. It didn't seem all that strange that he might send me a sign. His sexual power was so potent at this point, he could bend a spoon with one hand. He loved to practice on my spoons and tell me they "might be worth something someday."

The days trudged along, just barely. On the third day, I was motivated to tidy up but ended up just moving heavy boxes from one room to the other, kicking up dust and asbestos from the floor. This activated a chemical smell and something, some-where, was leaking. I had no service or Wi-Fi, so I spent a lot of my time deconstructing Seth's old texts for coded messages and imagined full conversations we'd have about the terms of our relationship and our true feelings for each other. My mind existed elsewhere at all times; even when I was with him, I was a step ahead, anticipating his needs, judging my performance. There could've been a dead body in that cabin and I wouldn't have noticed, or I would have, and immediately found a way to exploit it as a way to make me seem more interesting to him. *Guess what, I solved a cold case.*

I leafed through the boxes. Most of them were junk, but some of them contained handwritten letters, photographs, and old clothes. A better version of myself would be interested in her ancestry. She'd be curious about things that did not directly involve her. The many lives that preceded hers. Something, any-thing outside her agonizingly trivial text dramas or her belief that with enough effort, she could bend the universe to her whims, despite it having never once worked before. I forced myself to pick up a photograph from the pile to see if it might stir something in me: curiosity and focus, unmoored by obsessive thoughts. I held a sepia-toned portrait of a stoic-looking couple and their toddler. I envied their uncomplicated love, which I assumed to be a mutual agreement based on survival, shared resources, and a biological imperative to continue existing, despite all odds. I thought of my own survival as an abstract thing that only ever became obvious on airplanes or in hospitals or when I experienced some random body pain that the internet told me was cancer. The haunted photograph inspired a sober contemplation in me. I began to wonder: Did I really love Seth? Or had I just projected a fantasy onto him without his consent? Was he merely a man-shaped vessel to satisfy some unresolved pain within me? Did I ever want to truly know him, or did I prefer him as a fixed thing, unblemished by reality? If he knew, would he find my objectification degrading or the greatest honor of his lifetime? Was he maybe even a little bit ugly? Who cares! Life had a glimmer to it now. I felt high all the time. My crotch pulsed in sync with my heartbeat. I flicked the photograph back onto the pile.

Eventually I gave up on cleaning and sat on the balcony overlooking the forest and a few nearby cabins. In the distance, I noticed a heavyset, elderly man building a deck. I sat there for hours, watching him place planks on top of other planks, wiping sweat from his brow, standing periodically to assess his progress and admire his craftsmanship. He made being alive look so simple, enjoyable even. Surely, the Universe had led me here so that I might learn a valuable lesson about self-reliance and hard work. How satisfying it would be to accomplish anything at all. I watched the man until the sun began to set and the mosquitoes emerged in a voracious swarm. They were out for blood. If Seth were here, he'd kill them with his bare hands, then wipe their bloody guts on his sleeve. He never hesitated to strike my thigh or chest as hard as he could if he saw one on me. *Missed it,* he'd say.

The next morning, I remembered that I needed to continue writing. Lacking a plot or any idea of how to write a novel, I decided to document the progress of the man building his deck in my notebook as a warm-up exercise.

9:00 a.m.: Man searches for his hammer. "Where is it?" he mutters to himself. Man turns around and sees the hammer on the ledge.

10:04 a.m.: Man sees a squirrel.

12:45 p.m.: Man cuts a plank with a saw, then blows off sawdust and lines it up with another plank. He does this several times.

2:15 p.m.: Man removes shirt and wraps it around his head like a turban. Man spits on the ground but misses and it lands on his shorts.

3:05 p.m.: Man emerges from his cabin with a sandwich. Man eats half of it, then just sits there for a long time, throwing bits of bread on the ground. Birds gather. Man says, "Num num num" to the birds as they eat. The squirrel returns and he scares it away, saying, "Not for you!"

4:37 p.m.: Man accidentally bludgeons thumb with hammer, yells, "Christ!"

I watched the man suck on his throbbing thumb to self-soothe. Watching a man in a private moment of tenderness was oddly erotic to me. He reminded me of Seth. I suddenly wanted to tell this man all about Seth and their shared tenderness. I would tell him about Seth's proposition and ask the man for advice. He would nod and listen and tell me that open relationships were actually very progressive and cool now. I would ask to see his thumb.

I scanned the forest for other signs of life and saw none. I went back inside the cabin and whispered, "Hello?" Nothing. It became obvious what I needed to do.

I was familiar with the rules of seduction when it came to dating, but this was entirely new territory for me. Would I start by calling for help, then, once he came, explain my predicament? I'd assure him he had Seth's blessing to do as he pleased with me. Would he oblige, or would he be offended by my offer? Would he pay me for my services, or would I pay him? What if he wasn't attracted to women, or to one woman specifically (me)? What if he tried to attack me? I wouldn't fight it; I'd make my body limp to try to diffuse his lustful rage with consent. I imagined it wouldn't be fun to kill someone who wanted to die, who showed no fear in the face of it.

As I strategized, the man continued building, completely oblivious to my scheming. His life could change course at any moment; how thrilling for him. As our union became more possible in my mind, I noticed that his exposed backside was splattered with age spots: a telltale sign of liver damage. He was much older than I'd realized. He looked large, lumpy, and bruised, with the physical disposition of a potato. Paige would know exactly what to do in this situation. She'd beckon him over with an off-key Adele cover, her siren song. She'd tell him

about her secret apartment. When I opened my mouth to call
for him, only air came out. No sound. It was like screaming in
a dream, I couldn't do it. I tried again and there it was, a giant
mouthful of *hugck*. I spit it out. *Nope, nope, nope.*

I had another idea. I flipped to a fresh page in my notebook and
began writing a fictional account of the would-be rendezvous.
If I wrote it convincingly enough, I could trick Seth into believing it actually happened. It all came pouring out at once. Time
slowed. I felt trancelike, possessed:

> *It was a beautiful day, the mountains were . . . tall.*
>
> *It was late afternoon, and I was suntanning
> topless on the balcony when a man in the distance
> waved at me. I waved back and motioned him to
> come over. He looked around to be certain I wasn't
> waving at someone else, but there was no one else.
> He smiled and made his way over. He knocked on
> the front door and said, "Anybody home?" in a sit-
> com voice, and I said, "Yes, come in, sir." The man
> wasn't as attractive as Seth, but he was older and
> stronger and wanted me so very badly. I could tell
> by the curvature of his zipper. I stood up to greet
> him with a polite bow and he wasted no time, wrap-
> ping his hands around me and sliding them down to
> cup my bum cheeks. He made swirly motions over
> my jeans like a massage from someone who has
> never given a massage before, asking, "Is this ok?"
> I said, "Yes, harder!"*
>
> *He then instructed me to lie down on the cool*

hardwood floor and he lay down next to me. We held hands for several minutes. This man came of age in a generation when this was considered foreplay. As we both stared at the ceiling, he proceeded to tell me all the details of his life, spending a great deal of time on his past relationships and why they didn't work out and what he could have done better. He added, despite it all, he still believed in love. We sat together in silence until the man asked, "What are you thinking about?" and I said, "Nothing" but really, I was thinking about kissing him, with tongue. We turned on our sides and started kissing, but he did it in this new way that I was unfamiliar with and couldn't tell if I liked yet. He sucked the air from the inside of my mouth into his, gently bit down on my tongue, then pushed his tongue into my mouth to blow it back and alternated. He rubbed my arms vigorously as he did this. He told me he knew CPR and I thanked him for saving my life. This was role play, I think.

It was now dark and the man said he had a surprise for me and asked me to close my eyes. With my eyes closed, I heard rustling and movement. When I opened them, he was hovering above me, performing a choreographed striptease, removing each item of clothing and folding it neatly into a pile by the doorway. He was very fat and his penis was normal, but his testicles were enormous and distracting, I couldn't stop looking at them. He noticed me looking and told me it was genetic and there was nothing anyone could do. I nodded and told him I under-

stood. He asked if he could take off my pants, and I said, "I'll do it, because they're tight at the ankles and there's a trick to removing them." Once they were off, the man rolled on top of me and entered me in a manner I could only describe as feminist. He was so gentle that I barely felt a thing, but as he gained confidence, he worked up to an impressive hummingbird speed. He was really going for it and my legs had fallen asleep, but I didn't want to ruin the moment. Seth's presence hovered like a third entity in the room and when I told the man this, he said he didn't mind and that his spirit guides were also watching and I said, "Your who?" and he ignored me. After several minutes, I sensed him getting closer. Also, because he said, "I'm getting close." Finally, he screamed, "Christ!" and finished into a nearby ceramic vase.

He collapsed next to me on the floor and pushed wisps of hair from my face and asked if I would like to see a magic trick. I said, "No thanks." The man nodded and got up to leave. As he stood in the doorway, putting his shoes on slowly, he began to tell me about the war. "What war?" I asked. "The one in here," he said, pointing to his heart. As soon as his shoes were tied, he untied them and started over. I started to get impatient, wondering if I should say something. Finally, he pulled me in, kissed my forehead, and said, "Peace be with you."

"And you," I said, locking the door behind him. I showered thoroughly and went to bed; as I slept, a deep peace washed over me. I was a new woman

now, changed. Seth was right, I needed this. I should
have never doubted him.

Once I finished, I read and reread it, imagining how I would
recite it to Seth. I'd make a frame with my fingers and say,
"Picture this," and I would read slowly, alternating between
voices for dramatic effect. I could barely sleep just thinking
about what he'd do. Punch a wall? Propose? What did I want,
exactly? To expel this heavy wanting from my body? For him
to finally see me so that I could go home and sleep forever?
What a stupid thought. I wanted him, of course.

I made plans to meet Seth for dinner the night I returned
home. I could barely wait to tell him what happened, but I made
sure to tease it out slowly, saving it until after we ordered our
drinks. Each time he picked up his glass, I picked up mine. In
body language, this is known as "mirroring," an effective way
to build rapport. I was so eager to tell him that I almost hadn't
noticed his new haircut—his longish brown hair chopped to
nubs. It looked terrible. He must've done it himself.

"I did what you asked," I said, under my breath.

"What?"

"I did it. With a man. I wrote it all down for you."

Before he could respond, I took out my notes and read the
whole thing: *"It was a beautiful day, the mountains were . . .*
tall." I kept going; I never looked up once. The rush of reading
it out loud was turning me on. *"He noticed me looking and told*
me it was genetic . . ." When I finished, I looked up, feverish
and giddy. I waited for a response.

"Why are you telling me this?" he asked. His brows fur-
rowed until they became one.

"What do you mean? You asked me to."

"Yeah, it was a test."

"But you said—"

"I'm a little surprised. You, of all people," he added, tucking his phantom hair behind his ear.

"Wait," I pleaded. But it was too late; he was already pulling at the drawstrings of his hoodie. I watched his face disappear into a tiny black hole, and before I could tell him I had made it all up, the hole disappeared, and he was gone.

Can't believe "avoid sunlight" and "don't use your face" are legitimate skincare tips

To be honest, it's a little bit on us for calling it the "nervous system"

The spectrum of how ugly to how hot I can be truly scares me

Apricot face scrub buried at the bottom of my junk drawer: (whispers) *remember where you came from*

I call flossing my "tooth period" because I do it once a month and always bleed

hair on my head—gorgeous!

hair on my plate—I've been poisoned

The Cut is like "How This Babe Gets Her Skin So Good" and it's a photo of a newborn

Do parents ever wonder what their adult children's naked bodies look like?

The word *hemorrhoid* really captures the essence of what it is

My God, Your Face

The first thing she had me do was smell her sock. She removed her tennis shoe, peeled off her sock, and asked me if I trusted her. I did not. I had just met her—it was our first session. I didn't trust anyone, that was my problem. That and my condition. It was all over my chest and wrapped around my throat. It changed colors like a mood ring; red in sunlight, green when wet, blueish-purple when I was embarrassed. It hurt like a bruise. Google told me I was going to die, or maybe had already died and no one had bothered to tell me, like Bruce Willis in *The Sixth Sense*. I was seeking a second opinion.

She took her sock and pressed it against my nose. It felt damp and hot and smelled sweet, like yogurt. I couldn't move, so when she told me to breathe, I breathed. I was in shock; if she asked me to jump out the window or take off all my clothes, I might have.

The smell of her dirty sock rearranged my world so immediately that nothing made sense. Sense was elsewhere, on the other side of the door where a woman dressed in cheap athleisure flipped through old copies of *Us Weekly* and a bored receptionist watched a mounted TV playing a muted rerun of a game show with winners and losers and no one was confused about which one they were because they understood the rules of the game.

"There you go," she said, rubbing my back while ambient nature sounds played from a Bluetooth speaker on a shelf. I hadn't realized there were tears streaming down my face until she wiped them with her other hand. Exotic birds chirped over ocean breezes.

"Almost done," she said. "One more deep breath." Her voice was calm and deliberate. I took a breath as instructed. The room spun. I felt the inside of my mouth sweat, then I vomited into a trash bin. She continued rubbing my back, saying, "Thatta girl, good girl." She then handed me a glass of water and sat down next to me. "We'll keep working at it until you can handle it," she said. "The smell," she added. I was too disoriented to speak.

I swished water in my mouth and swallowed. My spit tasted like coffee and stew. "You know, disgust is a learned behavior, which means it can be unlearned. There is no such thing as a bad smell. You've just projected a lifetime's worth of memories onto the smell. All pain comes from memory," she explained, plucking out a strand of my hair, "even physical pain." Her face softened. "The good news is you can change these memories and create a new reality for yourself. One that is pleasurable, rewarding, and, most important, free. If you work at it hard enough, nothing can hurt you."

Vomiting left me with a euphoric feeling of emptiness; I hadn't done it in years. She handed me a tissue and explained that physical confrontation cut through decorum and allowed for real human connection. "Discomfort wakes up our animal. It brings us back into our bodies. Violence can be cathartic; look at war! People think it's just for men, but women need it, too," she said.

Dr. LaMarr's approach to somatic therapy was touted as "life-changing" and "not for everyone" according to her Yelp reviews. I had come about my rash, which could not be explained to me by my dermatologist, who recommended I explore psychotherapy, as the rash might be a symptom of emotional unrest. I hadn't considered it before; my malaise expressed itself more often as a tightness in my chest, styes, mouth sores, and constipation, but never a rash. The rash was new.

Sitting in Dr. LaMarr's office, I settled into my strange afterglow, feeling pacified. No one had ever cared enough to violate me. No one had caused me any real physical pain. I coasted through girlhood unharmed, with no sense of what I could endure, what I was capable of. She took notes while I looked around and waited for further instruction, like a good dog. The afternoon light made a glowing halo from the wisps of frizz around her head. I studied my surroundings. The wall behind her was covered in prestigious-looking certificates and the signed celebrity headshots you sometimes see in diners and barbershops. It was unclear if they were clients of hers or if she just collected them. She proceeded to ask me a series of questions:

Do you prefer the morning or night? Night

Do you believe in soul mates? No

Are you afraid of snakes? Yes

What's the worst thing you've ever done? Waste my
life

She claimed to have developed a complex system of symbols that correlated with memories. These symbols trigger the
same area of the brain as the memories they represent and can
be manipulated to represent something new and better. For
example, she suggested that I confront my money problems
by spritzing bills with my husband's cologne so that I might
treat them as sentimental objects and not something to just
give away carelessly. Whatever skepticism I arrived with had
been tamed by a desperate hope. There had been other spe-
cialists before Dr. LaMarr: allopathic doctors, distracted men
in lab coats who refused eye contact and left me inside win-
dowless rooms for hours, giving me vague, ominous guesses
that would need to be confirmed by more tests, but never were.
Scans came back "inconclusive," or worse, "unremarkable." I
wanted someone to name it—even if it was terrible or frighten-
ing. If it had a name, I could make a home in it. I could rest in
the certainty of it. Without a name, I took to hypnotherapists,
acupuncturists, chiropractors, homeopaths, and Reiki healers,
each with their own regimen of creams, supplements, special
diets, and spiritual ideologies. Each one predictably eager to
diagnose me with all manner of autoimmune, blood, brain,
and kidney problems, determined solely by inspecting my nail

beds, tongue, feet, aura, and breasts "for lumps." None of the names felt right.

After months of appointments, treatments, and bills, I tried living in denial, hoping that my body would catch up with my mind and move on. But my rash persisted. I tried covering it up with makeup and scarves, but it grew all around my ears and spilled across my forehead. With no other choice, I returned to obsessing with renewed vigor. I studied myself in every mirror, I kept lists of everything I ate, the hours I slept, my changing moods. I watched documentaries about people who survive against all odds: autistic men who climb giant rocks, swimmers without limbs, teens with cystic acne who get makeovers, addicts in recovery building community gardens. The human spirit could survive anything. People had gone through much worse and prevailed.

My husband, Graham, said he couldn't see it. He asked me if it was possible I was making it up. Sometimes I worried that his love for me was too strong, that it blinded him to my imperfections. That, or he actually didn't care at all. We'd been together for eight years; I suppose I should be grateful he had never once asked me to better myself. I wouldn't even know where to begin. My goal in life has only ever been to continue living, which is pretty impressive if you consider how many people have failed to do that. I've outlived millions of people by now, many of whom were probably far more successful than I'll ever be.

I asked everyone I knew, and they all said the same thing: "There's nothing there." No one believed me. I became paranoid and withdrawn. I watched big, pink continental splotches shapeshift across my body in the shower. I had unexplained back pains. I peed constantly. My teeth hurt. I sensed it was somehow all related. Dr. LaMarr was the only person who could see it. She told me it was bad, much worse than it looked. She said if I didn't get a handle on it, it would seep into my brain and turn me into a vegetable. I asked her why this was happening to me.

"You're too far out. Poor reception makes you weak, lowers your immune system," she said. She told me that when a soul takes a birth, it relies on its parents as an energy source to sustain it throughout its lifetime. Once those ties are severed, it's more susceptible to illness and decay. She asked about my childhood and my parents. I told her I preferred not to dwell on the past. I was an only child and was never close with my parents. That was all I said. What I didn't tell her was that they fled war and moved to the United States, seeking refuge in the suburbs of Long Beach where our realities split: theirs, a haunted nostalgia; mine, the vast frontier of AOL dial-up internet. I didn't mention how I grew up and moved to Los Angeles. Or how they prayed the rosary for me to find a husband and continued praying long after I met Graham. For years, a complex labyrinth of freeways kept them from visiting me. There were no big blowups, no dramatic endings, just the slow burn of time passing, people changing or not changing. In my defense, I was busy. I had a job and a life and went to the gym twice, sometimes three times, a month. This was normal adult behavior. This was the natural way of things. I told Dr. LaMarr some glossed-over version of this, quickly, so we could return to focusing on more urgent matters. My condition, for starters; or my seasonal affective disorder, or how Katie from work was a total bitch and ruining my life. Dr. LaMarr didn't seem to care about any of that. I glanced at her notepad and read, *ONLY*

CHILD, HUSBAND IS A LOSER, CALL MARIA BACK, PICK UP SOY MILK.

"What about your mother?" she asked. I told her that she died a few years ago. Breast cancer.

"You poor baby," she said. "Would you like a hug?"

"No thanks," I said. I knew better than to fall for her tricks. Dr. LaMarr was constantly testing me: slipping ice cubes down my back, shoving me up against the wall, and pinching the skin on my forearms as a way to confuse my nervous system.

A familiar heat rose from my neck. "My god, your face," said Dr. LaMarr. "It's all over your face." I could already feel it like a flat iron pressed into my skin. I looked up and saw Dr. LaMarr gripping her chest with her eyes shut.

"Hold on. It's your mother," she said, pressing her finger to her temple as if to channel the dead, "she has a message for you." She closed her eyes for so long I thought she'd maybe fallen asleep.

"She says she's worried about the drugs," she said, revealing the slit of one eye with a raised eyebrow.

"What drugs?"

"And your diet, she says you've gained a little weight. Is this true?"

"Not really."

"Maybe from the drugs?"

"I don't do drugs."

"Maybe someone is drugging you," she said, clasping her hands together, "without your knowledge."

"I don't know why anyone would."

"What can I say? I'm just the messenger."

It didn't sound like my mother at all. For starters, my

mother barely spoke English. She didn't believe in psychics and would never speak through one, even if she could. She was a devout Catholic. I was beginning to think Dr. LaMarr didn't know anything. But later that night, my mother came to me in a dream. She looked like Ukrainian figure skater Oksana Baiul, but I could tell it was her. We were in the middle of our routine, at the part where she skated into my arms for the big lift and twirl. I looked down at my feet and realized I'd forgotten my skates, but it was too late, she was already gliding toward me. I lifted her tiny body off the ground, and she floated up, up over the crowd. Up, up toward the ceiling, like a stray balloon. I reached for her, but I couldn't bring her down. She slipped out through a skylight and vanished. The crowd thought this was part of the performance and cheered. I sobbed and took a bow, doing my best to play along. I could not believe that she'd left me on Earth like this, with no practical wisdom, no family recipes, no inherited wealth. The only thing she ever taught me was that my own breasts could kill me from the inside out.

When I woke up the next morning, my rash had spread. It covered my body completely in a solid sheet of red, like a bad sunburn. I called my friend Pamela to see if she had any recommendations. Pamela was a friend from college with poreless skin who lived on a farm and hosted artisanal dinner parties for her homesteading influencer friends. I hoped to one day be invited to them. She suggested I try the Grembo—a hottub therapy that mimics the conditions of the womb, invented by her friend Dr. Rick, who believed that all problems could be traced to the emotional trauma of being exiled from your mother's body. The Grembo was lined with a sponge-like material and filled with an amniotic-fluid substance: a mix of baby urine, hormones, and antibodies. People traveled from all over the world to experience its healing effects.

"What about skin conditions?" I asked. "I have this rash."

"It will most likely aggravate any existing skin conditions, but your anxiety will disappear," she said.

I thanked her and told her we should catch up soon. She told me she was practicing boundaries this year and only committing herself to people and experiences that aligned with her divine purpose. "No," she said. "But thank you." After the call she texted me a link to an article she'd written called "My Year of No" for an off-brand Gwyneth Paltrow wellness blog. I told her that made total sense, even though it didn't, but almost nothing did anymore.

I tried making an appointment anyway, but Dr. Rick's receptionist said they were booked up for the next three years. I was clawing at my rash in frustration when I got an email from Dr. LaMarr. It read:

> 2153 S. Mariposa Ave
> Ask for Željka! Xoxo

I stared at the email, not knowing what it meant. Maybe Dr. LaMarr had given up on me, too, and now she was passing me off. I thought about my mother; about Oksana. I googled images of her: she was older now but still childlike, with a beautiful round Ukrainian nose. She didn't look like my mother at all, and yet I saw the resemblance. My rash throbbed, hovering over my body like an aura of pain. I grabbed my keys and drove to meet Željka.

The address sent me to the other side of town, down a long

gravel road to a dilapidated bungalow with the husk of an old Camaro left rusting in the driveway and a ripped white-pleather sofa sitting out on the porch. I knocked on the front door, and an old man in a bathrobe opened it. I asked for Željka, and he shrugged and let me in. She was sitting in the living room watching TV. From behind, she looked ordinary, kind of drab. She wore a gray sweatshirt and brown stretchy pants and drug-store slippers. It was only once she turned her gaze toward me that I saw her face. She wore heavy makeup. Her oily cheeks shimmered against the blue glow of the TV screen.

"Lady, what took you so long!"

"Dr. LaMarr sent me," I said.

"Good, good. Come sit." She patted the cushion next to her.

Once I sat down, a strange odor hit me: it was dog food, dry kibble—but there was no dog in sight. I wondered if this was another one of Dr. LaMarr's tests. Instead of being repelled by the smell, I made sure to breathe it all in, let it tickle my nose hairs and coat my throat. Feel it gag me. Eventually I got used to it and the smell faded.

"What you want, dear?" the woman asked. She rested the meat of her palm on my thigh.

I told her about the rash. "It's pretty much all over my body at this point," I said, treating her like a professional. She placed her other hand on the back of my neck and began rubbing.

I flinched and quickly stood up. I excused myself and told her I needed to use the bathroom. I walked down the long, narrow hallway and called Dr. LaMarr.

"I got your email, I'm with Željka—"

"Excellent. I've already briefed her on your situation," she said. "She makes excellent borscht."

"What?"

"Borscht. It's a soup: cabbage, beets. Lots of vitamins."

"I know what it is."

"Listen, she's affordable and very discreet," Dr. LaMarr said. "I've recommended her before."

"For what?" I asked.

"She's good at role play. Mother, nurse, witch, whatever you want, she can do it."

"You want her to play my mother?"

"Yes, and I give that rash a week, tops. Trust me, she's the best."

"You want some Canada Dry?" Željka yelled from the kitchen. I hung up the phone and walked toward the door. Željka blocked my path, holding a fizzy plastic cup. Under the harsh kitchen lights, she looked nothing like my mother. She looked much older, like her face had been carved out of an ancient oak tree.

"What happen to your face, baby?" she asked, pinching the butt of my chin.

"Oh, no thanks," I said, turning away.

"Listen, I help you for low price. Every day I call you, check up on you. Once a week, you come over, I cook you something."

I shimmied around her and our butts grazed. "You a good girl, okay?" Željka said. "You really good. I'm so proud of you."

"I'm committed to my inner joy right now," I said, unconvincingly, as I walked away and got into my car. I reversed out of her driveway and when I looked back she was still standing there on her porch, waving. Nausea bubbled up my throat and I swallowed it down, saying, "Yum" and "This is good" until it subsided.

———

Three days later, I was on my way to the gym when I got a call from an unknown number. It was Željka.

"How's my baby?" she asked.

"Željka?"

"Happy birthday! I send you something, okay? You gonna like it," she said, and hung up.

It wasn't my birthday, but the next day I received a package in the mail. It contained a dozen loose photographs of Željka. In one, she is sitting on the edge of her bed wearing a blue nightgown; in another, she is on the beach, her exposed arms glistening like two slabs of uncooked ham. In another, she is at an amusement park with two men who appeared to be her adult sons. They both had shaved heads and wore ripped skinny jeans. One stood awkwardly, and the other held up a backward peace sign, squatting. No one smiled.

Over the next few weeks, the mail continued. She sent me baby socks, loose pebbles, and a drawing of a horse. *Was cleaning and found some of your old knickknacks. From your childhood, remember?? Love you, girly*, she wrote. I threw them in the trash. I stopped answering her calls after that, but I kept getting mail: bills from a travel agency for her services, wire-transfer requests from foreign bank accounts, and letters from Željka's lawyer threatening legal action. My name was misspelled on every one.

I called Dr. LaMarr asking for help, but she told me I'd insulted Željka, her oldest friend, who'd only ever wanted to help me, and there was nothing more she could do for me. "You can't see the love that surrounds you," she said.

———

Dr. LaMarr was right. I couldn't see anything, I was so consumed by my pain, and also, my vision had recently started to blur. I took a long, aimless walk along the LA River to gather my thoughts and rehearse my fair, but honest, Yelp review for Dr. LaMarr. *Unpredictable. Violent at times. Mostly well intentioned.* Stillness had become unbearably painful, but walking kept my blood moving and out of trouble. I wore a long-sleeve shirt, a hat, and sunglasses. I put on my headphones and listened to a podcast about stimulating the vagus nerve to repair the mind-body connection. The guest expert had cured her hormonal acne through chanting, humming, and gargling. I squinted the sun from my eyes and let out a low hum from the base of my throat. *Mmmm.* I examined my hands to see if it was working.

Through my fingers, I noticed the blurry outline of a girl on Rollerblades speeding toward me. I watched as she swayed her arms to a song in her headphones and whipped past cyclists and dog walkers and a family trying to take a group photo. I preemptively stepped onto the grass to make way for her. She came into full view as she approached; her dirty-blond ponytail swung wildly in the wind and her knobby legs in bulky black Rollerblades glided across the pavement. Her eyes were closed as if she were in a trance and it looked as though she was headed straight for me. *Oksana*, I thought. *It's you.* I knelt down instinctively and put my arms out to catch her, but she flew right past me, shaking her high, prepubescent butt from side to side in cutoff jean shorts. Mortified, I quickly stood up and pretended to stretch my calves. No one saw me, but I held the stretch anyway to make it count.

I watched the girl recede in the distance until she was just a speck, then stepped over a freshly flattened lizard, clearing the flies that hovered above it, and continued walking. A group of middle-aged joggers shuffled past me taking shallow, labored breaths, their faces bright with blood. I gave them a knowing smile and a nod, as if to say, *I too have known great suffering.* Pain touched everything I saw. It was in the hulking man, violently rubbing his eye, tormented by an eyelash. It was in the ceaseless honking from a busy intersection in the distance, begging to be heard. And in the rival honk, wanting the same. A chorus of dogs barked. A pebble rattled in my shoe. A bug went in my mouth. Every living thing in pain, together.

I kept walking, smelling the smells of this pain. I inhaled weed and sweat. Rotting food from a restaurant dumpster. Wafts of dried pee. I breathed it all in like a human vacuum and metabolized it into the sound of *Mmm, yes.* I practiced breathing out the bad, vocalizing my exhales in a cathartic release. *Thank you.*

Love to tell other people to meditate and then never do it myself

I only write down dreams that reinforce my personal narrative and decide the other ones are meaningless/never happened

My boyfriend says I'm not allowed to be the next bachelorette "as a bit"

Very cool how getting off the drug known as birth control reconfigures your entire personality and makes you question the very concept of a self

Occasionally I try to send telepathic signals to my brother to wish him well instead of just calling him

Instead of calling something bad, you can just call it "performance art"

Every wife on that TV show *Snapped* is like, *Fuck, marry, kill . . . my husband*

I like to play God by sparing a bug's life

This Is Heaven

"Don't stop until you recognize me."

We do this every Sunday afternoon, as if our lives depend on it. Jordan strains his face like he has to pee, but he's holding it in. I watch him squirm and settle himself into a seated position on the floor. We're performing a meditation technique I half read about in a magazine and half invented myself based on years of self-taught online Buddhist study. How it works is you take an object and focus on it until it's no longer that object, but something else. It's a form of unlearning that loosens up your mental associations and frees you from attachments that no longer serve you. Depending on how advanced you are, you can turn something as ordinary as a toothbrush into a special healing wand or a sudden feeling of immense gratitude. I can do it with almost anything now. I can turn a stick of gum into a satisfying meal. I can look at Jordan's face and see my soul mate.

"Okay," he says.

We conduct the exercise by sitting across from each other on the living-room floor. I like to break him into parts and slowly work my way up to his whole being. It's like looking at a Magic Eye—revealing a depth that only appears when you're paying attention. I bet he takes me in all at once, the way he does with everything: how he inhales food like a hungry stoner, or in bed, the way he yanks my underwear to the side and jams himself in. There's no right way to do it other than sitting and staring until it's over. Meaning, we've found each other again. Sometimes he sees me immediately and has to sit and wait until I'm ready. The longest we ever went was around two hours, but that's because I got bangs and he was having a hard time finding me under them.

I begin with his lips. They are thin, bright pink, and chapped, and I can tell they're hiding something. I squint until all his other features blur and disappear and attempt to communicate with his mouth telepathically. After twenty seconds, the disembodied mouth starts laughing uncontrollably, excited by its newfound emancipation from the face. I remain calm and try to ask it things like, *Do you love me or are you just afraid to die alone?* and *Why won't you let me touch your asshole?* But it's too distracted to answer. It quickly grows confident, repeating "cunt" and "motherfucker" over and over again, like a tic. I realize the mouth on its own has nothing to tell me and place it back onto the face with a firm blink.

A strobe of afternoon light cuts through the window, illuminating thousands of dust particles descending upon our jute rug.

I swallow a cough and wonder how much dust I've eaten in my lifetime. Several pounds, at least. The microscopic film coats every surface of our modest apartment, the one we've shared for the last six years and never thought to leave because rent in the neighborhood has doubled in the last two years alone. Just like that, our apartment has become highly coveted real estate. I think about this whenever I hear the elderly widow above us farting loudly in her kitchen or screaming Slavic insults into her telephone. *Pizda materina!* "This is heaven. I'm in heaven," I repeat to myself as I crush another silverfish with a giant wad of paper towel only to watch it crawl triumphantly out of the trash can, its body disfigured and limping. We're royalty, in a sense, and even though we've done nothing to earn it, we agree that on a cosmic level, we have. Friends anxiously wait for us to leave: to find a duplex in the suburbs and move on with our lives. What they don't know is that we've agreed to grow old and die in this apartment together, no matter what.

Most couples never see it coming: that thing that blooms over years like mold, making them lazy and forgetful. It got so bad for our downstairs neighbor, Geoffrey, that he confused a woman he met online for his wife, Eleanor. He eventually moved in with this woman, claiming he was no longer convinced that Eleanor was who she said she was. Well, she was. I saw her yesterday. How do you just forget a person like that?

Some days I can see him so clearly, my husband, but then he shape-shifts into a child with a fever or a slob roommate or a chatty girlfriend. Or worse: an appendage of mine, some human-shaped growth with hair and teeth that spooks me every time it brushes against my leg in bed. We even have our

own language: a garbled baby talk that doesn't so much communicate meaning as evoke a general mood. *Pleebo*, *Boobkus*,
Moosh, and so forth. We are like two wounded children. My
therapist calls it "enmeshment." It's embarrassing, but I can't
stop.

Jordan never cared much for meditating but is willing to try
anything to save our marriage. Maybe *save* isn't the right word
for it, rather: *sustain*, *nourish*, *grow*. "Safe words," he jokes.
He's an obedient partner and agrees with me on nearly every
topic except when it comes to my body, which he worships
despite its obvious and well-documented defects. Specifically,
my most problematic areas: the cellulite under my ass; how
when I lie on my back, my nothing little breasts disappear into
my chest; the disappointing ways my skin betrays me despite
a rich diet of retinoids and sunscreen. His defense always feels
personal, as if I were offending someone who was not me—an
orphan or some omnipotent god figure. I can't trust that kind
of confidence.

As a rule, we approach matters of the heart with caution.
We both suffered the indignities of online dating after thirty
and emerged too wounded to talk about what we'd seen, fixat-
ing instead on easier topics like the state of our gut flora or
thoughtful ways to reduce our carbon footprint. Crawling, just
barely, off the battlefields of our twenties, we were embarrass-
ingly ill-equipped for the bigness of love. The brutal heft of
it. I couldn't bear it, not for a lifetime. I need a careful love, a
reliable witness. No one says this out loud, they just know it.
You get tired of chasing the ghost, and then you trust fall into
the arms of whoever will catch you. It's a survival skill, a way
to eliminate risk. I told Jordan my entire sexual history on our
first date, hoping that he'd find my display of forced intimacy

endearing, and not manipulative, as a former therapist once mentioned. Still, it took him years to reveal that his previous and only girlfriend left him for a female lifeguard, forcing him to reconfigure his jealousy to include both the male and female gaze. He avoids public pools now, says the smell of chlorine gives him a headache. It's an unwanted feeling, like a fear of dogs after an unprovoked attack by the family pet.

Ours is an uncomplicated love, aside from the occasional flare-up we offer each other that neither of us had asked for but must graciously accept: an email from Jordan's ex-girlfriend asking for her copy of *The Artist's Way*, or a recurring sex dream about a cousin that haunts me for weeks. Despite our precautions, we started losing each other under layers of performance fleece and reruns of British procedurals. Our sex, too, is predictable and choreographed. I could do it with my eyes closed and often will. I like imagining other people on top of me, like his father, so that I could be the one to give birth to Jordan and raise him to be more self-assured and independent. Less sensitive to criticism, also dairy.

When my mind wanders like this, I wiggle my toes to return to my body. I ground myself in space and time by relaxing my eyes to get a full view of the room without breaking my focus. The first thing I notice is an industrial Steampunk-looking lamp that needs a special bulb I never got around to buying. I thought it was cool just a few months ago and now every time I look at it, I want to hurl it out the window. How could I have been so wrong? I usually have discerning taste, but occasionally I surprise myself with an impulsive chevron print or something macramé and worry that I actually have no idea who I am or what I like. I strain my eyeballs to the edge of my periphery where a clock sits on a mantel, but it's just a white orb with no numbers. How long has it been? I'm already bored, so bored, so bored.

The sound of Jordan shifting his weight brings me back and I un-relax my gaze and bring my focus back to him. Hello, hi. I'm here. I look down at his chest and notice he's wearing my beige sweater. I like the way it drapes over his pointed shoulders. I like a thin man, almost sickly looking. It makes him look so graceful, like a dancer. We share clothes, mostly neutral-colored cotton basics from Uniqlo; that way we don't have to expend energy picking out what to wear in the morning. It's more efficient since we both work from home. Jordan scores film and transitional music for reality TV, and I work part-time for an environmental advocacy group. So, while the planet cooks and world leaders threaten global annihilation, we've resigned ourselves to an indoor life, thoughtfully constructing our own private paradise in uncertain times.

Sometimes I worry we've done too good a job and we'll never want to leave again. Our efforts to safeguard against loneliness made us too dependent on each other, causing a self-perpetuating loop. The more we are together, the more we shut out the world, the more we distrust it, the more we need each other, etc. I'm finding it harder and harder to go outside when everything I need is right here. Every room has been optimized for maximum efficiency and comfort: a black-and-white dish set, a single bread knife, a fake fig tree by the window, a tweed loveseat and glass coffee table, and a closet filled with expensive Canadian wool blankets. We're both inspired by Kanso and Wabi-sabi design, but Jordan made me get rid of our bonsai tree out of a sensitivity toward cultural appropriation. At the start of every season, we like to reset by purging all our nonessential belongings and surrounding ourselves with objects that evoke joy. The goal is to eventually want for nothing. The goal is to be free.

This controlled environment works for now, but what about the future? Who will we be? My future self is capable of anything and I hate her for that. I've heard stories about men who emerge from botched brain surgery as pedophiles, and no one knows why. Or those women who smother their husbands with pillows or sleepwalk into the ocean. When I shared my concerns with an online chatroom for advanced meditators, a few of them suggested I incorporate the drug Ecstasy to encourage deep feelings of empathy and connection with my partner. Jordan had never done it and the one time I did, I slow-danced with a coat rack alone in a hotel room, sobbing. I remember it being cathartic. I eventually managed to procure some pills from my niece's boyfriend, Chad, but whatever he gave me must have been cut with amphetamines, because instead of meditating we took turns picking at the shower grit, scrubbing the walls, and wiping dust off the venetian blinds until there was nothing left to wipe. I stayed up all night listening to the sound of Jordan slapping his dry tongue against the roof of his mouth while I heard a symphony coming from inside my own brain. I'm worried I caused us permanent brain damage.

I look down at Jordan's folded legs and try not to laugh; nothing is funny, but my restless body is filled with so much energy that it sometimes expresses itself inappropriately and without my consent. The sitting is so uncomfortable it's impossible not to laugh or cry or hum a little tune. My body will do anything to cut through the silence. Jordan almost laughs, but it dies in his throat, choked out by his enormous Adam's apple. I imme-

diately think of the saddest thing I can think of: Jordan as a
toddler waving goodbye to his mother as she pulls out of the
driveway and never comes back. His baby cheeks pressed up
against the foggy glass. "Ma-ma!" he screams in an empty living room. This never happened, but it helps me to recalibrate. I
return his gaze with renewed seriousness. I fix my eyes on his
nose and wait for a revelation—some recognition of our truest
selves, and by that, I mean the best versions of ourselves, the
ones that were advertised to us, promised to us in front of God
and everyone we know. I think if we look hard enough and
really focus, we can remember who those people are and how
to coax them out. Maybe we'll discover we're sex positive or
into vape culture; I'm open to all possibilities.

I stare into his eyes, which are wide and expressionless like
a curious toddler's or a benevolent monk's. His eyes are always
watching me in a sort of all-loving, all-knowing way. "You've
got an eyelash," he'll say, "make a wish!" then present it to
me on his finger, things like that. He has monitored my every
move over the years—from the way I incorrectly lift an Amazon package (legs, not back!) to the irregularity of my menstrual cycle to the way I walk slowly "on purpose"—as if he
were taking notes for a research study on the most inept woman
alive.

In retaliation, I take secret pleasure in making him cry. I'm
not proud of it, but I've accumulated a greatest hits of insults that
can make it happen on command. I'll say things like, "You've
told us this one already," after he shares another depressing
story about his dad's beloved Jamaican hospice nurse to all our
friends over happy-hour drinks. When he later tells me I hurt
his feelings, I'll roll my eyes and tell him to grow up, which
makes no sense since he's seven years older than me and has

high cholesterol. I'll mention that, too. I know it's coming when he looks up at the ceiling to keep his tears from falling, hoping they might reabsorb into his head. The look of anguish and betrayal on his face transforms him and he once again becomes a stranger to me. Immediately I fall at his feet and beg forgiveness. "My sweet Boobkus! Remember me?" Making him cry for sport is both immensely pleasurable and physically unbearable; it's the closest I've ever felt to being in love.

"Now?" he whispers.

I shake my head, no.

His face barely even looks human now, more like a mound of clay. I rub my eyes and look again. When I do, another man's face appears, someone I've never met before. He looks as menacing as a serial killer or a lonely youth pastor. I start to worry that I'm hallucinating, that I've gone too far and lost my grip on reality. I believe this happens to advanced sitters, but as a novice, it startles me. I look down at the ground and work my way back up again, hoping to snap out of it, but this time I see my college boyfriend Rico flexing his bicep and looking constipated. "Sup," he proclaims. It's just like Rico to show up like that, in a manner that feels forced and nonconsensual. I blink again and there's Jordan looking back at me, totally oblivious.

Let me think: Jordan. Love of my life. I search inside the creases of his eyes, his defined jowl. I stare at the pink mole protruding from the side of his left nostril. Every time I look at it, I have a deep animal desire to rip it off. He looks panicked but hopeful, as if he fears being lost forever. I panic, too, but don't show it. I'm determined to see him, really see him. Who am I looking for, anyway? I want the old Jordan, still perfect and unencumbered by my petty judgments. This was the same Jordan who had yet to discover my night terrors or my eczema or student loan debt. The Jordan who inspired me to take up reading for maybe the first time in my life, just to impress him. *Tolstoy? Yes, looove it. Him. Love him.* The Jordan whose car seats and armpits and bath towel smelled like some heavenly combination of cologne and sweat; it gave me a druglike high. It made me want to breathe until I passed out.

Suddenly I hear what sounds like a synthy electronic beat playing through the vents, and just like that, I remember the night we went dancing in a dark club, or rather I was dancing and he was sort of hovering over me, holding my hips, swaying awkwardly from side to side. We never go dancing—we aren't those people—but we decided to try it one night after dinner, the way tourists might wander curiously into ornate cathedrals hoping to spontaneously feel the presence of God. "What if it's fun?" he proposed, looking drunk and cross-eyed. Once we entered the club, we quickly realized that we were surrounded by sexy youths and professional dancers, and our version of dancing wasn't funny at all, it was humiliating. "I thought I was good!" I shouted. "But I'm actually bad!" He took my hand and twirled me to the tune of an imaginary polka beat as trap music thudded our rib cages.

"You're the best one here!" he said. I fell into his arms and wept.

When I come to, he gives me a confused look, which I assume means that he's lost me. I'm taking forever, and it reminds him of how slow I am at most things. I forgot that I'm also being watched and the realization horrifies me. Is my mascara doing that thing where it smears around my eyes and makes me look goth? Do I look too much like his mother now? Does he wish I looked more like her? What's my hair doing? Did I even try to fix it? I feel exposed, as if all my flaws are on display at once, even the internal ones. I wonder if it shows on my face: my secret browser history. The contents of my manifestation journal. That ancestral rage in my blood that emerges randomly, like when playing cards. Or how I've changed, seemingly overnight, and I don't know how to stop. Can he see, too, that I'm trying? That I want to be good? I relax my face and perform a childlike smile.

The longer I sit, the less I recognize him. Even little things lose their context, a side effect of staring at anyone for too long. What are bodies? And what is a hand, anyway? Is it a hand, or is it a family of fingers? I imagine him dying in front of me. This hiss of his last breath, his lifeless body. It's an old body, with spots and craters and pustules all over it. I'm afraid to touch it or go near it. I'm afraid of its coldness, its strange smell. I sit and wait and watch until he slowly comes back to life, filling up with blood, growing younger. I watch the spots disappear, and he is himself again, breathing effortlessly. I'm relieved, but I can't unsee it: how it ends, right here in the living room.

The distance between us grows and grows until it becomes an ever-expanding, gaping canyon with exquisite vistas. Jordan is a dot, barely visible to the human eye. I sit on the edge of a cliff and wave violently in the hopes that he might see me. If I can't find my way back, then what? What happens to two people separated by some abstract, unmeasurable distance? My Buddhist video tutorials taught me that meditation, or really any kind of intense, singular focus could cure anything: anxiety, food allergies, you name it. I briefly consider the possibility of being wrong.

The sun is setting. We hadn't thought to turn on the light and it is getting dark, but neither of us can move. Moving doesn't even seem like an option. The man in my living room scratches the tip of his nose. The problem is his nose isn't where it's supposed to be, it's been grotesquely flipped and jumbled like a cubist painting. His one eye hangs low on his left cheek and his ear floats above his head. It's as if my brain has taken his individual features and scattered them at random. I sit waiting for the night to erase him in a sheet of darkness.

"You still there?" I ask.

"Yeah, are you?"

"Yep."

"Can I turn the light on?" he asks.

"Please!"

Jordan gets up and flicks on the light switch while I rub my legs and come back into my body. Then he looks at me. "Well?" he says. "Did you see me?"

I never did. Not once. He says he does every time; says it's easy.

"Yeah," I say, "I saw you."

He smiles, then looks down and notices a giant brown beetle sauntering across our laminate tiles. It senses it's being watched and freezes. Without saying a word, Jordan slowly picks up his slipper and crushes it with an impressive blow. When I get up to look, the beetle's amputated antennae are still twitching and its iridescent shell has torn into bits of cellophane, covered in goo. I stand back and watch as he wipes up the guts with a paper towel and washes his hands meticulously, like a surgeon. I know I might never really see him, but I want to spend my whole life trying.

My mom used to tell me that the apocalypse would
be nice since we all get to die together

Should be illegal for distant relatives to engage
with your art (This isn't for you!! Look away!!!)

I have an out-of-body experience anytime someone
reads the birthday card I wrote them in front of me

Hilarious how most of my decision-making
comes from the ghosts of my ancestors who dwell
inside me

Despite all my rage, I'm still just a girl in a plague

Daddy's Girl

It was my first home: a crumbling little bungalow with crusty carpeting and uneven floors that simulated the feeling of being on a cruise ship. The refrigerator moaned in agony; once I thought I heard it say something like "Fill me." Or maybe it was "Kill me." Somewhere a dying smoke detector chirped in concert with it. The toilet was locked in a perpetual flush mode. The little compost in the yard where I dumped cantaloupe innards, potato skins, and expired meats had recently attracted a family of rats. I worried they were closing in on the source, using refrigerator noises as sonar or a mating call. Meanwhile, a swarm of termites feasted on rotting wood in the garage. Hosing them down seemed only to make them grow stronger and multiply. I was outnumbered.

I called my dad, who I only ever consulted on practical matters concerning the material world, like how to undent a car (punch it) or install an illegal cable box. Beyond that, we barely spoke. My dad worked as a contractor and was surprisingly virile for a sixty-two-year-old Bosnian man with a bloated stomach filled with undigested sausage. He was, in essence, a real man. How do you talk to a real man? You don't. But if you must, be clear. Enunciate. If he yells "What?" over your question, calmly repeat yourself. If he does it again, give up. Go ask someone else.

I felt a flutter of nerves as the phone rang because he never figured out how to save my number, so whenever he picked up he was already irritable in anticipation of a scam call. I was relieved when it went to voice mail. "It's Dani. Can you come over? I need some help with house stuff. I don't know what I'm doing." I sighed wearily. My tone was a little helpless—childlike. I was like a snake charmer luring him in with my weak feminine incompetence.

He reliably showed up the next morning, wearing a stained Chicago Bulls T-shirt tucked into his faded work jeans and a wallet holster hanging off the side of his belt, looking sleepless and deranged. His walk was unselfconscious and aloof, like an animal's. I imagined he regarded his body for its utility, not as some decorative form on which to display his personality. I was just glad to see him wearing a shirt. His personal style didn't bother me, but I feigned embarrassment in front of outsiders like my friend Laura, who happened to be in the kitchen helping me unpack the last of my boxes.

"Tata, this is Laura."

"Nice to meet you, sir!" Laura sang.

He ignored her and instead kicked at the loose plaster moldings in the entryway. He never cared to meet my friends. He only ever knew the basics about my life; mostly that I lived in sin with my American boyfriend, Gems (James) and that I had a job "in computers." Like most immigrant patriarchs, he held me at a distance. This wasn't a bug but rather a feature of his parenting style. Slavic dads believe that showering children with love and attention is dangerous; if you want your child to grow up strong and self-reliant, you have to shock and confuse them through negligence or by setting arbitrary rules without explanation. For example, he used to berate me for walking around barefoot on the cold kitchen tiles. Cold feet lead to inflammation of the liver and the brain, which leads to death. So does wet hair. Most things lead to death. This would often lead to an unrelated history lesson about the war and the thousands of active land mines buried in his village back home. "You tink day go barefoot?" he'd say. I couldn't make the connection. Navigating his moods was like a game of chess, in that I had no idea how to play chess. He had a selectively inflated sense of my capacities, treating me as if I should know as much as he did. As if I were a fawn, capable of walking around and foraging immediately after birth. When I was around six or seven, he would ask me to make him an espresso, and when I'd tell him I didn't know how, he'd say, "Vat are day teaching you in dat school?" and I'd say, "Photosynthesis," then run to my room before he could punish me for talking back.

My dad wandered from room to room like a psychic picking up on the presence of spirits. He rattled doorknobs and knocked on walls, making mental notes of the repairs that were needed. Occasionally he'd make a little sound, a little knowing huff or grunt, as if he'd discovered a clue, some fault line or sign of shoddy craftsmanship.

"I never knew you had a dad," Laura said.

"What?"

"You never talk about him."

"Who talks about their dad?" I said, knowing she did. All the time.

"Your dad is so tall," she said.

"He used to play basketball."

"Professionally?"

"No, just in the driveway," I said. "Are you done with this box?"

From the sliding-glass door I could see my dad laying out his measuring stick in the yard. Periodically he would pause and write something down on a yellow notepad, then return to surveying the area. Maybe he envisioned a lap pool or a rock garden. Or a boccie ball court or a gazebo. It was the first fatherly gesture I'd encountered in years. I was so moved, but I did my best not to show it in front of Laura.

"Doug says he wants to take us out later," she said, staring at her phone. Doug was Laura's dad.

"No!" I said, and flinched involuntarily, like I was having a mild stroke or a small object was being thrown at my head. I didn't mean for it to come out that way; it just crawled up from the depths of my bowels and ejected itself from my mouth before I had time to stop it. I overcorrected by adding, "Just kidding, you know I'm obsessed with him," hoping it would creep her out enough to not want to invite me. Instead she just laughed it off, meaning she was one of those women who secretly thinks her dad is hot and desperately wants other people to point it out.

Doug was in town for the weekend and was staying in her apartment. He did something supposedly important in music publishing and loved socially conscious rap music and was "very cool"? I only knew this because Laura always found a way to bring him up in conversation, and also I met him once at a sushi dinner for her birthday last year. I remember he wore a white Levi's denim jacket and tapered jeans that had this weird metallic sheen to them, which I honestly think should be illegal to wear past a certain age. It did nothing to distract from his sad eyes, thin lips, and weak chin; he had the degenerative bone structure of a melted wax figure, which made him look frail and impotent, overly domesticated. He asked me intrusive personal questions about my job and the future, which he referred to as female. I found his pop-culture fluency grotesque; he filled his brain with pseudoscience and useless gossip but lacked basic survival skills. He admitted he was "more of an indoorsy guy" and confessed that he'd only ever been "glamping." I wanted to scream at him to go build a deck or to punish us for disrespecting our mothers, but instead I just listened quietly as he shared some boring story about Laura having hiccups onstage during her school play debut. "Remember that, sweetie?" he said, bathing a piece of sashimi in soy sauce. Was this some form of child abuse? I'd seen crying children dragged out of supermarkets by their dislocated arm sockets, but I'd never witnessed anything like this before. I searched the deep void of Laura's pupils for some sign that she needed to be rescued, but they were obscured by a curtain of fluttering store-bought lashes covered in mascara goo. I don't know, she seemed fine.

———

My dad came back into the kitchen to tell me he could finish renovations in two weeks. After berating me for buying a "problem house," he let out a defeated sigh and rattled off a list of supplies he would need to order. It sounded like an incantation: steel pipes, drywall, traps, insulation, valves, window treatments, his friend Goran, electrical cords, rocks, tiles, and paint. As he spoke, I began spreading liverwurst over bread and cutting up the assorted cured meats I purchased for special occasions, to lay out as a ceremonial offering.

"I have a sendvich in da car," he said.

"It was nice meeting you, Mr. Brr-cheech," Laura said, in a put-on, almost offensive-sounding accent. It's a habit she picked up after spending a summer abroad in Bulgaria.

"Okay," he said, digging around in his pants in search of his keys.

He left without saying goodbye or providing me any further details. I stood at the door, watching his truck back out of the driveway and leave behind a cloud trail of exhaust like a vanishing magician. Poof, gone. As his daughter, I occupied the liminal space between blood and other. We were too close as family but too different as people to exchange niceties, so we've abandoned both in favor of a comfortable fantasy world with no expectations. I would never ask him about his feelings, and he would never pry into my personal business—or worse: be proud of me—in an attempt to take unearned credit for my success. It also meant he would never have a smartphone or a social media presence or an email address, and that alone rendered him blameless in my eyes. He was a real person, and his ambitions remained earthbound and humble, not in the accumulation of pithy likes and followers online. I never had to worry about a friend request or, God forbid, a poke.

"I'll have some," said Laura, fingering the meats. She suddenly agitated me in a feral way, and I resisted the urge to kick her chair out from under her. Something about being around my dad made me regress into a child. I stuffed a piece of bread in my mouth before I said anything I'd regret.

Just after eight o'clock, James returned from work. He was dragging a giant Amazon package that had just been delivered.

"How was work?" I asked.

"Hell. Sarah never showed up for her shift."

"Want some help?" Laura yelled from the kitchen.

"What did you get?" asked James.

"Pantry shelf, for storage. I can handle it," I said, straining to turn the hefty child-size box onto its side.

"I can do it," he said. James had a physically demanding job as head chef at an upscale tapas restaurant downtown, so by the time he came home, he was too exhausted to help me with house stuff. He was also less enthusiastic in general because the house was mine, so he assumed the role of tenant whenever possible.

"That's okay, Laura can help me."

"No, I want to," he said.

"Okay, go for it, the instructions are in the box."

"I know that."

I spent the next two hours watching James's fruitless search for the missing D screw and then foolishly skip to the next step without it. The entire living room was littered with bolts and washers, Bubble Wrap, and tiny wrenches.

"Fuck!"

"What?"

"I tightened the bolt thingy and a piece of my skin snagged on it, look."

I examined the bruised flesh and determined that my boyfriend was too soft for this world. Seeing him helplessly splayed out on the floor reminded me of the time he called 911 after taking an edible because he thought he was dying. I'd watched as a paramedic who looked to be his age hoisted James onto a stretcher and wheeled him into an ambulance. James had kept calling out for me, but I'd been too high and embarrassed to acknowledge him. When I picked him up from the hospital an hour later, he was sipping apple juice from a straw, looking like he'd seen a ghost. Like he'd really gone through something harrowing. We never spoke of it again.

My dad would've assembled the shelf in twenty minutes, no problem. I once saw him start a fire with only a toothpick and the singular determination of a lifetime of repressed male rage. It wasn't entirely James's fault; he hadn't grown up under Communist rule and probably never had to eat his own pets to survive. James came from a nice suburban American family and, like most privileged boys I grew up around, his suffering was entirely self-inflicted. He had chronic anxiety and panic attacks, as if deep down he knew he'd been spared from real tragedy, which meant it was always looming and he had no sense of how big and how catastrophic it could be. Benign stressors and minor calamities had ravaged his health—he blamed his poor digestion on athletic performance anxiety from childhood sports and blamed his mild stutter on his fear of public speaking. I texted my dad, *James needs help with a shelf, can you fix it?* A few minutes later I added, *It's Dani.* He never responded, probably because I stupidly mentioned James, who my dad never formally acknowledged existed. It wasn't personal, but

James and I weren't married, so my dad didn't want me to confuse his response with some kind of approval of our godless union, which was a sin according to his genetically inherited Catholic beliefs. It was probably for the best; he would've just asked me why I'd wasted my money on garbage IKEA furniture when I should be investing in high-quality wood furniture that would last a lifetime. It didn't matter if it was ugly or outdated as long as it was indestructible, water-resistant, and looked like it had been carefully handcrafted by German elves.

On the first day of renovations, my dad arrived before dawn with his friend Goran, a retired electrician and my dad's lifelong apprentice, even though he was way too old and feeble to be doing any sort of manual labor. They got to work demolishing the interior of the house while Balkan turbo folk blasted from a boom box in the living room. Goran had a bony build, a patchwork of reddish broken capillaries all over his face from overexertion and alcoholism, and an approval-seeking glint in his eyes, as if he'd waited his entire life for someone to tell him what a good boy he was. I once asked my mom what the deal was with him, and she'd told me that my dad handled some business disputes for him back home, something to do with land inheritance and deeds. She'd made it sound just boring enough for me to lose interest. Growing up, I'd heard whispers about my dad's reputation—people used to call him "Punisher" for some reason. I thought it sounded cool. He wasn't violent, except for when he was watching soccer or playing cards with his friends in the basement. He only ever threw a shoe at my head once for calling my sister a bitch (even though I technically said *binch*, not *bitch*), but otherwise he never hurt me. I sometimes wished he'd break my nose so I'd have an excuse to get a nose job like my friend Ivana, but he refused.

My dad's face looked older now; his hair had grayed in patchy spots across his sideburns and along his jaw, and he had deep frown lines resting in perpetual disappointment. Besides his bloated belly, he had giant muscular arms with bulging veins from years of physical labor. He looked like a bodyguard or a misunderstood ogre who doesn't know his own strength and destroys everything he touches. I left for college at eighteen and never returned, and I probably only saw him six or seven times throughout my twenties. Every time, we would awkwardly greet each other, avoiding direct eye contact like two people who'd been abducted by aliens and were not yet ready to discuss it. I never thought it was unusual; if anything it was a sign that I was independent and had outgrown his services as a basic-needs provider.

So while my friends' fathers memorized the names of their professors and monitored their credit card activity and the relationship status of their exes and crushes, I was free to do as I pleased. I respected my parents for not meddling in my life; they had better things to do, lives of their own. My mother was always busy in the kitchen, steaming up the windows with her bean stew or roasted pig with boiled potatoes and cabbage. Our refrigerator was filled with plastic-wrapped meat-and-cheese platters, sweet buns, and walnut rolls, ready for the rotating cast of church friends and relatives who happened to stop by. She had a raspy, world-weary smoker's voice that made everything she said sound harsh and sensual and, above all, true. She was like a village oracle, imparting advice on what to eat, what to feel, who to trust. But her bravado softened around my dad. I don't think I ever once saw them touch. The details of their relationship were none of my business, so I never asked. I admired their pragmatism, their loyalty to marriage, unblemished by the volatile unpredictability of feelings. Everyone else in the world seemed obsessed with this idea of a soul mate, which is why most people end up miserable, divorced, and alone. My parents had prepurchased their side-by-side burial plots years ago so they could continue not speaking, together, in the afterlife.

I watched my dad rip down drywall with the ease of a banana peel while Goran dutifully tried to keep up and remain conscious. I tried to stay out of the way by doing laps around my new neighborhood. I quickly noticed that most houses on the block were also in disrepair. The house across the street had hung a Bob Marley flag as a curtain and had a mountain of empty bottles and scrap metal piled up in the yard. A few blocks down was a house occupied entirely by cats. Dozens of them, crawling out from open windows, clawing at an old leather sofa like a giant scratching post. It was disgusting. The farther away I walked from my house, the less safe I felt, as if I were leaving Earth's atmosphere and being sucked into a black hole of unfamiliar streets, strange smells, and unfriendly faces. I would've felt fine if James were with me, not that he could fight, but his height alone was enough to function as an adequate human shield against predators. Alone, anything could happen. I could vanish like those college girls did on TV. No one would ever find me, and I'd end up being memorialized on a popular crime podcast months later. I only hoped that my death would be immediate and not drawn out over days and weeks trapped in some pervert's basement. I accidentally locked eyes with an elderly man hosing down a flower bed in his yard and let out a tiny silent fart, which sometimes happens when I'm nervous or afraid.

I decided to turn around, but I walked back slowly to give my dad space while he was in the zone; I didn't want to interrupt the artist at work. This felt like a new chapter for both of us, and I was trying hard not to ruin it. I really wanted to recalibrate from the lingering stink of our embarrassing past—I doubt he remembered, but I could recall at least three formative instances that still haunt me to this day. The first: When I was five, I had a spontaneous panic attack over my discovery of death as a concept. I was sitting at the kids' table during my grandfather's funeral reception and started involuntarily hyperventilating. If my parents died first, I would be forced to live with my godmother Biserka, a miserable lady who smelled like Vaseline and prayed constantly. I would've rather died with my parents than live with her. My cousin Jure had asked me what was wrong, and I told him the truth: He was going to die. His parents were going to die. Everyone he'd ever known would also die. No one knew when or how. It could happen tomorrow. Right then, even. He'd started crying like a baby, drawing attention to our general area. My dad had picked me up and carried my tiny convulsing body into the parking lot, where he told me to stay outside until I could "be normal."

Another time, when I was eight, I saw what appeared to be my dad's bulge through his swimming shorts at a public pool and burst into tears. I was convinced a creature had crawled into his pants and was attacking him from the inside out. My mom tried her classic "you didn't see nuttingk" trick, but I knew what I saw.

Or the time when I was twelve and decided to embark on a tennis career after watching the tennis scene in *Clueless* (where no real tennis occurs, but not the point). After I dusted the banister, washed the cars, and confessed my sins to a framed picture of the Virgin Mary, as instructed, my dad took me out to a nearby court for my first lesson. Halfway through, I'd noticed that my school crush, Kevin, was watching with his friends, so I started making these guttural moaning sounds every time I hit the ball to signal that I was both familiar with sex and good at it: "Ughhhhhhh! Oooof! Huck! Yes!" This, of course, was a lie, but I'd watched enough movies to know about the sounds people made. My dad, infuriated by the boys' leering and giggling, had flung a racket at Kevin and his friends in the way you might scare off a flock of pigeons. We continued our lesson in silence. I never played again after that.

On the walk back to my house, I could hear a faint polka bass line under a symphony of drilling, banging, pounding, and slicing. The house was already half-gutted, and plumes of asbestos and drywall dust hung in the air like vapor from a fog machine. Goran was collecting garbage and debris while my dad sawed a wooden plank with no protective eyewear and his bare hands narrowly avoiding the spinning steel blade. My house was in ruins, and I told myself not to worry, that a caterpillar eats itself inside a cocoon and needs time to transform. My house would soon morph from its goo state into something beautiful. Goran's persistent cough was mildly concerning, but I gave him a thumbs-up to let him know I appreciated his willingness to risk his life to install my crown moldings and Sonos speaker system.

That evening, James and I dragged an air mattress into the kitchen to sleep, but the sound of a loose tarp flapping in the breeze kept us up all night. I said it was kind of fun, like camping, and he told me it was "the worst night of my life." We splurged on a hotel two nights later because James was allergic to dust and had broken out into hives. He was especially sensitive to the toxic lead particles. I let out a few fake coughs to make him feel better, but I was fine. I had built up my immunity from years of breathing in construction dust and secondhand smoke.

James did his best to avoid the house, due in part to allergies but also because his morning routine—which included a methodical twelve-step coffee-making ritual set to the sound of a political podcast—seemed inappropriate while elderly foreigners worked tirelessly in the other room. "I refuse to be emasculated in my own home!" he told me, his impassioned declaration losing steam once it reached the words *my own home*.

In my dreams, I fantasized about James and my dad growing close through some safe proxy topic like sports or historical events or their shared contempt for the general concept of women. I would welcome it, even at my own expense. There was so much to choose from: my sociology degree; my criminally overpriced Prius lease; my mumbling, inaudible girl voice. But it needed to happen naturally; I could never force it.

One morning I was sitting at the kitchen table checking my emails when my dad called out for me.

"Danijela!"

"What?" I said, carefully navigating the obstacle course of plywood and paint cans in search of him. He was on his knees, priming the living-room wall.

"Nuttingk, never mind," he said.

"What is it?" I asked, unsure if he'd heard me.

"Ništa!" he said. (*Nothing!*) His English wasn't perfect, so I wondered if he wanted to ask me something but didn't know how to say it. This happened once when I was in high school. He'd called out for me to get him a rag to wrap around his foot after he stepped on a giant rusty nail, which was poking out of his running shoe. I'd panicked and brought him a box of Band-Aids, and he just looked at me and muttered something to himself. I'd watched as he pulled out the nail and hosed off the wound, then limped back to his car and continued working as if nothing had happened. I was stunned; it was like those movies where the robot villains get shot and they're totally fine. They don't even flinch; if anything, they seem amused.

My inability to learn the language of my people had undoubtedly brought shame to my family. It was a total rejection of my ancestry, my own blood, and God. In my defense, learning another language is hard and boring and did nothing to get me closer to my ultimate childhood goal of becoming a famous supermodel slash dancer slash figure skater. The only thing that successfully wormed itself into my brain were lyrics from the popular eighties Croatian pop band Magazin. I'd memorized all their hits growing up, only half knowing what they meant. It was always something about dying for love or dying from heartbreak or jealousy or being ugly or lonely or both. I liked the joyful desperation they had—meaty anthems about longing to be loved. My favorite of their lead singers, Ljiljana Nikolovska, embodied the ultimate woman: powerful, yet feminine in her black power suit, with a harem of sexy, accordion-laden bandmates surrounding her at all times. I envied her commanding fluency of her native tongue and sang along, convincing

myself I was her until the song inevitably ended, when I'd once
again be exposed as a fraud.

My dad preferred Narodna music, a type of repetitive,
sleepy folk music played at weddings so that old people can
dance. Those songs are more patriotic and festive, usually
about country loyalty and getting drunk and naming off various small towns and villages. He also enjoyed the remixed
versions, where an electronic beat thrums beneath the song's
quivering string instruments in a cheesy attempt to modern-
ize it. I respected his unapologetic love for classic folk tunes,
untouched by fleeting trends or the opinions of others. I preferred it to the heady, long-winded monologues Laura's dad
had about *Pitchfork* reviews and the authenticity of vinyl versus laptop DJs. No one cares, Doug!

Two weeks passed in a fever dream of wood shavings, carpet-
fluff debris, and drywall chunks; the house was complete. The
walls were freshly painted, the carpet ripped out and replaced
with hardwood, a wall knocked down to reveal a giant living
room, the bathroom retiled, and the refrigerator silenced. There
was a sterile purity to it, the ghosts of tenants' past buried and
forgotten under layers of wood and paint. I wandered around,
smelling the chemical newness of it, amazed by the airy feel
of the open living room, which made all the furniture strewn
about now look like cheap kid's toys, unfit for a real adult dwell-
ing. I suddenly understood the appeal of handcrafted German
furniture. Goran soothed his cough with a menthol cigarette
while my dad gathered his remaining tools, and a disembodied man's voice wailed, "*Večeras je naša fešta*" (*Tonight is our
party*), through tinny boom box speakers. I cautiously handed

my dad a blank check, and he made a confused face, as if I'd presented him with a dead fish.

"Nah, nah, nah," he said, handing it back to me.

I knew he wouldn't take my money, but part of me wanted to test his reaction. The more offended by the attempted business transaction, the more it really was an act of love. My dad loved me, and this house was proof.

As they packed up, I went about installing my newly purchased Japanese paper lantern in the kitchen by balancing on a chair and hammering an upside-down ceiling hook.

My dad looked over at me and shouted, "Ayyy, not like dat!"

"Like what?"

"Move!" He took the hook and twisted it in by hand.

"I was going to do that," I whined. "God!"

"Isuse Bože," he casually pleaded with Jesus for strength. What he really meant was: *Your stupidity bewilders and exhausts me.* We both laughed through our teeth, our mutual annoyance bubbling over until it became unbearable, like actors forgetting their lines. He raised his hand in jest, pretending to smack me, and I shook a dishrag like a matador's cape in playful self-defense. Goran walked in with the last of the garbage bags, and they loaded my dad's truck while I stood there watching. Then they got in the truck and drove away. Any memories of their efforts were compartmentalized and swiftly forgotten to make room for the next day's bathroom reno or cabinet install. Poof, gone.

Alone, I opened all the windows to air out the lingering paint stink and reconfigured my furniture in a pointless attempt to accommodate the new layout. Something was off. An eerie draft whistled from an unknown source, cutting through the quiet. I walked around trying to find it. I soon realized it was nothing, it was a ringing in my ear that had always been there. James came home later that night and wandered around, obviously impressed but holding back.

"All very nice, they did a good job," he said, emotionless. The house was less his than it had ever been; he wandered about with his hands in his pockets, acting the way a tourist or a window-shopper might, restrained and curious. He kept his shoes on.

"Something is off, though, right?" I said.

"Like what?"

"I don't know, it feels unfinished . . ." I trailed off.

"Well, now we need to decorate it, hang up some artwork, get some plants in here."

"Yeah."

"You can do whatever you want now," he added.

I nodded, trying to convince myself.

The following evening, Laura and her dad popped by unannounced. Through the peephole, I could see Doug cradling a bottle of wine and a box of doughnuts, wearing a distressed Pink Floyd T-shirt that was made to look old but was actually an eighty-dollar reprint from Urban Outfitters. I only knew this because James had the same one. Doug saw my blinking pupil through the hole and said, "Open up, girl!"

I stepped back, gripping my throat with pity and dread. Doug had that aura of loneliness that every divorced dad I knew seemed to have. He and Laura's mom had split three years ago, so now he was on all the dating apps that Laura used, and they both found this hilarious. At one point he even matched with her, as a joke. His opening line was "I hear you've got a pretty cool dad!" When she showed me, I closed my eyes and died, and she continued existing in the world, unharmed by the horrifying exchange. I'd said nothing because Laura was the only person in the world who knew all my secrets, like that my mom hired an exorcist to treat my ninth-grade depression instead of just putting me on birth control like everyone else.

When I opened the door, Laura and Doug cradled me in awkward side hugs, took off their shoes, and wandered around to marvel at the remodel. Doug had a gross cold sore on his lower lip with too much ChapStick on it. He wore thick black glasses to distract from his infected mouth, which he sucked on anytime he caught me looking. Laura twirled around like a child, sliding her dirty socks all over the living room. "Wow," she said.

"You know, I've been thinking about a kitchen remodel myself. You think your dad would be up for it?" Doug asked.

"My dad can do anything," I said.

"Great! Can I get his info? Does he have a website?"

It felt like a slur. *Website*. Ha! Stupid Doug.

"No. I can give you his number, but he's got a six-month waiting list," I lied. It could've been true. It felt true. I knew my dad was in high demand because you couldn't book him unless you had a referral. Even then, it wasn't a guarantee. I gleefully recited his number while Doug tapped it into his phone. I couldn't stop staring at his weak, girly wrists. I imagined them snapping like chicken wings. *Good luck!*

I sat and listened as Doug talked about a music documentary premiere he'd attended over the weekend. He kept name-dropping elderly musicians who I'd never heard of but who were supposedly iconic and still huge in South America. He connected his phone to my Sonos speaker and started playing one of their songs, saying, "You've definitely heard this one before." I played dumb so as not to give him the satisfaction, then ate two doughnuts to keep my mouth occupied so I wouldn't have to talk as much.

I excused myself to the bathroom while Doug and Laura sat in my living room discussing their shared struggles with body dysmorphia. Doug blamed social media, while Laura blamed the patriarchy. After a few more sips of wine, they both blamed Laura's mother. I sat on the toilet counting the white shower tiles and thought about staying in the bathroom until they got the hint and left, but I knew they weren't the type of people to pick up on hints, so I told myself I would go back once I reached the hundredth tile. I noticed a tiny chip in the corner of the eighteenth tile, so I got up and started picking at it, but it had been superglued to the wall. I looked through my drawers, found a metal nail file, and began chipping away at the surrounding grout until the tile loosened and popped off. I inspected the tile carefully, then slipped it into my pocket. The missing tile looked obvious, so I took the file and removed the entire row to match, making it worse. I continued with the next row of tiles until I heard a knock.

"Knock knock," said Doug.

"One second," I said. I pocketed the remaining tiles and flushed the toilet to make a sound.

"I need to use the loo," he said in a goofy British accent.

"All yours," I said. I squeezed the tile shards in my fist and returned to Laura, who was in the living room tearing a doughnut into smaller pieces so she wouldn't eat all of it.

"Don't let me eat this," she said, taking another bite.

"Okay. Don't," I said.

"Fine, just one more bite," she said. "I'm so bad!"

I noticed a fly buzzing around and started swatting at the air with my hand like a maniac.

"What are you doing?" Laura asked.

"There's a fly," I said, grabbing a slipper.

"So what?" she said.

I thought I saw it out of the corner of my eye; it was resting on a circular mirror hanging on the wall. I lunged at it and smacked as hard as I could. The mirror collapsed and shattered on the hardwood floor. There was a loud clap followed by a shimmering waterfall sound.

"Whoa, are you okay?" asked Doug, wiping his hands on his predistressed jeans.

"I got it!" I said, presenting the fly guts on my slipper.

"You broke your mirror. Bad luck," said Laura.

Doug and Laura helped me put the bigger pieces in the trash, and I swept up the rest.

"Well, you could say tonight really ended with a bang, ha ha," said Doug, dabbing ChapStick on his sore.

"Are you going to eat the rest, or should I just take them?" Laura asked, holding the half-empty doughnut box.

"You take them," I said.

Doug asked Laura to drive because he was "a little buzzed." His hug lingered a beat too long as he swayed me from side to side until I broke loose and thanked them both for stopping by. I locked the door behind me and felt compelled to return to the bathroom to finish what I had started. I knelt down on the shower floor and went to work, chipping away to reveal an ugly layer of dried glue. It gave me the satisfying sensation of picking at a scab. James came home from work an hour later and found me cross-legged on the floor, sweating.

"What are you doing?" he asked.

"They fell off," I said, showing him the collection of loose tiles.

"Really? Because it looks like you're removing them," he said.

"Well, yeah, because they were loose. I had to," I said.

"Okay, well, I'm going to bed." He looked tired and smelled like fried fish and armpit sweat.

"I'll be there in a minute," I said. I pretended to stand up, then I grabbed my phone and sat on the edge of the bathtub to call my dad. I knew he was asleep and wouldn't pick up, so I could leave a message. I waited for the beep.

"Tata? It's Dani. I think you need to come back. Some of the shower tiles came off. Also the mirror broke, I don't know how. And the toilet is clogged; I think Laura's dad did it. He was in here for a long time. When you come over, I'll show you."

Acknowledgments

To Ryan Hahn, for everything. To Andrea Nakhla, my muse, my best friend. To Kenny Laubbacher, my brother and forever friend. To Lori Tipton, my spiritual advisor. Thank you.

To my agent, Marya Spence, you were the first to spark a small hope in me and you were patient enough to watch it grow. Thank you for your mentorship, advice, and hilarious audio-message pep talks. You are the coolest of them all. Thank you also to Mackenzie Williams, Natalie Edwards, and everyone at Janklow & Nesbit. Thank you to my editor, Anna Kaufman, whom I immediately recognized as a like soul. You approached my work with endless enthusiasm, wisdom, and a sense of humor; for that and many other reasons, I'm deeply grateful to you. Thank you also to Zuleima Ugalde, Madeline Partner, Alex Dos Santos, Annie Locke, Kayla Overbey, Robin Witkin, and everyone at Vintage.

I'd also like to thank Kristina Baumgartner, Lizzie Rose, Allie Rowbottom, Jedidiah Jenkins, Annabel Graham, Hannah Beresford, T. Kira Madden, Meredith Talusan, Leah Dieterich, Chelsea Hodson, Jonathan Hyla, Jillian Kliewer, Mara Roszak, Taylor Rice, Andrea Actis, Anjelica Armstrong, Sharaya Summers, Anna Burton, Jana Piazza, Justin Bauer, Grace Mitchell, Brandon Tauszik, Matty Lynn Barnes, and the whole Local Natives fam. Thanks to the Banff Centre, CBC Books, and the Canada Council for the Arts for all your support.

To my parents, Kaja and Joso, and my siblings, Ana and Adam. I love you beyond words, time, space.